SIERRA HOTEL

A NOVEL OF THE VIETNAM WAR

SIERRA HOTEL

A NOVEL OF THE VIETNAM WAR

Kent McInnis

TIREE
PRESS

an imprint of

THE OGHMA PRESS

OGHMA

CREATIVE MEDIA

Bentonville, Arkansas • Los Angeles, California
www.oghmacreative.com

Library of Congress Cataloging-in-Publication Data

Names: McInnis, Kent, author.
Title: Sierra Hotel/Kent McInnis | Sierra Hotel #1
Description: First Edition. | Bentonville: Tyree, 2021.
Identifiers: LCCN: 2021940152 | ISBN: 978-1-63373-722-8 (hardcover) |
ISBN: 978-1-63373-723-5 (trade paperback) | ISBN: 978-1-63373-724-2 (eBook)
Subjects: | BISAC: FICTION/War and Military | FICTION/Historical |
LC record available at: https://lccn.loc.gov/2021940152

Tiree Press trade paperback edition September, 2021

Cover & Interior Design by Casey W. Cowan
Editing by Gordon Bonnet & Amy Cowan

Published by Tiree Press, an imprint of The Oghma Press, a subsidiary of The Oghma Book Group. Find out more at www.oghmacreative.com

To Captain Jack R. Harvey (KIA Vietnam),
Barbara, and Kelly

PREFACE

AS A YOUNG TEENAGER I kept a diary. I continued the practice until joining the military. I switched to letters which I later retrieved from friends. After leaving the Air Force, I returned to my diary. Writing down these events served to burn the memories into my brain.

This novel is based upon personal observation. Rob Amity's experiences as a pilot on the homefront were shared by many, although they were not the stories that combat veterans would bring home to adulation or, in the case of Vietnam, condemnation. The dialog is not always polite. The actions are sometimes unwholesome and immature. Events I depict are based upon firsthand experiences or observations. Some characters are based upon common legends all young pilots learn in their first year.

Pressures put on members of the military by detractors during the Vietnam War were unforgivable. For those men who joined to avoid the draft, their forced commitment was no different than their fathers' dilemma in World War II and Korea. We had our dreams dashed, while cultural forces pulled us in multiple directions. It was a nation in conflict with itself. This is that story.

ACKNOWLEDGEMENTS

A BOOK IS NEVER WRITTEN in a vacuum. My mother, Betty, blessed me with strict standards of grammar. My father, Marvin, taught me by example how to tell a tale and make it entertaining. My older brother, Marv, spent nights in our bunk beds sharing with me what he had read that day from his latest book.

Many former and retired airmen shared stories, both true and legend. I value the experience of men being thrown together in pilot training. As the Laredo AFB Undergraduate Pilot Training Class 71-06, the Rio River Rats, we worked together to either sink or swim. Of the more than eighty who started in our class, fifty made it to graduation. The bond among these men has held for 50 years. All but a handful spent some time in Vietnam. This is their story as young pilots-to-be.

I owe much to Dr. Hugh Strickland, my closest friend in the Air Force when I was an instructor pilot. We shared many days of laughter, frustration, and drinks. Hugh achieved the same dream I also desired—to become a veterinarian. He reached that goal for both of us.

Order of Daedalians is a fraternity of military pilots with whom I have shared many happy dinners over twenty years. Their experiences made writing about Vietnam that much better. Lt. Col. Glenn Schaumburg shared his firsthand experience flying a B-52 in the Christmas bombing of Hanoi in 1972. Col. Larry Hoppe flew F-105 Thuds over North Vietnam in 1967 and provided me with invaluable information about methods, armaments, and specific missions targeting SAM sites.

Finally, there is Cheryl, my precious wife, who has always told me that I could make it as a writer.

1

I STARED INTO THE EYES of a red-faced and angry captain that I had nearly knocked out of the sky in a midair collision. It would have worked out better for me had I outright killed him.

The captain growled, trembling with rage. "Some son of a bitch broke out of the traffic pattern at Barfly and came so close to hitting me that I could read his tail number."

He looked straight at me, for I was that S.O.B. I wanted to respond with a face-saving retort, but the captain was right. I had really screwed up.

Four years earlier on my departure for Air Force pilot training, my father told me that if he had to choose between fighting in combat against the Japanese or facing an abusive superior officer, it would be a tough call.

"But I suppose if you're lucky," he said upon further reflection, "your commander will be the worst enemy you ever face."

So today was my lucky day.

It started so innocently earlier that day when I tried to solo out my Iranian student pilot.

From my T-37 cockpit I spied the familiar practice landing field on the horizon. This part of south Texas was a dry isolated spot where the hot autumn South Texas sun radiated unobstructed onto the bleached desert grass, cactus, and mesquite. Four bored and frustrated U.S. Air Force pilots, who would have preferred flying jets rather than talking to me, waited for us in their glass-enclosed runway supervisory unit, a sort of mobile air traffic control tower. They were listening for my next call over the radio that announced Axon two-two and my Iranian student were on our way to a full stop landing. Ironically for me, my experience at the auxiliary landing field had always been a pleasure. When jets were not landing, the field was silent, except for sounds the desert made through the distant call of a bird or the gentle rustle of a warm wind. Today, I planned to leave the plane, watch my student fly his first jet solo, and enjoy a quiet period of peace with my flight buddies in the small RSU.

We were speeding across the northern horizon at a right angle to the direction of the airfield runway. Inside my cockpit, my Iranian student pilot would have benefited from the vantage point of the pilots on the ground, for he had no clue where he was.

"You missed your five-mile call!" I said as we turned right to line up with the runway.

"Yes, sir," he said in his Persian-accented English. *"Axon two-two, five-mile straight-in!"*

"Get your head out of your ass, Mossare."

"Yes, sir."

"Do you see the runway?"

"Yes, sir."

Mossare lifted his colored visor for a better look. What I could see of his face around his oxygen mask looked as green as his gloves.

"Why are we heading thirty-degrees away from the runway?"

"Yes, sir."

"When are you going to line up with the runway and make your gear check?"

"Yes, sir."

I was getting more concerned now. He had known English only a short time. Mossare was already a washout from his previous class. This was a second attempt to get him jet-soloed. We were not communicating, given the stress he was under.

"Mossare, are you still with me?"

"Yes, sir!"

"Then call gear check! Get your head out and get us lined up."

"Yes, sir," the Iranian said, his hands trembling in the green leather gloves. *"Axon two-two—"*

He would have finished the transmission except for the gurgling sound he began making. I looked away from him just before he lost his lunch. He hadn't even tried to remove his oxygen mask. I took control of our jet immediately.

"Axon two-two is on the go. Departing traffic," I radioed to the pilots below us.

I pulled the nose up, added power, raised the landing gear, and began the bumpy climb to 3500 feet for our return home to Laredo Air Force Base. Passing 1500 feet, I skirted by another T-37, making its initial approach for an overhead landing. The jet's two pilots turned their heads in surprise as I climbed past them. We were close enough to them that they may have seen Mossare's vomit-smeared face mask. I did not have time to wave.

Mossare sat in the left seat choking, making no effort to help himself.

"Get your mask off, Mossare!"

I finally decided he could not talk but must have wanted to say "yes, sir" to me. I reached over, unhooked his slimy oxygen mask, handed him a barf bag, turned off his intercom, so I would not hear his retching and choking, and switched my own mask to 100% oxygen to eliminate the foul odor.

"Let me demonstrate a return to the home drome," I said. "You take it easy."

He gave me a look of relief, mouthed something that must have been "yes, sir" in Farsi and spewed more Thanksgiving leftovers in his lap, missing the barf bag completely.

Mossare's pilot skills were bad enough, but his airsickness just compounded things. I had seen him drive a car. He was a danger to everyone on the road. He and two of his fellow Iranian cadets had never driven a car until they came to Laredo Air Force Base. So why was he trying to fly airplanes when he had not yet mastered driving? It was because America promised Iran some pilots. The Shah bought our airplanes, so we had to train their pilots. This hazardous mission, we instructors joked, might be a close second to the real danger of flying over North Vietnam.

As we flew back, I added full military power to the twin jet engines to bring us home to an early landing. In a way it was a good deal. I seldom flew the airplane myself. This was a rare chance. I slowed the craft to 200 knots, descended to a level off at 1000 feet above the ground, and called the runway supervisory unit on the home strip. As we passed over the inside runway, I pulled the power back and simultaneously broke into a right 60-degree bank turn to place us in the opposite direction downwind. After rolling out of my pitchout turn, dropping my speed brake, landing gear, and flaps, I started a shallow descending turn to the runway for touchdown.

"Axon two-two, gear check," I radioed, *"full stop."*

I was always good at these traffic patterns, but I never got too many awards for my touchdowns. I passed over the threshold of the runway, hoping I might perfect my roundout technique and flare before touchdown. No such luck. I hit the ground firmly, as usual. Steering the airplane off the runway and taxiing back to the parking ramp, I was glad to get the canopy opened. Breathing 100% oxygen tended to irritate my throat. Now I could breathe fresh air and dilute the stench inside.

Cadet Mossare said nothing. His embarrassment could only get worse. As I pulled into the chocks, a crew chief was already laughing. He waited for me to cut off the engines.

"Lieutenant, do we have a problem?"

I turned to look at Mossare, who was trying to unbuckle his shoulder harness without further spreading his mess.

"I need something to clean this mess up," I said to the crew chief, pointing to the pungent cockpit.

"Right away, sir." He began jogging toward the squadron building.

"Hey, Sarge!" I called after him. "This bird have a turn time?"

He stopped, turned, and nodded affirmatively then ran on.

"Mossare, someone else is flying this bird in fifteen minutes, so you spend that time cleaning. They'll bring you some soap and water. I'll fill out the 781. Okay?"

"Yes, sir." What a worthless answer that was.

"You've got to clean this cockpit up before you come in."

"Yes, sir."

"Give me a break," I said to myself, wondering if he understood me at all.

I proceeded to log our flight in the Form 781 that we carried in the plane. I noticed the sergeant carrying a bucket back with him. He was still laughing at the young cadet, and I knew how he felt. It was funny to me, too. The crew chief handed Cadet Mossare the bucket of water and some cleaning rags.

"You must have really given him a wild ride," the sergeant said, turning to me. "Loops and all that?"

"No." I laughed. "This was supposed to be a solo flight. Traffic patterns only."

"That means you get to do it again."

"Right you are. Thanks for the bucket."

"Yes, sir."

I headed for the chute room, taking my parachute off one shoulder to help cool my back. The long walk across the white cement parking ramp was like a hike across the burning sands. The sun's reflected heat sent shimmers through my view of the squadron building in the distance. It often reached 130 degrees on the ramp and taxiway even in late November. I was soaking wet by the end of the walk back. It would feel good to get inside where it was cool. Once inside I hung up my parachute and wiped the sweat from my helmet and oxygen mask in a cleaning ritual designed to ensure my safety. After hanging up my helmet, I stepped into the hallway, past the operations desk, and into my home away from home, A-Flight.

I entered the flight room to the usual scene of flight-suited pilots standing and sitting at the nine tables situated throughout the big room. Each instructor's table had four to five chairs, enough for his three students. The pale green cinder block walls held several two and three-foot-high replicas of class patches worn on a student's flightsuit from earlier classes.

A large chalkboard on the back wall had a line drawing of a pregnant woman with an arrow pointing to her large round belly, which said, *AIR*. The name, *SUZY*, was underneath. To the left was someone's tasteless poem about the uses of napalm.

At the front of the room stood a dirty, chipped, wooden podium with our red 3640th Pilot Training Squadron arm patch, depicting an eagle tossing two eaglets out of their nest.

Two slogans over the door leading into the instructor's briefing room and to the right of the current weather map read:

If you feed a monkey enough bananas, you can teach him how to fly.

And below that:

If they can make penicillin out of moldy bread, we can make a pilot out of you.

Captain Hal Freed was first to meet me as I surveyed the Ragtop flight room. He burst into laughter, reading the frustration displayed on my face. "Rob, you look like you just got spanked by the opposition," he said loudly. "You want to give me my five bucks?"

I reached into my unzipped pocket and pulled out a sweaty, limp, five-dollar bill. I slapped it into his hand in sincere disgust.

"I thought for sure I could solo him the first time," I laughed. "For once, Freed, you can't top what's happened to me!"

Then I tried to tell Freed and the others in the room what the Iranian had done. I wanted to be kind to Cadet Mossare. For his sake, I needed to tell my story before the poor fellow got back from cleaning up the airplane.

I scanned the faces of the five other instructors in the room. Freed, a tall, tawny, and confident ex-fighter pilot by the doorway, Captain John Alexander, our A-Flight commander and my close college friend, Captain Vicente Nuñez, our resident mestizo who had forgotten how to speak Spanish, Captain Jim Starchweather, the squadron hippie and expert on illicit chemicals, and skinny, hyperactive, Captain Johnny Wise. Depending upon how their flights had gone today, their expressions ranged from boredom to elation to dejection.

"Well, guys, we were only doing traffic patterns. Mossare had done two satisfactory landings, but Barfly told us to break out of traffic. The trip around to line up for a straight-in must have unnerved him. He forgot to call at the five-mile point. Worse than that was when he called for a gear check but stopped in mid-word. I looked over at him. Was he having a heart attack or something? He never bothered to take his mask off. First thing I knew there was puke dripping out from around his mask."

The group of students and instructors gathered around me laughed and groaned in unison, a few even turned and walked away in disgust. I continued.

"I broke out of traffic immediately and took him back home. I couldn't wait to get out of that airplane." I shuddered at the thought of it.

"Did you have a near miss with another Tweet, Rob?" Freed asked. He was cautious with the way he asked.

I had forgotten about it. "Yeah, come to think about it. Yeah. Maybe a little too close."

"You must have climbed out immediately, then."

"Oh, crap!" I realized for the first time the procedural error I had committed. "Who was it?"

"The worst possible."

"Hell! How many know about this? Everybody?"

The group around me all nodded, yes. I knew now that I was in big trouble. I asked my next question with only a single word.

"Military?"

"Military." The whole flight knew. They all seemed to say it in unison.

"Oh, crap!" My words elicited more laughter. "How did word get here so fast?"

"Military radioed in just after it happened," Freed said. "I'll tell you. He's pissed. I can't help you on this one."

The instructors and student pilots departed from around my table like I was a newfound leper.

2

AS A BOY OF EIGHT, I liked many things. But at the top of my list were airplanes and girls. About the time I suspended my first plastic model airplane from the ceiling of my bedroom with nylon monofilament fishing line, I went on my first date with a girl. I was in fourth grade. Even at that young age, I saw the possibility that romancing girls would be a more achievable aspiration than flying airplanes. It was a tossup as to which would be more expensive—or more dangerous.

As a nine-year-old, I had already reached the pinnacle of romantic success. I convinced my eight-year-old girlfriend to go to a movie with me. Once we were alone in the back of the darkened theater, we joined as one to experience the ecstasy of sharing a single Coke with two straws.

In high school I honed my skills. I learned to dance. I learned how to kiss. I learned that not all girls were a good match. I did all right in high school. And when I left for college at Oklahoma State, I took with me a reputation as an honorable gentleman. I was not sure that was my desired goal. The bad boys always seemed to get the prettiest girls.

As for flying, it remained only a pipe dream. I gave up hanging my model airplanes, afraid that it looked like a childish interest. I had never flown in an airplane. It seemed intimidating. Convincing myself that I had a fear of heights and flying, I concentrated on studying hard in school, pursuing girls, and delaying the Selective Service draft board.

I was fortunate in college to start my freshman year rooming with my best friend, John Alexander. We met as grade school boys in summer when his family moved onto our block. A year and a half older than I was, John took a liking to his young neighbor. We found ourselves getting up early most mornings just to begin our daily high adventure. We shared a common interest in girls. Because of our age difference, he had a taste for older girls. We never had to compete. Our friendship strengthened into a brotherly bond all through high school and for two years of college.

I MET SUZY IN FRESHMAN English class on my first day of classes at college. Williams Hall was an old un-air-conditioned building that was torn down in my senior year. I took a front row seat directly in front of the lectern because I wanted to be successful as a student. It was 1964, and they were already drafting the flunk outs. The professor's first words were instructions to get out a pencil and paper. He had us immediately write an essay. That was the first day—not even a warmup lecture. We had an hour to do it and could leave when we were finished. I wanted to do well, so I invested the whole hour writing a masterpiece. Just thirty minutes into the hour, this willowy goddess of virtue walked up to the professor, handed him her essay, and left the room. She was incredibly gorgeous! Five feet, four inches tall. Long, straight, streaked blond hair clipped in the back. Her clothes were both stylish and proper. Though it was in the nineties on that hot September day, she did not sweat. She did not even perspire. Her eyes were the most dizzyingly beautiful green. Her figure was well proportioned, though a bit thin for my tastes. My dad had suggested to me when I left for college to pick the skinny ones for marriage because the ones with the big boobs never stopped growing. He used to say, "this year's prom queen becomes next decade's homecoming float." Well, Suzy was the first girl that I met who was thin but a real turn on. So, while most guys, usually including myself, were mentally stripping girls naked, I mentally put meat on Suzy's bones, picturing her naked in future years.

For the next English class two days later, I was fifteen minutes early. I sat on the second row on the side by the door and waited in ambush. She was the last student to enter the class that day. In fact, she walked in with the professor himself. I soon knew why. He had been waiting in ambush for her, too. The first thing he did after everyone took their seats was to hand out our essays. That's when I learned why she was the last one in the room. There was only one "A" given in the whole class—Suzy's. Fourteen of us got "D's" and twelve got "F's." He awarded no other grades. I was one of the lucky ones with a "D." I glanced over my shoulder to look at Suzy on the back row of the class and fell in love that very day.

I caught up with her after class. "Tell me your secret?"

"Didn't you hear him tell us what he wanted in an essay?" She had a most captivating smile—oh that smile.

"No, I was too busy looking at you all hour." I was abnormally bold that day.

From the very first, my main attraction for her was her intelligence, her jaunty self-confidence, and her off the wall sense of humor. It was my initial discovery that a girl's brains were a turn-on, not only their bodies. What was most pleasant to discover, we had a mutual attraction that surprised us both.

During the first semester of my freshman year, I lived in the dorm. Second semester I moved into a rented apartment with Alexander. John was a very serious student who worked very little to get all "A's." He was out of the apartment all the time. That made him the perfect roommate. He was two years ahead of me, which meant I profited from his experience. After my initial "D" in English that first day, I held my own in school, thanks both to John and Suzy.

In my sophomore year, John's interests began to expand to women. He said I had such a good deal with Suzy that he was going to search for someone just like her. He always asked her if she had a sister. She didn't. We double-dated a lot. There was never any question that Suzy and I were close, not yet that close. We may have had our own apartment, but I never had the nerve to take advantage of it with Suzy. Mom told me I wasn't to do that. My dad had been more direct. "You get a girl pregnant, and I'll kill you!"

In those two years we dated, my dad's prediction came true. Suzy grew a body that was a dream come true. Oh, how she could turn heads! She looked good in anything she wore. Her complexion was as clear as a commercial. And then I blew it.

MY JUNIOR YEAR STARTED OUT with Suzy sick. She missed going to the Howdy Dance, where new students could come to mix in and match up with other students. Our attendance had been a two-year tradition with Suzy and me. I hated to break tradition, so I went by myself.

I was by myself for about twenty minutes before I met Jane. From the first sight of her, it was pure lust, not love. Jane was a freshman, her high school's prom queen, and everything else for that matter. The moment I fixed my eyes on her voluptuous profile, I decided to tempt fate. She had an element of danger about her, but I might have been safe from her had she not immediately reciprocated my attraction.

She was barely five feet tall, all legs, and had breasts that were so big around that they not only met in the most marvelous cleavage but could hardly be contained to the outside. Yet, she was not at all fat. Miniskirts were just then becoming widespread on campus, having gained notice only since spring break the year before. She was one of the few girls who knew how to move in one. Like Gypsy Rose Lee, Jane could show everything without ever exposing anything. She was a master manipulator of men's minds. That night while dancing she would raise her arms up and expose the best pair of legs on the floor. Her yellow cotton halter dress caused men to make hasty side glances whenever her arms went up again. They could look at her legs, or they could check out her chest, but they couldn't do both. Her hair was a light fiery red, worn in a pixy cut. That served to expose a most slender and tempting neck, which emerged from the sensuous form of her bare shoulders. I loved following the lines of her neck all the way down to her toes.

Jane was one of those girls whose picture never would do her justice. I never could get that sense of her animal attraction unless it was in person. It was the way her brown eyes could cover my body like an artist strokes paint on a canvas. It was her expressive fluidity in those luscious lips that never would hold still. They seemed in a perpetual, yet infinitesimal, quivering quest to touch. When she kissed me that night, I was a goner. No one either before or since has kissed me quite like Jane. She had a way of consuming my whole face in her mouth, as if she had not eaten in days. Her passion knew no limits—horny twenty-four hours a day, every day of the year. It was stupendously fun while it lasted.

It was the typical move of a stupid man who couldn't control his hormones. This handicap is simple to explain. Man, unlike woman, has two primitive brains—the *medulla oblongata* and the *baja oblongata*.

Suzy was naturally upset, but within six months she was thanking me. Alexander had found the next best thing to Suzy's sister. John graduated and left for a career in the Air Force. Sadly, what he took with him was a wife, the first woman I ever fell deeply in love with.

The draft board greeted me a year later. Jane dumped me. She said I should go to Canada. It was clear she would never follow me there. So, I put my girl hobby on the back burner and decided to renew an interest I had put on ice for a decade. I followed the lead of my childhood friend and applied for Air Force pilot training. Why not? What better way to overcome my fear of flying?

Mom and Dad were proud of me when I told them. Mom cried as I boarded the airliner for officer training at Lackland AFB in San Antonio, Texas. To my surprise, I had more fun there than I ever had in college. I soon experienced a comradery I never knew existed. We sank or swam together. I liked that part of my training.

After getting my commission as an Air Force second lieutenant, I had a week before needing to report to Laredo AFB for pilot training. I hurried home to see my parents, then rushed up to Stillwater to see Jane and say goodbye. She was noticeably distant but did promise to come see me in Laredo, Texas.

Pilot training was a happy time. We all thought we were hot stuff. We learned that the phonetic alphabet had secret codes. "Sierra Hotel" was code for "Shit Hot." We all aspired to be that—shit hot fighter pilots. To strap ourselves into a jet airplane and blast into the air all alone in full afterburner did not hurt our self-image one bit. The stress of classrooms, deadlines, and occasional flight emergencies only brought my classmates closer during our fifty-three weeks of training. We described our situation, our base, and our behavior in the secret numbers called the Falcon Code. If I had been ignorant of life before, that myth was dashed in the first two months of training. The Officer's Club became the greatest classroom experience of my formative early adulthood. Strippers every Friday and an occasional Saturday Champagne brunch made the "O Club" the greatest place a bachelor could dream of being.

To my great fortune I learned that Suzy and Captain John Alexander, now also an Air Force pilot, got an assignment to Laredo as an instructor pilot. He soon was elevated to Flight Commander in the same Ragtop Flight where I had been a T-37 student. By then, I was at Randolph AFB learning how to be an instructor pilot in primary jet trainers. John, keeping our friendship a secret, requested that the squadron assign me to be a Ragtop IP.

That's how I now found myself in my flight room with students and in a real pickle. I successfully let down my best friend from boyhood, made my first inexcusable mistake as an instructor pilot, and chose the meanest badass on base to infuriate.

3

I DECIDED TO BURY MYSELF in paperwork in a futile attempt to hide from what I knew would be next—a Military confrontation. After going to the snack bar to get a thirst quencher, I sat down at my table, peeled open a can of cold Dr. Pepper, and pulled out Cadet Mossare's gradebook. As I opened it up, each red "Unsatisfactory" visually jumped out like a stop light.

It was routine to give a passing grade to a solo student if he failed to kill himself in the air or on the ground. Flying with an instructor, though, meant the student got no mercy. On a dual flight, if the student attempted to murder the instructor more than five times in an hour, he would be in store for a "pink." A "pink" was a big red "U" for unsatisfactory in the gradebook.

Mossare's gradebook in the early stages was never too full of black letters. It was routinely colored with red "U's" like broad brush strokes. This gradually evolved into black letter grades as his improved skill allowed. Mossare had progressed to the point that, although it had required twice as many hours of training, he was ready to solo. He was lucky on this ride. He puked before finishing the mission, so it could be graded as "incomplete." In this case a black "I" was far more desirable than a pink.

As I glanced across my table to the door, Mossare entered the room. The sight of his dark-skinned, green face made me laugh. The sweat still flowed off his forehead, and I sensed the tension he must be under. Laughing was my release.

The poor guy had learned English only six weeks before arriving in America for pilot training, and he was doing fairly well. I wondered what he felt inside. He understood English well when on the ground, but under stress, he resorted to his native tongue.

"Monday we'll do it for sure," I said to him as he walked over to sit down. "Don't even think about it this weekend. Just relax. These things happen."

"My lieutenant will make me think about it, sir." Mossare's voice was very soft. "I will have to work hard to prepare for Monday."

"Well, tell your lieutenant to take a hike," I said, knowing he would never relay that message. "He's an ass."

The lieutenant that Mossare feared was the only officer among the Iranian student pilots at Laredo. All the rest were only cadets, not to be commissioned as officers until graduation from pilot training. There were rumors about an Iranian cadet the year before who failed to solo. The lieutenant had sent him packing, and no one ever learned his fate. The other cadets treated his existence like some state secret. The rumor went around that, upon his return to Iran, he was executed. Cadet Mossare took his lieutenant seriously.

I looked up as the hulking forms of my other two students appeared in the A-Flight doorway. They stood just inside, surveying the human landscape, a wall-mounted class patch to their right depicted a flying Schlitz Beer can captioned You Only Go Around Once. The taller student smiled, nudged his stocky friend, and pointed in the direction of Mossare. After picking up a folder with their flight records, they walked over to the table. The large hand of the taller student slapped Mossare on the back.

"Well, Sorry, ol' buddy. Did you solo?" Fred Picks said in a loud voice.

"I've been waiting to throw this camel jock in the tank all month," another stockier student said cheerfully. He referred to the tradition of throwing newly-soloed jet pilots into the watering tank adjacent to the squadron building.

"Camel jocks aren't getting out of being dunked," Picks said to him. "Right, Sorry?"

"I'm not a camel jock!" Mossare's voice betrayed real irritation.

"Hell, yes, you are. Sorry. You got nothing but sand and camels where you come from."

"I'm not Arab. I'm Persian! We have snow in Iran, not sand, you dumb—you dumb—Buffalo Jock!"

Several eavesdroppers broke out in cheers for the beleaguered Iranian. It was his first known good comeback. Laughter and the term "Buffalo Jock" repeated over and over filled the room. Mossare needed that, I am sure, as he continued to recover and hide out from his lieutenant.

"Well, how is the rest of the crew?" I was looking at my two second lieutenant students. "Still uninjured after tripping the surly bonds of space alone once more?"

"Lieutenant Amity, sir, I survived again!" stocky Ted Ark said, his sly grin giving me much to wonder about what he really had been doing while unsupervised in the practice areas.

"Sir, did he solo?" Picks persisted in his query, again slapping Mossare on the back.

"No," I said matter-of-factly.

"Well, dang," Picks was holding both of Mossare's shoulders in his large hands. "Get with it, Sorry. We gotta throw you in the water before it all dries up."

"We'll get Mossare soloed on Monday for sure. I'm not worried. Too bad I can't drink any of my booze this weekend, though. I was counting on it."

I wasn't desperate for another bottle, but it made them feel like I appreciated their gift. Besides the water tank dunking tradition for new jet pilots, another tradition was the presentation to the instructor of a bottle of high-grade booze. It was a reward for having the balls to leave the student alone in the aircraft before his solo. It was the one risk that, if my judgment proved poor, would get me strung up, or worse yet, court-martialed. Of course, the student could be dead. That, too, might be bad.

"Hell, sir, Ark and I just soloed less than a month ago. Have you polished off the stuff we gave you already?" Picks made an impression of mock surprise. "Dang, sir. You need to slow down!"

"Oh, for crying out loud. I can't even drink the crap you gave me. Tequila and rum both give me a headache. If you remember, I asked for Wild Turkey or some Chivas."

"Picks said he was going to get you the good stuff," Ark said, "but he couldn't pass up the bargain price on what he got."

"Less than two bucks a bottle," said Picks with obvious pride, as he stuck a wad of chewing tobacco inside his cheek.

I looked up at the two of them standing behind Mossare and pointed a finger at each of their chairs. They sat down dutifully, Ark laying his gradebook to my left.

"Cadet Mossare, go home and relax," I said to him. "I'll see you early Monday morning. Now go."

Mossare gathered his books, pulled himself out of his chair, snapped to attention, and saluted me smartly.

"Thank you, sir," he said softly.

As he left my table to walk to the door, his dreadful Iranian lieutenant blocked his exit. The officer had an inquisitive look, which quickly turned into a disagreeable frown.

I focused my thoughts on Mossare's plight. I was truly worried for him. I should have pondered the next step to take with my Iranian, but my two American students interrupted.

"Lieutenant Amity, sir," Picks broke in. "Captain Military was looking for you."

"And he seemed pissed off about something," Ark said.

"Oh, great. This is going to be one fine lousy day."

"Why would that be, sir?" Picks continued. "How could it be a lousy day? You've got us here."

I looked up at Second Lieutenant Fred Picks recalling as I often did that he was not a normal student. Although Picks was an excellent jet pilot, he earned a degree of infamy in other notable ways. He had unusual habits that turned my stomach. We were both graduates of Oklahoma schools, but while I came from Oklahoma State, Picks went to the University of Oklahoma. No one was sure who was more representative of the state—the real Okie.

Picks chewed tobacco wherever he went—whatever he did. He carried a clear cup half full of tobacco spit everywhere, setting it down under everyone's nose as if it were a cup of coffee. While people turned green, he turned everything around him tobacco brown. I figured that if I ever threw up on him, he would never notice anything different. While friends might sneeze and say, "excuse me," Picks would fart and excuse them. Although his fellow students tried ridicule, it never bothered him. Today was no exception as my students turned from my troubles to each other.

"Hey, Picks," Lieutenant Ark said. "Get that soggy turd out of your mouth!"

"This ain't no turd, man," he drawled in his exaggerated Oklahoma country boy manner. "This here's good quality stuff."

"How did a city boy ever learn to eat that stuff, as you call it?" Ark said.

"Hell, everyone enjoys a chew where I'm from."

"Speak for yourself, Picks." I had no desire to sully my own reputation just because we were both from Oklahoma. "Don't count me in with your crowd. Nobody I know in Oklahoma City carries that dribble around in a cup."

"Picks suffers from diarrhea of the mouth," Ark cracked.

Picks snorted laughter. "Pretty good. I like that… but you guys are missin' the pleasure of a good chew. It's somethin' a man can appreciate… like the services of a good woman."

"Can you imagine Picks kissing some broad?" Ark chuckled. "It would be an act of poor taste."

"It's never stopped me." Picks spat more brown saliva into his clear cup.

"Only at Boy's Town. Right?" I said. I proceeded to put routine marks in Ted Ark's gradebook to log his solo flight.

"You guys can't knock somethin' you've never tried." Picks moved his cup around to add emphasis before pulling the plug out of his mouth and dropping it gently into his collected spit. "There's everythin' you'd ever want… right there across the border."

"Like the clap?" Ark joked.

"Hell, no!" He pulled a cigar out of its clear plastic wrapper and poked it into his mouth. "Those whores are clean. They get checked once a week."

"What if you're there on the seventh day?" I wanted to knock some sense into him.

"I never worry. Besides, the prices are too good. You can find some real bargains out there."

Fred Picks was big on saving money. At mealtimes he hung around tables like a dog at a hamburger stand. He would stumble into the Officers' Club for breakfast each morning and eat for free. He waited for someone to get up from a table, then he pounced on the scraps in the plate, like a starving cur. Migrating to another table he would consume bites of egg, toast, or bacon, then drink any milk or juice available. Finding a coffee cup, he might fill it full of deserted, stale, and cold coffee from numerous tables, then graciously accept refills from the horrified waitresses. Picks became a master at making those around him lose their appetites. It meant more for him to eat.

"If you're really into bargains, why don't you eat dog food?" I handed Ark his gradebook. "You'd save some money that way."

He pondered that suggestion. Then his eyes grew wider, like a lightbulb lighting up in his head. "That's a good thought. I haven't done that since my senior year at OU... Big Fred the Big Red!"

"How did you take a date out to dinner? Take her to the grocery store for a twenty-five-pound bag?" I held my hand out for his gradebook.

He removed his cigar to laugh heartily, exposing twenty-six perfectly straight and stained teeth. He placed in my hand his brown-stained and dog-eared gradebook. It looked like something that came from a restaurant waste bin. Picks was well over six feet tall, heavier than most, wore his hair cut Marine Corps style, and smelled like day-old sweat and stale tobacco. He never smoked a cigar. Instead, he chewed it. Throughout our conversation it became shorter. He used his cigar like a child would a candy cane—sucking and chewing it out of existence. Picks laid the last of the butt on the table and pulled a plug of Red Man Chew out of a pouch in his pocket.

"You ate that cigar, didn't you?" I was in amazement.

"Guess I did." He stuffed his mouth full of tobacco again.

"Why don't you swallow that chew? Then you won't need that cup."

"I can't swallow that, yet," he muttered. "I still get sick. My goal, though, is to fly a whole mission with a plug. So, I'm teachin' myself to eat it. You might say I'm in trainin'. I can't carry a cup in a jet plane, you know."

"No, I suppose you couldn't."

"Oh! Let me show you somethin'." Picks pulled out his wallet. He slipped out a picture of a beautiful blond with a slender, top heavy figure, outfitted in a low-cut, red, thigh-high teddy.

"You seen her before?" Picks slowly waved it before my eyes.

I shook my head. In the month since I became his instructor, nothing anymore surprised me.

"She's an Oklahoma girl."

"Your sister?"

"My fiancée."

I paused briefly in genuine puzzlement.

"You?" I couldn't disguise my horror.

"Why not?"

"You're gross and disgusting! That's why!"

"She's says I drive her wild." He laughed at his own cockiness.

"I would agree with her on part of that." I handed him back his grade-book. "Picks, you drive us all crazy."

Looking down at her picture, it reminded me of my own girl back home. Jane had no intention of either marrying me or even visiting me in Laredo for that matter. I was jealous as hell.

And then out of the corner of my eye, a pilot's silhouette filled the doorway to the A-Flight room.

4

FRED PICKS SPAT ONCE MORE into his clear plastic cup, then got my attention by waving the putrid mess in front of my face.

"Sir," he said, looking alternately at me and at Cadet Mossare. "I think Captain Military wants you."

"I know. I saw him."

There, sure enough, was the C-Flight Commander standing in the doorway in his usual Prussian posture, chin tucked in tightly, eyes sternly penetrating, and hands nervously clenched at his side. Standing at attention, Captain Military offered us a special, yet always unpleasant diversion. Though his real name was not Military, no one called him anything else, not even our squadron commander, Colonel Meneur. It was *not* a compliment. The captain stood so still and straight that his face turned red and began to tremble from the strain. His mustache was never trimmed evenly, which helped make one eye appear more evil than the other. His oily black hair always pushed the limit of regulation length. He wielded his rank over lieutenants like an ax. It would not be long before my own promotion to captain. When that day came, my greatest joy would be in calling him captain but without adding "sir!"

"Yes, sir." I quickly stood and walked over to the doorway. "I can tell someone's in trouble."

"Who flew Alpha two-one-four?" It was meant more as a challenge than a question.

"Let me check the schedule here." I could feel my heart pounding with the knowledge that I had just landed Alpha two-one-four with Cadet Mossare.

"Why? What happened?" I hoped he couldn't tell I was stalling in the hope of gleaning some idea of what direction he would go.

"Some son of a bitch broke out of the traffic pattern at Barfly. He came so close to hitting me that I could read the tail numbers." His voice growled and trembled with rage. He stared straight at me. "And I think I'm talking to the one who did it!"

I swallowed hard, remembering Cadet Mossare's airsickness on himself, the smell of vomit in the cockpit, and my decision to depart the practice landing field at Barfly just as Mossare threw up again, this time on himself and the floor of the airplane. It was an understandable distraction to cause me to forget proper exiting procedures, but, yet, Captain Military had a right to be angry. The fact that he was justified made it even more painful to confess. I had done a stupid thing, which could have caused an accident and possibly a death. I kept thinking that, if I were to collide and kill another pilot, I had made a good choice in Captain Military. The fact remained, though, that it was a near miss. I could not have picked a more despicable character to come so near yet leave still living. Why could it not have been a new instructor or a solo student? At least with them I could ignore the whole thing or, if necessary, blame it on them.

"Am I right?" Military's anger increased. "Did you fly Alpha two-one-four?"

"When was this?" I was nervously attempting to squirm out of his tightening hold on me. "Was that the third period of takeoffs?"

"The fourth." The tone of hate in his voice intensified as did his merciless expression.

I decided to trade my pride for embarrassment. "I'm afraid I'll have to bite the bullet on that one, sir."

He stepped threateningly close. "You should do more than bite the bullet, Lieutenant Amity."

"I'm sorry about that. I...."

"Sorry, hell! You came so close I could read your tail number and count the pimples on your ass. You're not sorry. You're an *idiot!*"

He turned around and marched out of the A-Flight room leaving all of us in an awkward silence. I hated being busted in front of my peers. Even worse was that my three students knew now that I wasn't perfect. Freed got up from his table and walked over to me as I turned my back on the doorway.

"That bastard should be shot," Hal said in his slight Georgia accent. His words had an instant soothing effect. My own anger and humiliation were washed away by those words of defense. I knew I was not alone in my contempt for Military. Many in my squadron expressed the same sentiments. They were always said in humorous terms, but the truth was that Captain Military was a real prick. Captain Military, would have made a good cartoon character. Every one of his personal traits was out of proportion to reality. Captain Military always kept a burr in his underwear to ensure that no one would ever like him. His eyes could cut down the toughest of students on the flightline. The young student pilots would salute and say "Yes, sir," then turn their eyes away in disgust. Everyone must have hated him. He was so cruel that he once threatened to leave his pregnant wife if she had a girl. And so, the stories went. He liked to tell funny jokes to students and then launch verbal attacks on them when they laughed or otherwise lost their military bearing. He was so nasty and hateful he even detested himself.

His father, an old weathered full bird colonel, once announced a surprise visit to the base to visit his son. It was awkward for all of us to watch. There was too much formality, excess military courtesy, and extreme coolness between them. But when the colonel made a suggestion, the captain interpreted it as an order and hopped to.

"I want to fly one of your airplanes." His father's command was granted.

That evening, when they took off, the area controller assigned them, not the regulation areas of east-one through east-eight, but "all of east Texas," to honor Colonel Military, who was the only full colonel airborne within 150 miles. Captain Military was humiliated.

"There seems to be a lack of radio discipline at your base, Captain," his father said after they landed.

Captain Military responded with only a feeble "yes, sir." His father evidently was satisfied with his son's flying skills because after that comment, the colonel said nothing at all. His son seemed pleased.

The year before, when Captain Military arrived at Laredo to start training students, he had been greeted with groans from the other instructors who knew him, such as A-Flight Commander Captain John Alexander. A calm, tall, imposing, curly, blond-headed man in his middle twenties, Alexander knew Captain Military personally.

"We went through pilot training together," Alexander had reminded me. "As a second lieutenant, he would go out of his way to make someone salute him. He would go across the street and half a block down to tell a two-striper he didn't get a salute from him. I swear the closest they ever got to each other was fifty yards. Military made him hold his salute at least thirty seconds before returning it with his own.

"I tell you, there's nothing quite as obnoxious as a butter bar who thinks his rank means something. The worst thing that ever happened to the Air Force, after giving Lieutenant Military an officer's commission, was awarding him pilot's wings. And to add further insult, he FAIP'd to a UPT base as a T-38 IP. Can you imagine him as an instructor pilot in a supersonic trainer?"

Captain Alexander leaned forward with eyes brightening further. With a raised index finger, he indicated a memory he would cherish for years.

"You won't believe what he did then. He was promoted to first lieutenant about the same time as he qualified as an instructor. He used to stop captains who were not pilots and tell them they had to salute him because he wore pilot's wings. The top brass dressed him down for that one rather early in his career. But that didn't stop him. He tried to go down a grade and make fellow first lieutenants salute his wings if they were not pilots. They'd only laugh at him. He never could get it through his head that he was the joke of the base."

Alexander laughed, remembering the grand finale to his tale.

"Logically you'd think he'd get wise and stop there. Wrong! He figured, since he was an instructor in the T-38 and it cost more and went faster, that T-37 IPs should salute him. He went out of his way to walk by the T-37 squadron building, looking for instructors or students. He made the fatal mistake of trying to get one pilot to salute. When he tried it a second time, the T-37 instructor decked him. Laid him flat on his ass right there on the sidewalk."

"Who was it? You remember?" Alexander led me to the punchline. "Man, I'd love to shake that guy's hand."

"Oh, I remember, all right because it hurt like hell." Alexander gave me a wide grin and extended his hand to mine. "I'm the guy who put the lights out on that son of a bitch!"

5

COMING OUT OF THIS PLEASANT daydream, I noticed Freed still staring at me. My recollection of Captain Military had occurred with lightning speed, like those "life flashes before my eyes" near death experiences one reads about. My friend just looked at me and chuckled. I turned in a daze and returned to my table to regroup the shambles of my pride with my students.

I sat back down in front of Second Lieutenant Ted Ark, slumped in his seat, the sweat still dripping down his forehead. His dark green Nomex flightsuit was saturated with a sunny days' worth of perspiration brought on by two flights, each of an hour and a half. A body odor of stale sweat and Old Spice cologne hung about him. His expression was one of happy cockiness. His manner told me my criticisms of his flight skills were welcomed. Ark always hungered to achieve better performance. His sandy short hair was matted down from his flight helmet, making it appear darker than when dry. He sported a coarse afternoon stubble on his chin and cheeks, with a sandy blond mustache halfway to being fully grown. I was amused, as I glanced across the table at this stocky young man, knowing I was in charge of this gorilla and had his future success in my weaker hands.

"What's on tap for you tonight, Ted?"

"Honey's coming down to see me tonight from San Antonio." Ted grinned.

"Who's Honey?"

"You know her," Ark had a gleam in his eye. "You saw her last Friday."

"I did?"

"Here's her calling card." He pulled a well-worn pink card from his wallet and tossed it across the table to me. "Look familiar?"

The pink card was illustrated with a nude woman leaning against a large champagne glass with bubbles bursting above her head. The card read:

Have a party with Honey

or

One of her friends!

Beneath that was a telephone number in San Antonio. I remembered her now. She was a large-breasted woman in her late 20's, perhaps a bit older than me. But she was a looker. She reminded me a lot of Jane, my semi-ex-girlfriend back home. Jane was one of those gifted physical specimens who knew all the right ways to move. Honey, too, was a great talent.

"She stays with me when she works in Laredo," Ted Ark said.

"No kidding?" I was genuinely surprised. "Did this just start?"

"Oh, about four months ago. We met in OTS before I got here."

"How come all you ugly guys get all the beautiful women in town?"

"Hidden talents!" Ark pointed a thumb at his chest. "Besides, I'm a *gringo*. Honey doesn't like to date Beaners."

Beaner was the local *gringo* name for the Chicano residents of south Texas. I never used it. The locals had been too kind to me to think of them any other way than as just plain good old Americans. I was in the smallest of minorities. Even Vic Nuñez called himself a Beaner.

But I was more interested in Ark's calling card from Honey.

"I'm finished here." I stood up and extended my hand to Ark. "Let me see Honey's card again. You going to C-Fight to watch the training films?"

"Yes, sir! Always ready!" Ark said eagerly while handing me Honey's business card.

"Hell, Ark, I'm a *gringo*, too," I said, still staring at the card. "Where did I go wrong?"

"I said already. I've got hidden talents."

"Yeah, yeah. So, I settle for the vicarious thrill of a training flick." I buried my head on the tabletop and pounded a fist. "I'm so lonely!"

"Hell, sir. You're just jealous."

He was right, of course. I was envious of his free love and his charisma and his animal instincts. Although I had a token girlfriend, too, Jane was 700 miles away. Besides, she probably was not loyal. I was shy. What a deadly combination. For the short term, my adventures with women were only on stage or on 16-millimeter film. And this was such a night.

Every other Friday evening was stag movie night at the flightline. The duty for these "training films" rotated on a volunteer basis among all six of the flight rooms. The students of a flight would provide a keg of beer, usually Miller or Bud. Never Pearl. The stag films came from Mexico or one of the Scandinavian countries. On alternate weeks we flew early morning hours and quit in the middle of the afternoon, which seemed as good a time as any to conduct training in macho beer drinking and repetitiously dull dirty movie viewing. Every other week was frequent enough for this rite of manhood. Any more often and we might have thought of ourselves as too perverted. Besides, on alternate weeks, we were watching strippers late Friday at the Officers' Club. It was a duty for every shit hot pilot or wannabe in the Air Force. We usually watched the movies for an hour or so, drank ourselves silly on draft beer, then went home loose and horny to annoy our wives or girlfriends if we had them. I'm sure the women were thrilled.

It was a pleasant diversion for nearly all of us, whether married or not. There were a couple of Jesus freaks who never drank the beer or glanced at the projector screen. There was even a student who, after spending an evening with us squadron perverts, left the proceedings never to return. He later said that he had found Christ. I am glad we could help. For many pilots the Friday night beer and movie ritual had all the trappings of an organized religion, complete with dogma.

The primary ritual centered around the keg of beer. Some aspiring macho instructor would announce to all the students that no one could leave the flight room until the keg floated in the barrel of ice. The apparent object was to get everyone drunk. I never stayed until the keg floated. Even as a student, I wasn't intimidated enough to play the game. But many stayed and later complained. Some instructors even hoped a student would get drunk and pee on the floor. Part of being "shit hot" during this student ritual was to not leave the room for any reason, including urination. Alas, nobody ever peed on the floor, and most instructors left before the keg floated anyway. So only the fools sat around drinking beer, holding their bladders, laughing while in pain, but secretly wishing they could go home and plunder their women.

Captain Military's C-Fight students were hosting this late afternoon. Ark and Picks followed me into the hall where we picked up my IP buddy, Captain Freed.

"Let me get my coffee cup," Freed said in his self-assured movie star voice. He was what every fighter pilot wanted to look like.

"Bring mine." I knew the beer man usually failed to bring an adequate supply of cups to these social functions.

Freed emerged with a coffee mug in each hand. Ark and Picks would have to fend for themselves. I had a lot of pride in my mug. It was a symbol of power and belonging. It identified me as an instructor complete with our squadron patch, appropriately portraying an eagle kicking the young fledglings out of the nest into the air. Below the eagle was printed, "LT AMITY" with "Rob" on the other side. Thus, properly equipped, I led the foursome into the smoke-filled and darkened room. The light from the hall cut across the movie screen as I opened the door to C-Fight.

"Shut the door!" someone said.

"Ragtop weenies aren't welcome!" another said, referring to our A-Flight nickname, Ragtop.

"Blow it out your ear!" I cracked as my three companions stepped in behind me.

The hallway light slowly disappeared as the door closed behind us. I had enough time before the door shut to see that there were no seats or tables left. It was standing room only with only wall space left leaving a vantage where the movie screen lay eighty-five degrees to our line of sight. As my eyes quickly adjusted to the darkness, I counted nearly sixty men crammed inside. There sat Captain Military supervising the projector, while, nearby, the squadron operations officer, Major Cooke, sat slouched in a chair, a cup of beer on his belly and that stupid look on his face that he always seemed to have. Behind those two sat or stood the many instructors and students, eyes transfixed with beer-filled bladders. The movies were now so routine that rarely did they arouse any genuine interest. But to students, the stag flicks in such massive quantities were a new experience. Their comments proved just original enough sometimes to make these sessions entertaining.

"Now let's see an unusual attitude recovery!"

"Now he's in idle!"

"No! He's dropped his landing gear!"

"Look at the size of her flaps!"

"Those aren't flaps! They're speed brakes!"

The jokes soon grew stale. Eventually the crowd viewed in silence, except for the whir of the projector or the hack of a cigarette smoker. I turned away to fill my coffee mug once more with beer.

Abruptly, the projector popped and cracked, then the blasted film broke. The crowd cried a single voice of protest, and the machine stopped.

"Somebody get the lights," Captain Military gruffly ordered.

"Somebody get the projectionist," a brave soul said in the dark as the room moaned in nervous reaction.

Ted Ark, being nearest the switch, turned on the lights. As soon as my dilated eyes could see in the relative brightness, Captain Military's eyes fixed on the four of us. He seemed in a queerly jocular mood. When he spoke, he surprised me even more.

"Hey, you're not in my flight." Military looked at Ark from across the room. "Any students outside my flight can't come in."

The C-Fight crew roared their approval with various boos, whoops, and chuckles.

"Unless they come over and report to me in a military manner," the captain continued.

I laughed along with everyone else. Ark, like all four of us, was at ease with his joking.

"Yeah?" Ark grinned to match Military's own rare expression of amusement. The stag films evidently had worked their magic for once on the son of a bitch. Just when things seemed so pleasant, Military stood up.

"*Yeah?*" He bellowed like a drill sergeant. "I don't think you understand me, Lieutenant!"

"Sir?" Ark stared at him with surprise.

The last chuckles died out as Military stormed over to stare directly into Ark's face.

"If you want to stay in here, you can report to me in a military manner. Otherwise... get out!"

The room went completely silent. Everyone seemed to gawk in amazement. Buddies looked knowingly at each other with bewilderment or disgust or amusement or horror or embarrassment. Ark stepped loosely to attention but gave no other signal of intimidation. Picks, on the other hand, kept himself casually propped against the wall but nearly swallowed his plug of chewing tobacco in nervous reaction. The silence ended, not when Captain Military opened his mouth to yell something, but when Ted Ark spoke first.

"No, sir. Thank you, but I was just leaving."

"What about you, Lieutenant?" Military turned toward Fred Picks.

He jumped off the wall into a position of attention, his breathing abnormally rapid.

"No thanks. I'll stick with him."

"Sir!"

"No thank you, sir."

"You're perfectly willing to stay."

"No, sir. We'll go," Picks repeated.

"Then get out!" he ordered. "Somebody get the lights."

I wanted to leave, too, but stayed to avoid a public expression of protest. When the film finally finished, Freed and I walked out after getting another free beer. To my dismay, Captain Military followed us out the door.

"Lieutenant Amity."

I turned around. "Yes?"

"Were those students from your flight?"

"Sure were."

"You better talk to them about showing some respect."

"I thought you were making a joke," Freed said.

"I was until he opened his mouth."

"I think you fooled all of us," I said. "It's easy not to take any comment seriously in the middle of a stag flick."

"That 'yeah' he gave me was disrespectful. I won't tolerate that. See these bars on my shoulder?" He pointed with his right thumb. "I'm a Captain, United States Air Force, and I expect some discipline. You talk to them."

"I will, but I think they got the point."

"On second thought," he said, pointing a finger toward his office door, "I want to see them first thing Monday morning."

"I'll try, okay?"

"Your ass will be in a sling if they're not, Lieutenant. And another thing that bugs me." He hissed at me and stepped closer until he forced me to inhale his beer-polluted breath. "The first word I want to hear from you starting now is 'sir!' Get your act together, Lieutenant. You got that?"

"Sir." I said it as sedately as I could.

I then clicked the heels of my flight boots and slowly brought up a salute in an affected manner of pseudo-respect.

The captain did an about face without returning my salute and marched back inside to his dirty movie.

His behavior gave me sudden inspiration as Freed and I glanced at each other in disbelief.

"I've got a great idea, Hal." I walked Freed down to the snack bar to buy some supplies.

"You want a banana, Freed?" We stood halfway through the snack bar door.

"Not really." He held up his coffee mug. "I never chased beer with bananas before. Besides, that idiot asshole made me lose my appetite."

"Well, here. Take one anyway." I tossed one to him, then began to peel my own. "I don't care if you eat it. Just give me the peel."

"What the hell are you doing, Amity?"

"Follow me, and I'll show you." I stuffed my mouth full of banana, chewed quickly, and swallowed. "We need to get some strong industrial tape."

As I led him down the hall to the Ragtop flight room, I explained my idea. Freed jumped at the chance for sweet revenge. We found it no problem at all to sneak our way into Captain Military's office while the rest of the squadron sat in the next room drinking beer. Now and then laughter poured out when something appeared on the screen that they found entertaining. Freed stood guard as I entered the pretender's office domain.

The first thing that struck me about the tyrant's office was the egocentrism of the decor. Second Lieutenant Military getting his butter bars, Second Lieutenant Military receiving his pilot wings, First Lieutenant Military receiving his silver bars, and Captain Military receiving his silver tracks. There were pictures of him in front of C-130s, F-4s, T-38s, and T-37s. There were two dozen similar photographs. Although married, his wife's picture was nowhere. His desktop was stark and spotless except for a small picture frame featuring himself in graduation robes. Nothing else of significance was in his office.

Quickly I crawled underneath his desk and taped the banana peels in the two far corners of the knee space, where no one would find them for months. Moving rapidly out from under the desk, I stood up and spied a closeup wall photo of Captain Military saluting with the American flag waving briskly behind him. I tilted this hero picture crooked on the wall, then tiptoed out the door.

"I saw a picture of Mussolini like that once," I whispered to Freed.

"Yes. Even the mustache looks right."

"Let's clear out," I whispered again, panting nervously. "The weekend ought to work miracles."

The whir of the projector was still the only noise in the hall as Freed slowly, silently shut the door behind us.

6

I PEDDLED HOME ON MY ten-speed bicycle to my less than spacious Bachelor Officer Quarters. This was to be one of those lonely Friday nights. Freed had a date. The fighter pilot always had a date. He was charmed that way. The contrast between us was noticeable in the way we approached women. Freed would make things happen, while I waited for them to happen. He quite often lectured me about my lousy technique with women. I was not a very good student. The truth was that I was a sucker for the moment. Sadly, for me in Spanish-speaking Laredo, Texas, which was 86% of the population, there just were not that many moments.

The disparity between Freed and Alexander was just as obvious. Alexander had been my friend for many years. We had roomed together at Oklahoma State University in Stillwater. While Freed made things happen, Alexander always had good things simply fall into his lap. At least that is how it appeared. Unfortunately for me, but not for him, Alexander had married my ex-girlfriend. Suzy fell into his lap, or more precisely, I dumped her there. Alexander was lucky that way.

As I surveyed my quarters upon my return, the flick of the overhead lights reminded me of how dismal my dwelling really was. The Air Force had enforced wattage limits of light bulbs, both for safety and economy. They did not consider the potential expense for psychiatric bills brought on by dim bulb-induced depression.

I managed to cope long enough to write one more futile letter to my girlfriend-in-name-only, Jane. Among many other barren bits of drivel, I wrote, "I still offer you my open invitation to come visit me here. I'll be glad to pay your airfare down."

Who was I kidding? She had said to me we were history but, having nothing else to do in this isolated town, I did many foolish things. It did not help knowing she offered me a counter invitation to come to see her. So, with these visions of hope for a miracle, I spent this Friday evening writing friends, reading, and watching television, which was mostly in Spanish.

Many Air Force pilots dreaded weekends. What was there to do when unable to fly? The reality of our lives forced its way in on these Saturdays and Sundays. If he would ever be honest, the average pilot during the Vietnam War would much rather be somewhere else. But the lure of flying elevated most to the level of a divine addiction. There is a common theme among all pilots, whether addicted to flying or longing to be elsewhere. "It can't get much better than this." For me it never has.

TWO DAYS LATER I SAT lazily in a chair in the officer quarters of John and Suzy talking about dreams of a life beyond this. Their on-base housing was spartan by any measure. Built by the lowest bidder, everything was dingy, colorless, and dark. Lighting was more like a cheap motel than a warm inviting home. I measured cheeriness by how many lamps they purchased to compensate for the meager ceiling fixtures. The Alexanders needed to purchase more. Their furnishings came from across the border in Nuevo Laredo, where furniture makers would create custom pieces for bargain prices. Bright colors were most popular for their customers. Greens, blues, and yellows added some joy to the gloom of the homes officer families lived in.

The service seemed like such a permanent interruption of my aspirations. Nothing would ever be like it was before Vietnam. School plans interrupted. Career dreams permanently altered. Women I thought I loved torn forever from me.

There across from me sitting in a large beanbag chair was Suzy. I had loved her always. This reality depressed me over and over. Somehow, despite being within days of becoming a mother, she made that cheap vinyl mushy beanbag chair look like classy real leather. She sprawled across most of its length, comfortable with my presence. As I looked into her eyes, I sensed she knew it—that I still loved her. After all, in years past I had told her that often. That was before the fashions of today. If Jane had not worn those short skirts, today would have been remarkably different. I still could vividly recall the way Alexander's wife looked eight months before, as the first warm days of spring arrived in Laredo. The surety she had in her own self-image flourished in a way I had never known in college. She had worn a colorful floral halter top tied together seductively at her ribs. Her white polyester bell-bottomed hip-huggers framed long slender legs and a trim waist which caused men to pause breathing. Glancing discretely at her navel, I reminded myself of my major blunder of my college youth. If fashions had been like this on campus back then, I might be her husband today.

"Here, Rob," Alexander said from behind me, interrupting my daydream.

"Thanks." I took a gin and tonic.

Even though John and I were the closest of friends, we kept this fact semi-secret because John was also my boss as flight commander. It had been only by the oddest of circumstances that we had been brought together once again at Laredo Air Force Base.

"Suzy was telling me about this takeover of the mess hall on base," I said.

This was Sunday afternoon, the day before I had to return to flying once more. My frequent nose bleeds were a concern to me. Flying was causing me worry. I held up a copy of the day's Laredo newspaper. It reported that several black airmen at the base had taken over their own mess hall to protest the shortage of black women willing to socialize with them. The article reported that the airmen had to go 150 miles north to San Antonio before they felt welcome—some reference to Mexicans and white women not being very friendly.

"Those guys won't have their careers any longer after this," John said, "assuming they wanted a career to start with."

"What would they do on a remote assignment? They should try going to Incirlik Air Base. See how they get along with the Turks. I hear they're real understanding about their women."

"The real tragedy is that our base commander probably will be gone by Monday morning. He just took over his job. It can't be his fault, but heads will roll."

"You're right. It doesn't seem fair."

Suzy looked at us with frustration in her eyes. She was an extremely compassionate woman.

"Have you thought what would drive those airmen to do such a desperate act? How would you feel, Rob?"

John turned his head to look at me. I met his eyes for an instant. The same thought simultaneously collided in our minds. I burst out in laughter, watching John reflect my amusement, as if I was watching myself in a mirror. The laughter continued uncontrolled for half a minute. I rolled to one side, grabbing my side.

"What's so funny?" Suzy asked over the cackles, half in consternation, half in jest.

I struggled to control my laughter long enough to speak. "The way my love life's been lately, I might as well be a soul brother in this town."

I joined John in a new round of hysterics.

In truth it was hard on everybody who was male and single. If you knew Spanish, you were set. If you did not, your odds of any love life were much better the farther north you traveled from Laredo. In contrast, John and all other married men had an advantage. They brought their women with them. They did not need to know Spanish. I had taken a conversational Spanish course at Laredo Junior College, but I was not very good.

Suzy got up ungracefully from her sofa and stepped closer to lay a hand on my shoulder. She rubbed it in a manner that unwittingly brought back painfully those memories of opportunities messed up. Oh, that Jane. Jane had been my undoing. No, in truth, I had been my own undoing. Maybe Suzy was already in love with John before I met Jane. It just proved again how smart Suzy was and how dumb I had been.

"Do you ever hear from Jane?" John's laughter diminished to a chuckle.

"Are you kidding? I'm afraid she's not much for letter writing. I've asked her to come down to visit me, but she seemed pretty much against it. Something about refusing to associate with anybody contributing to killing people in Vietnam."

"That doesn't seem very fair," Suzy said. "It's not your fault. It's just such a hateful time."

"Well, it could be worse," I said. "She has invited me to visit her on campus. She just refuses to come to a military base."

"Does she think it's a den of evil?" From her expression, it was obvious the question was tongue-in-cheek.

"Probably so."

"She doesn't want to be confused with the facts." John raised his arms in a what-me-worry pose. "She doesn't want to find any humans down here. It might ruin her image of the Air Force as those evil baby bombers."

Suzy admonished her husband. "John, you're talking about Rob's girlfriend. Perhaps he doesn't feel that way."

"No," I said. "John's right. I think Jane was a wasted investment. It's time I left this part of my life and found me someone who will love me back."

I don't think I had ever loved Jane. She was pure raw red-haired animal attraction. I had only a vague clue what love was. Suzy was love. Love lasted. Jane did not.

Suzy surprised us by suddenly sitting up and putting a hand on her swollen belly. "I feel the baby kicking. Here, feel."

She grabbed my hand and pressed it firmly against her swollen belly. The sensation of another living being pushing against my hand was eerie. The baby seemed to sense my presence, pushing back against my fingertips. I shared an odd bond of closeness, as the woman I still loved pushed her hand down on my bare knuckles. This unborn child fathered by my closest friend now pressed up from her belly into my palm.

7

"DAMN GNATS!" CAPTAIN MILITARY CURSED. It was Monday morning as Lieutenants Ark and Picks stood at attention before him.

Alexander and I hid around the corner in hopes of a peak and to pick up the rantings of the C-Fight commander. We had no trouble hearing as his voice echoed through the doorway and out into the halls of the squadron building. His authoritarian harangue began to attract a large crowd, and we spent much of our time waving students out of the way. The instructors collected around the door like dogs around a bitch in heat.

"Sir is what I want from you before anything else comes out of your mouths!" Military swatted away a pair persistent fruit flies. "You got that, men?"

He didn't wait for a reply but proceeded to spew more venom.

"You're just two stupid lieutenants, nothing more! Hell, you can't even fly airplanes, but you don't think your shit stinks, huh?"

Major Cooke joined the group. He just stood there in his curiously witless way, making no effort to flex his rank to break up the gathering.

"When you get to be a captain, I'll leave you alone, but until then...."

The crowd suddenly parted as the squadron commander joined the eavesdropping throng. There was ambivalence among us. No one knew whether to leave or stay. Colonel Meneur had one consistent quality which made him an excellent leader. Although he occasionally could be a horse's ass, he still earned our respect all the same for his even-handedness.

"Okay, men," he ordered in his deep, resonant voice. "Back off from here. Move it!"

"...and I want you to report to me every morning until...."

Colonel Meneur waited for the masses to disperse, then he took a renewed interest in the bombastic, ranting discourse coming from the flight commander's office. He moved commandingly over to the doorway and paused for a brief second facing Captain Military. The colonel was at first puzzled to see the captain flailing his arms around in the air as he ranted. The colonel, only five feet, four inches tall, stood with his hands propped against his stocky body, then swelled his frame to its maximum size, as he further filled his Nomex flightsuit with authority. With his face now the same color as his sandy-red hair, he spoke.

"Captain Military!" He roared thunderously, carrying his order into the hall to its farthest corner. "Shut the *hell* up!"

The shock was immense. Not a sound came from anybody—not from the captain, not from the colonel, not from the mob. The colonel just stood there a moment and glowered into the office as my two students, Ark and Picks, tried in vain to look serious. When Captain Military started to reply, Colonel Meneur turned around and walked quickly back into the hallway toward his own office. He passed us with a scowl that appeared to dare anyone he encountered to show amusement. With little delay, Ark and Picks emerged from Military's office and walked rapidly past the men gathered to listen. They fled more out of fear of laughing than out of fear of the captain. With Colonel Meneur gone in his office, Alexander broke out in muffled laughter. The two lieutenants turned with a nervous smile, then dashed into the Ragtop flight room, laughing uncontrollably.

"Damn those gnats!" Military hollered into the hall again, as a crash sent shards of picture frame glass out the doorway with his screams. He then muttered in a more restrained voice, "How in hell did these bugs get in here?"

I caught a quick glance at Freed, my banana-eating buddy, who returned my look with his own quiet smile.

8

WE RETREATED FROM THE HALLWAY to our flight instructor room, where Alexander pre-briefed us on the day's events, before we came out to greet our waiting, sleepy students. Alexander was the benevolent type when it came to command of a flight. He was as fair and laid back as one could get. Our A-Flight had the first launch of the morning, and he had assigned me the weathership. It was my first time to get that honor. Looking at the schedule, my student, Ted Ark, was in for a treat.

As we entered the main flight room, the students came to attention. I stepped to my table and received the three formal salutes of students Ark, Picks, and Mossare. I was glad to see the latter still among the living. I casually returned their salutes with my own and a smile. We four sat down with the rest after a formal report from the ranking student to Alexander. The students briefed us on the weather, the day's bulletins, and other such forgettable trivia. The weather sounded interesting. With the briefing over, Ark and I quickly slipped out to our aircraft to do our preflight checks in the dark. We promptly found ourselves number one for takeoff.

With engines at full throttle and brakes released, the small Cessna T-37 twin jet began its early Monday morning takeoff roll. The horizon was well defined by the sun's faint glow in the distant east under a thin cloud layer. The runway was still shrouded in darkness. At 65 knots the nose wheel left the runway, and at 90 knots the aircraft became airborne. Holding the horizon on the lower third of the windscreen, it accelerated. Gear up. Flaps up. 500 feet above the ground and 200 knots. We climbed on our way.

"Laredo Departure, Axon two-two, airborne," Ted Ark radioed.

"Roger, Axon two-two, radar contact." The radar controller's voice was tinny. *"Maintain runway heading, report VFR on top."*

"Axon two-two," Ted said to acknowledge.

I looked ahead at the clear early morning sky forecasted to be overcast.

"Ted, do you see any clouds near us?"

"No, sir."

"Well, why don't you tell them we're VFR on top?"

"Laredo Departure, Axon two-two, VFR on top," Ted called without hesitation.

"Axon two-two, roger, report departing frequency."

"Roger," I said. *"Be advised that takeoff leg is now totally VFR. Axon two-two, departing your freq."*

"Axon two-two, roger, good day."

I quickly switched the radio from channel four to channel nine, the Maytime frequency for T-37 aircraft. It was Maytime's responsibility to assign practice areas, monitor the weather, and keep track of each aircraft's position.

"Maytime," I called. *"Axon two-two."*

"Axon two-two, go."

"Roger, takeoff leg is clear. I'll tell you more when I get out to the areas."

"Roger."

Every morning some lucky flier got to takeoff before sunrise to report weather conditions in the practice areas. A student never learned much, but it was always fun for the instructor. We continued to climb, turning eastward. In the distance a large layer of clouds formed.

"Let's make a three-sixty and see what's behind us," I said to Ted.

I cranked the jet into a tight sixty-degree bank turn, bending my head back behind my shoulders to get a better view of the horizon, which now appeared above my canopy. Thick downy clouds rolled in from all directions, like ocean waves in slow motion.

"Looks pretty bad," Ted said.

"Yeah, fairly cruddy." I keyed the radio. *"Maytime, Axon two-two."*

"Axon two-two, go."

"I'm about 12,000 feet, and it looks like Laredo is in a big hole. I'll give you bases and tops in a second."

"Roger, what's the coverage on the clouds?"

"About nine-tenths."

"Copy nine-tenths."

"Sir? Why did you say nine-tenths? It looks more like ten-tenths to me."

I looked at him and started to chuckle, remembering what my own instructor had taught me three years earlier.

"What's the term overcast defined as?"

"Nine-tenths or more coverage." His reply was automatic.

"Okay, Ted, if they ask me to check the bases and the tops of the clouds, how can I do that when it's a solid overcast?"

Ted looked down below us to the heavy layer of clouds that were now passing under us. "I don't know, sir. You can't fly through the clouds."

"So, we find a hole to fly down through, right?"

"Well, that would make us legal, I guess?"

"Ark? Do you see a hole?"

"No, sir."

"What do we do then?"

"I don't know."

I rolled the T-37 inverted and pulled the nose down in a sharp descent. Continuing the roll back upright, I pulled the throttles to idle. We approached the cloud tops heading east like we would for a runway landing.

"You make a hole. You never want to say more than nine-tenths overcast, or they will ask you how you could check cloud layers without breaking VFR rules. It's called CYA, Ark. Cover your ass."

Ted just nodded. The engines were now relatively quiet. The sun was about to peek out from below the horizon, putting a cottony-soft diffuse pink lighting on the cloud tops. We were all alone in the air, not another aircraft within fifty miles.

It was as if the clouds had an altimeter. The tops were uniformly 10,000 feet. As I approached them, I added power to maintain airspeed. The nose began to rise with the extra thrust. We leveled off with the belly just skimming the cloud tops. The ever more brilliant pink cloud layer was like a vast sea. With no land in sight, there were only ocean ripples of flaming red.

"Fantastic," Ted said softly.

"It's beautiful up here, isn't it?"

"It looks like I could get out on it and walk." There was awe in his voice. "It's so smooth and thick. It's beautiful!"

"We'll float along here and enjoy it a minute. It won't happen again soon enough."

The carpet of clouds raced under us, leaving a wake like water under a speed boat. Was this where dead pilots went? If this were heaven, I would never be afraid to die. It reminded me of John Gillespie Magee, Jr.'s line about reaching out and touching the face of God. By golly, God was right here with us.

Gradually the pink clouds went pale into white. The first glaring rays met our eastward glance, breaking forever this once in a lifetime spell of aloneness with the Almighty.

"Let's make us a hole in the clouds and check the bases of these things." I reduced engine thrust. "Besides, Ark, if we were to ever collide with another airplane up here, it would be because we're both trying to go through the same hole. Surely, he won't make his own hole exactly where I'm making mine."

Before going into the undercast, I glued my eyes to the attitude indicator to ensure the plane stayed right with the world. The craft bounced slightly as it first penetrated. We descended 200 feet, 400 feet, 600 feet, and finally 800 feet before breaking out underneath the now gloomy cloud layer.

"*Maytime, Axon two-two,*" I radioed.

"*Go,*" came the short reply.

"*It looks like the layer covers all of the east, north, and south areas. Tops—ten thousand feet. Bases—ninety-two hundred feet. VFR below that.*"

"*What's it like back toward the field?*"

"*It appears you'll be overcast shortly.*"

"*Thanks, Axon two-two. You're assigned east-one. Status is now Dual Only.*"

"*East-one, Axon two-two,*" I said, looking at Ted Ark. "Now, Ted, let's get some work done."

9

INSTRUCTING INSTRUMENT PROCEDURES IS THE meat of flying. It is both the most complex and the most boring. A monkey can learn to fly when provided an adequate quantity of bananas, but a whole plantation would not produce a good instrument monkey. It takes real desire. It is ninety percent of flying military aircraft. If not executed correctly, an actual journey into cloudy and hazardous weather can be deadly.

Ted and I began the dull, repetitious work of perfecting his instrument cross check. He slipped a cardboard hood under the visor of his helmet to blind him from the view of the outside. The object was to concentrate only on the aircraft instruments and gauges. Looking outside was cheating. While Ted glued his eyes on the inside instrument panel, I continually cleared outside the aircraft for other objects. Birds, civilians, and other military aircraft were all potential hazards.

"Okay, Ted, let's descend to 8500 feet on a heading of zero-two-zero and slow us to 160."

Ted reset his J-2 heading indicator so that 020 degrees appeared at the top. He began a slow medium-banked turn of thirty degrees to the right. At the same time, he pulled his power back to sixty percent and started to slow down. When he approached 160 knots the nose dipped slightly, descending us at a constant speed.

Ted had to constantly monitor four necessary gauges in his instrument cross check. The most important was the attitude indicator. Next came the heading indicator and altimeter. With these three the aircraft could be controlled. There was a fourth gauge which determined how quickly control arrived—the airspeed indicator. Ted's basic instrument cross check was theoretically, attitude—heading—attitude—altitude—attitude—airspeed—attitude—then repeated constantly. The worst mistake was to fixate on one or two gauges and forget the others.

"Ted, what's your heading?"

"Oh, hell!" He gently rolled the plane into a turn back to the left. "I only went past it fifteen degrees. That's an improvement."

"I suppose," I said as he rolled the wings level while passing far below 8500 feet.

Ark noticed that after rolling his wings level his rate of descent decreased, and the airspeed slowed down. He started to lower the nose to compensate when the altimeter grabbed his attention.

"Sh... my cross check's not at its peak yet."

"Don't climb back up." I knew that climbing back up would only eat up limited time and fuel. "I want to see a descending level off. Try 7500 feet."

"Yes, sir." I was pleased that somehow he managed to arrive near 7500, 160 knots of airspeed, and a heading of 020 degrees.

"Only took five minutes, a thousand feet, and a hundred pounds of fuel."

"Do you want a level-off check, sir?"

"No. Start a vertical-S alpha, and I'll do the checks. We're running out of time."

Ark set the power on the twin jet engines at ninety-three percent. The craft started a lazy climb at 1000 feet per minute to 8500 feet. Then he descended at the same rate but with the power reduced to maintain a constant 160 knots.

"That's not bad. Close your eyes."

I took the controls from Ted and put the plane in an unusual attitude—nose high, wings level, and nearly stalled out from rapidly decreasing airspeed. With a hood blocking his vision of outside the cockpit, I ordered him to take the controls from me.

"Recover!"

"I've got it!" He opened his eyes to again see what the instruments told him. First he checked his attitude indicator, then slowly added full power while banking the T-37 to 30 degrees. The nose immediately fell below the horizon. Rolling the wings level again, he announced completion of his recovery.

"Okay, Ted. Take your hood off and rest your eyes. I've got the bird."

"You've got it," he said dutifully, taking a deep breath to relieve the tension.

"Look at those clouds down there!" I said in surprise, realizing they had formed below me in a matter of minutes. *"Maytime, this is Axon two-two."*

"Axon two-two, go ahead."

"I see some scattered layers forming below me. It's moving in pretty rapidly."

"What tops, Axon two-two?"

"One minute." I rolled the Tweet over into a dive. Approaching 2000 feet, we hit the tops. *"It's got tops at about twenty-two hundred. Bases appear fairly thick, but it's still clear between here and the home drome."*

"Roger, Axon two-two. We'll have another launch in a few minutes to check out take-off leg. Status is still Dual Only."

"Roger." I put in full power to regain our altitude.

Once back upstairs, I decided it was a good time to have Lieutenant Ark practice the emergency procedure for runaway trim. The trim tabs on the aircraft are used to stabilize the jet's forces on the control stick. I can trim up the aircraft, take my hands off the stick, and maintain any attitude I desire. It is the aircraft version of cruise control on a car. If the trim ever goes too far off a desired position, it takes a great deal of muscle on the stick to maintain aircraft control. I ran the trim on the elevator full nose up then pulled the circuit breaker on the student's trim button to simulate an electrical short, as well as make sure my student could not easily correct the problem. When I had it just right for a simulated emergency, the force on the stick was about forty pounds of pressure toward my stomach.

"Can you take the stick for just a minute?" I tried to be nonchalant.

"Yes, sir, I've got it." He grabbed the controls.

"You've got it," I let go.

The stick slammed Ted's hand between his legs, instantly pitching the nose of the T-37 up at a force of three Gs, three times our body weight. Ark put in full power and banked the plane into a dive. The airspeed rapidly increased, adding heavier backward forces on the stick.

"Now what are you going to do?"

"Is this runaway trim, sir?" Ark was already breathing heavily.

"What do you think?"

Our airspeed continued accelerating, having the same effect on the stick's backward pressure as car speed has on one's hand when held out into the wind.

"What are you going to do?" I asked again. I was puzzled by his response.

His silence was broken only by the staccato sounds of panicky breathing. He let the nose go up to an excessive attitude. We rocketed in altitude by two or three thousand feet before stalling out. Now nose down and still at full power, the plane began to descend at a tremendous rate.

"Are you there, Ted?" I tapped on his helmet.

There was no response.

"Do something!" I said.

He did. He pushed on the throttles for more power. Fortunately, there was none. It was already at 100%. We were now in 45 degrees of bank and excessively nose low. When the airspeed approached 300 knots, I realized the strength required to keep both of our two sticks from snapping back into our stomachs must be enormous. If Ark unexpectedly let go of the stick now, the resulting G force would certainly be enough to break the wings off. I panicked. I quickly pulled the throttles to idle, which he should have done at the first, and coached him out of his mess.

"Let the nose come up nice and easy... so we can slow this mother down!"

His arms were now trembling from strain.

"Sir, you've got it!" He finally let go of the controls completely.

The force was still too much. The stick partially snapped back as I grabbed it. Ted, now slouched from exhaustion, was pushed by the G force even lower in his seat just as I shoved the stick partially forward. His face mask jammed onto the stick, which held firmly between his oxygen mask and his clear helmet visor. He tried to pull loose, but the stick went back with him, pulling the nose of the aircraft up, thus, adding further G force.

This forced his eye socket onto the control stick. Each time he tried to free himself by pulling back, the renewed G force jammed his eye deeper onto the control stick.

"A-a-a-a-a-h-h-h! Help me! Dang! It hurts! A-a-a-a-a-h-h-h!"

"Pull your mask off." I was running the elevator trim back to neutral to relieve the control stick pressure. "Unhook the damned thing!"

"I can't!"

"Unhook it!" The aircraft was now totally out of control in a spiraling dive, quickly gaining speed.

"I can't!" His voice sounded hopeless. He pulled his head back once more. *"A-a-a-a-a-h-h-h!"*

"Grab it! Jerk it!" I ordered. I then reached over and released the bayonet mount, which separated his mask from the right side of his helmet.

I could hear, almost feel, the sigh of relief as Ted snapped free. He raised his head cautiously just as I pulled the newly freed stick back and to the right to recover from the dive. We skimmed over the top layer of clouds, which had risen from 2200 feet to over 5000 feet. The force of my pull up pushed Ark back down, his helmeted head banging against the cockpit instrument panel.

"What happened?" He reconnected his mask after realizing I could not hear him. Again, with mask and mike connected, "What happened?"

"You okay?" I rolled wings level at 8500 feet. He simply nodded. "How in hell did you ever get graded anything but unsatisfactory for runaway trim? For crying out loud!"

"Sir." He spoke in a low, sheepish tone. "I've never done it before."

"Don't give me that crap, Ark! I remember your grade book. I spotted four or five entries for runaway trim. A couple of Unsatisfactories. A couple of Fairs."

"I just know that I've had a lot of IPs fly with me lately." Ark was still out of breath from his ordeal. "They all forgot to have me practice runaway trim. So, after each flight, we pencil flew it."

"What a bunch of crap. That could get you killed. Who the hell flew your last mission?"

"Captain Alexander."

"Ha!" I nearly choked. "Alexander? Holy Cow! I didn't know flight commanders ever screwed up. How's your face?"

"I'm okay, sir. My eye's a little sore. That's all. Say, I'm sorry I screwed up."

I turned the plane to exit the area.

"Next time you get runaway trim, Ted, slow the airspeed. Hell, you must have been holding back two or three hundred pounds on that stick. If you'll just slow to 110 knots, you can run the trim up or down all day and notice very little difference in stick pressure. Okay?"

"Yes, sir."

"Turn to your emergency procedures," I pointed to the checklist strapped to his leg. "Read about runaway trim, page fourteen, while I get us out of here."

"Maytime, Axon two-two, departing east-one," I radioed.

"Roger, Axon two-two." The voice sounded like Colonel Meneur's. *"Be advised. The status is now Standby."*

"Axon two-two."

It sounded like a weather recall was coming. The rush of anticipation gave me goosebumps.

10

WE RAN INTO A SOLID mass of clouds less than one mile from the border of east-one. I keyed the mike.

"Maytime, Axon two-two."

"Go ahead, Axon two-two." It was Colonel Meneur again.

"My VFR route is blocked completely. I'll need to go over to Approach Control for vectors."

"Roger, Axon two-two. Be advised this is a weather recall. Contact Approach Control on channel one-three."

"Channel one-three, Axon two-two." I switched my radio to the new frequency.

"Ted, you ready to get an instrument demonstration?"

He nodded as I pressed the mike button on my throttles.

"Laredo Approach, Axon two-two, eight thousand, five-hundred."

"Axon two-two, roger," a voice that sounded like it came from the inside of a tin can responded. *"Squawk zero-four-zero-zero and ident."*

I changed the digits on the transponder by my knees from 1200 to 0400 and pushed down the spring-loaded IDENTIFY toggle switch.

"Axon two-two, radar contact. Fly heading two-six-zero. Descend to six-thousand."

"Two-six-zero, six-thousand, Axon two-two."

I simultaneously turned to correct my heading and reduced power to sixty percent, both to descend and to slow down my airspeed.

"I'll try to tell you as much of what I'm doing as I can," I said hastily. "Ask any questions you can think of. And you can help me, too. Any time he calls out a heading to us, you reset that heading in the J-2."

"Two-six-zero," Ted said, reaching for the heading indicator.

"Axon two-two, Laredo weather, one-hundred variable, three-hundred overcast, visibility one mile, winds one-five-zero at ten, landing runway one-seven, altimeter two-niner-niner-seven."

"Two-niner-niner-seven, Axon two-two."

"That altimeter setting is the most important item to reset now." I returned to my teaching mode. "If we set that wrong or failed to reset it, we'd sure be sorry—when our altimeter said we were 500 feet above the ground, but we landed on someone's roof."

The first wisps of cloud began passing by the windscreen as we leveled off at 6000 feet.

"As soon as I see us approaching the clouds, I start giving half my attention to the attitude indicator and half to the outside. That way, when there's nothing to see outside, I know what's going on inside, and my eyeballs will be adjusted to working in close quarters."

"Shall I do an Approach to Field Check?"

"Good idea. I might forget it."

"Axon two-two, turn right heading three-five-zero, downwind."

"Three-five-zero, Axon two-two."

"Ted, notice, when he said 'turn right,' I started my right turn even before he gave the exact heading. He wants it done now, not later. If we turn too late, it will foul him up."

"Axon two-two, missed approach instructions: maintain runway heading, climb to two thousand feet, then proceed direct to Laredo VOR. Maintain this frequency."

I madly searched for my ballpoint pen. *"Axon two-two, roger."*

"Quick, Ted. Write that down. No! Damn it. First set 350 on the heading indicator. Okay, now write runway heading, 2000 feet, then direct VOR."

Ark nervously pulled a pencil from his sleeve pocket, then wrote it down on the back page of his checklist.

"Shall I read missed approach back, sir?"

"Is it right?"

"Yes, sir."

"Forget it, then. Just keep it handy."

"Okay, sir."

"Did you hear what they told us the weather was?"

"Three-hundred ceiling?" He was clearly guessing.

"...variable to one-hundred. Why is that important?"

"It's going to matter about how safe we land?"

"Bull! We can't legally land below a 300-foot ceiling in pilot training. If it's lower, we'll have to go missed approach! Our controller may be hinting something else."

"Like what, sir?"

Suddenly, the airplane buffeted as it hit its first solid wall of clouds. From all appearances, the plane was suspended motionless in this homogenous shroud of white. Only the whine of the engines and the steady buffet, caused by variable cloud densities, indicated to us we were actually moving forward at 160 knots.

"What'll we do then about this 'something else' you're talking about?" Ark asked while gawking with amazement at the sea of white clouds we had intentionally entered.

"If we go missed approach, you mean?"

"Yes."

"Oh, we're not going to go missed approach."

"But if the ceiling goes below 300...?"

"I have X-ray eyes that can see through any cloud layer between 100 and 300 feet. Works like a charm every time." I was not about to admit to him that this was my first real weather landing.

"I don't get it, sir."

"Ark, if I see the runway, I'm going to land. Have you checked the fuel?"

Ark gazed a second at the fuel gauge, turned the handle left then right to see what fuel remained in the wing tanks, and finally announced, "The wing tanks are empty."

"Then our center tank fuel is all we have left. It's time to get this mother on the ground the first time." I finally got the point across.

"*Axon two-two, descend to two-thousand, two hundred, ten miles from touchdown.*"

"*Two-thousand, two-hundred, Axon two-two.*"

"We're going to maintain 160 knots until we're headed to the runway and inside ten miles. He should keep us informed of our distance as we go along."

"*Axon two-two, turn left heading two-six-zero, maintain two thousand two hundred feet.*"

"*Two-six-zero, two thousand two hundred, Axon two-two.*"

"Now we're on base leg, ninety degrees off runway heading. We can expect a forty-five-degree dogleg turn shortly. We'll slow to 140."

"*Axon two-two, turn left heading two-one-zero, descend to one thousand seven hundred feet, seven miles from touchdown.*"

I slammed the landing gear handle down. "*Two-one-zero, one thousand seven hundred. Axon two-two.*"

Then the voice over the radio changed to a new controller.

"*Axon two-two, this is your GCA final controller. How do you read?*"

"*Loud and clear, Axon two-two.*"

"*Roger, you're loud and clear, also. You need not acknowledge further transmissions.*" The drag caused by dropping the landing gear was slowing us down. I quickly added power to hold our airspeed at 120 knots. "*Turn left heading one-eight-zero. This will be a precision approach to runway one-seven.*"

"From now on, Ted, keep quiet unless you see the ground or the approach lights." I lowered the flaps to half, compensating with pitch and power for the added lift.

"*On course. Approaching glide slope. Four miles from touchdown. Turn left heading one-seven-zero.*"

I put in a ten-degree bank to correct to the new heading and kept my eyes glued to the four primary instruments. Attitude, altitude, heading, and airspeed were most critical from now on. The controller started an almost continuous flow of information.

"*Left of course. Turn right heading one-seven-two. Three miles from touchdown. Turn further right heading one-seven-four. Now on course. Turn left to one-seven-two. Two and one-half miles from touchdown. Begin descent. On course. On glide slope.*"

I lowered the speed brake and adjusted the power to average a rate of descent on the vertical velocity indicator of 700 to 800 feet per minute. It was too shallow a descent.

"On course. Above glide slope. Adjust rate of descent."

I reduced power on both engines by one percent. The effect was immediate.

"On course. Heading one-seven-two. On glide slope. Heading one-seven-two. On course. On glide slope. On course. One and one-half miles from touchdown. Excellent glide slope."

"Did you hear that!" I said, drowning out for a brief instant the controller. "Excellent glide slope? What about my course? Come on, pal. Say it to me."

"Heading one-seven-two. On course. Excellent glide slope. One mile from touchdown."

"Give my course some credit, chief!" I was yelling now, paying particular attention to my altimeter as we approached the minimum descent altitude of 300 feet. "Where in hell is the ground?"

"One half mile from touchdown. Heading one-seven-two. Excellent course and glide slope. Heading one-seven-two."

"Hear that?" I cheered in triumph. "He said excellent!"

The first patch of ground steadily passed under the right wing as we went below the 300 feet minimum altitude. Just as quickly, the ground vanished in more low clouds. We glided to below 200 feet.

"On course. On glide slope. At decision height. If runway not in sight, execute missed approach." Our altimeter indicated 150 feet above the ground. He was cheating a little bit to help us, too.

Finally, we broke into the clear above the runway.

"Yee haw! Hot damn! We've got this baby on the ground now!"

"Out of sight!" Ted said. "I wouldn't have missed this for anything!"

"Careful now, though." I was more serious. "This last hundred feet is where we earn our flight pay."

I dropped down to the runway, chopped the power, and slowly pulled back on the stick to round out the touchdown. I was barely aware of the GCA controller still talking me down to solid earth.

"GCA, Axon two-two, runway in sight." We hit the ground with a declivitous thud.

"Axon two-two, contact tower on landing roll. Excellent approach, sir. Good day."

"Axon two-two thanks you for your help." My reply sincerely given. Then I went to radio channel one for Tower.

"Did you hear that, Ted? Excellent approach!" I hit his arm. "How about that?"

"Tower, Axon two-two, landing roll."

"Axon two-two, cleared to the ramp."

"Axon two-two, roger."

"How about that? What do you say?"

"That was pretty good, sir."

"Pretty good?" I said mockingly.

"Shit hot, sir!" We continued our taxi to the parking ramp. "That was shit hot!"

11

THE LOW CLOUDS QUICKLY TURNED to fog. It stayed WXOFF the whole week—a total-sock in. As it turned out, I was one of only two pilots to fly that entire week. Still, it had taken its toll. I was glad for the week to rest my sinus condition that got worse with every flight. I was at the stage where after every flight my teeth ached the rest of the day. Only upon waking in the morning would the pain be gone.

This was the beginning of the students' advanced instrument training, which I never liked. It required training the students to do penetration turns, a four to six thousand feet per minute descent from the holding pattern. The rapid descent was over 10,000 feet in about two minutes. It was a killer. As we would begin our drop from altitude, I quickly had to divide my time between the Valsalva maneuver to force air back into my sinuses before they ruptured and getting Ark and Picks to increase their rate of descent. They never seemed to grasp the importance of getting the nose down.

The radar controller would clear us to leave the holding pattern. We were to begin a rapid descent in a predetermined direction away from the navigation beacon called the VOR. The rate of descent was critical. Our approach plates, those three-dimensional roadmaps of the sky, told us to make a 180 degree turn back toward the VOR, as our descent passed through a certain altitude. It was important to keep the rate of the drop at four to six thousand feet per minute or we would be off the radar screen before we reached the critical altitude to make our turn back. No matter how I admonished Ark and Picks to lower the nose, their penetration turns invariably brought them ten miles farther out than they should be. I would look up and see a 3000 feet per minute descent, personally push the nose down for them, then go back to forcing air into my nose. They might achieve 4000 feet per minute but never more. I figured perhaps they were afraid to fall so fast. For whatever reason, they were the worst students I had ever seen in penetration turns.

These instrument maneuvers were not the only assaults the Air Force inflicted upon my sinus condition. Spins were bad enough, but the other event I dreaded was Commander's Call, which without fail occurred anytime weather grounded the squadron. Colonel Meneur liked to smoke. He inspired over half the squadron to join him. Tobacco smoke not only irritated my throat and lungs but caused a swelling of the sinus cavities in my head. The pain was instant. The cigarette smoke of Commander's Call would ground me from flying if the fog did not.

On Tuesday, the fog thickened. I brought a book titled *The Second International Great Paper Airplane Flying Contest.* Our flight spent the whole day turning paper into the numerous airplane designs, which had won different contest categories. There was the paper airplane with the longest duration aloft, the longest distance flown, et cetera. We made them all. It was great to see our country's professional pilots hard at work acting like kids again.

On Wednesday, Freed showed films he brought back from Vietnam of his F-105 Wild Weasel missions. In addition, we checked out a film from the base library of the TV documentary series, Air Power, about the American fighter escorts over Germany in World War II. I was ready to volunteer for the F-4 after seeing those movies. Everyone wanted to be a fighter pilot. Thank goodness we were socked in for the whole week or every formation flight we flew would have degenerated into a dogfight.

That afternoon Alexander called me into his office. He handed me a typewritten paper.

"Rob, read this and see if you think it's any good."

"Ah ha! *Tweet Talk.*" I guessed correctly, referring to John's weekly column in the Laredo Air Force Base newspaper.

"Tell me if the idea works. See if you get it."

I sat back in the chair by his desk, propped his article on my right knee, and began to read.

TWEET TALK
by Capt. John Alexander

Many times, pilots hear their wives complain that they cannot imagine why the flightline draws their men away like magnets. When they do come home, sleep is next to impossible. It seems that all night she wakes up to the cry of "RECOVER!" "I'VE GOT IT!" and "IF YOU THINK I'M GOING TO GIVE YOU MY CALL SIGN, YOU'RE CRAZY!" By morning hubby gets out of bed sweaty and exhausted.

Here is a tip for the wives that might bring togetherness back into flying. Make yourself into the cockpit controls. Your feet are the rudder pedals, your right forearm the throttles, and your left forearm the stick. You must both sit on the floor facing each other. Now go through a traffic pattern stall series or maybe some acro. Also, if you surprise him with runaway trim, it can become very romantic. Over the top maneuvers are strictly prohibited.

WARNING: Inadvertent or intentional spin recoveries could cause serious bodily injury.

Tonight, when the fly boy drags home after dark, give him a good supper then make his eyes pop out when you say, "KICK YOUR TIRE AND LIGHT MY FIRE!"

"Hell, John." I sent the article spinning onto his desk. "That's great! Being a miserable bachelor, it's hard for me to connect, but I'm sure all you married types can relate. You and Suzy do tests of your columns, or is this just BS you pulled out of your ass?"

"Sure we've done it." John acted defensive. "We test market all my articles."

"That wouldn't leave you much time to write."

"Hey, she's pregnant. There's plenty of time, now." John had an exasperated grin.

We both laughed. I couldn't speak for John, but a woman swollen with child was not one of my turn-ons. On the other hand, she was still good looking for a pregnant woman.

"You're lucky. You know that, don't you?"

John laughed. "What's that mean?"

"I mean, you seem to be perfect for each other, John. It's obvious you have the hots for each other. You finish each other's sentences. Things like that. It's really nauseating."

"Well, Rob, you'll be happy to know that having this baby of ours will probably screw up the whole thing."

"What a pair."

"What a trio, you mean," Alexander corrected.

"Trio? What? You two and the baby?"

"No, I mean the three of us college freaks." John laughed. "Don't forget, you introduced us."

"You mean you *stole* her from me."

"I think she might have just simply volunteered."

"Hell. Volunteer? She had no choice." I chuckled. "I dumped her, like a fool. It probably wouldn't have mattered. She had fallen in love with you the moment you two first met."

"I think Suzy saw you and me as just two peas in a pod. The only difference was that I was the marrying kind. You weren't."

"Well, that's changed. It's lonely as hell here. I'd poke a snake if it'd have me." I paused. "Oh, I think she made the right move. After two years of dating me, Suzy knew better than to take a chance on good old Rob."

"She's the reason I don't take chances. I want to be able to kiss her hello in the evenings."

John was now smiling. He always did when he talked about Suzy. The two had been married nearly four years. I still remembered with shock their announcement to me that they were getting married right after John got out of Officer Training School. That was only a few months away. They wanted me to be their Best Man. It had been only three months since I had dumped Suzy for Jane. Yes, with me out of the equation, it was love from day one. Years later, they still made goo-goo eyes at each other. At parties they rarely stayed separate for long. They were fine friends of mine when separate but were unequalled as my companions when together. Their personalities complemented each other's. I found it impossible to imagine them as two separate people. It was natural to think of "Suzy and John" as a single word, while odd to say one name only. I meant it when I joked that I wished there were another woman as wonderful, attractive, and loving as was Suzy. What a fool I had been. It was not as much the woman as the relationship that I envied. Why they enjoyed me as a single man, I could not say? Maybe, unlike most of their associates at Laredo, I understood the very special nature of their partnership.

At John's first Ragtop party, after he was promoted to flight commander, he challenged everybody, in one of those childishly enjoyable party games, to get with partners and imitate their favorite mating animal. But, of course, everyone was too inhibited to demonstrate. That was exactly what Suzy and John hoped would happen. For the next hour they kept us intermittently laughing and gasping for air as they demonstrated the different mating techniques of gorillas, paramecia, sea cucumbers, gouramis, elephants, dinosaurs, and barnacles. They performed them all with the precision of a ballet. Their whole sequence came with a maximum of sound effects at critical moments with exaggerated movements. It was funny to me because their abandon at parties contrasted completely with John's caution at work.

I ended my momentary daydream. "Look, pal, you're becoming obsessed with this taking chances BS. You know, that's what's killing lots of the GIs in Vietnam. They get too careful."

John waved his right hand. "Yeah, yeah. I know all that. You'd worry, too, if you had a pregnant wife due to deliver this week. Go get one of your own, and then you'll understand."

"I don't think either one of us likes to fly anymore. Your caution. My sinuses."

"That's not true… but every time I'm assigned a flight my heart moves up into my throat."

"It must be love."

"If I could line you up with a woman, you'd know more how I feel."

"Hell, John, you've always been cautious of everything. You wore that blasted seat belt in your car all during college. You made me wear one when I rode with you. Only you wore seat belts in college. Nobody else! If they had 'em, you'd wear a seat belt to ride a horse!"

John's cheeks blushed. "But I'm alive. Whatever I did must have worked."

"You're right, I know, but lighten up. Relax. Try to enjoy flying again. They're paying you to do this. What more expensive hobby do you want for free?"

"Okay, I know." John stepped back outside his office. "I'll try to have more fun. You win."

As if by afterthought, he halted his exit, paused, and turned back to me.

"Just promise me something?" There was a nervous chuckle in his voice.

"What?"

"If I ever become a crispy critter, don't let her see me. I might not be having a good day."

"Who? Suzy?" What an odd time to chuckle?

"If I buy the farm, don't let her see me."

"What kind of idiot talk is this?" I tried to be a little sarcastic. "You have a damn death wish!"

"Just random thoughts from a paranoid pilot, okay?" He was not joking.

"Sure, John. Whatever you say."

He seemed a little flustered. "Oh, forget it."

"What you need is a wild party."

He laughed. "Good idea, Rob. I'm going home to my pregnant wife."

With a wave he stepped out of his office into the flight room. A paper airplane zoomed high over his head.

12

WEDNESDAY CAME AND WENT. I woke up in the early morning to the same weather. I peddled my ten-speed bicycle to work in the dark before the clock read 0500 hours. It was good to breathe the air of early morning. Predawn Laredo always had the faint smell of tortillas frying in a cast-iron skillet along my route. It made me hungry by the time I walked in the door of the squadron building.

I charged down to the snack bar to get a bachelor's breakfast of a banana and Dr. Pepper. I carried it down to Ragtop Flight where the early morning chatter had gotten unusually loud.

"Okay, you guys," Freed casually announced on this foggy Thursday morning, holding a poster marked off into grids. "Put your bucks here. Right here."

On the wall behind him was a large replica of a class patch with two copulating cougars and the caption, "We get ours." How appropriate.

Freed proceeded to tape on the wall by his desk a rather large chart with neatly drawn lines formed into forty-eight squares under the words, "Alexander's Baby Pool." For the price of a dollar we all had the chance to guess the time of birth of Suzy's and John's baby. Hal had designated each square as a thirty-minute time block from 0030 hours to 2400 hours. At the bottom of the chart Freed had clarified that a time selection also included the twenty-nine minutes that preceded. His own name appeared in the first time square of 0030 hours.

Alexander threw in a couple of dollars, penning his name in the blocks. I did the same. The best time blocks went rapidly. When Hal asked Colonel Meneur to participate, our squadron commander complained about the lousy choices left. He then bought one for himself and one for his blank-faced operations officer, Major Cooke.

The colonel gave us a wry smile. "He'll pay me for it. He just doesn't know it yet."

The carnival atmosphere prevailed throughout the day, with Freed spending most of the time soliciting further investors from the hallway. The thick morning fog failed to lift, so by 10:00 a.m., the flight status board lit up *"CANCELLED."* Alexander chalked on the board in large letters *"WXOFF."* The whole room cheered.

WOXOFF days were spent normally in mindless amusements. We had viewed the motivational and training films. We had made paper airplanes by the scores. We had even resorted in desperation to instructing students on flying procedures. These pursuits continued until instructors excused students or the last takeoff time of the second period went beyond thirty minutes. At noon, Colonel Meneur decided it was a good day to talk to his instructors and staff. At lunch time the squadron was usually full of both the morning and afternoon shifts.

"Clear out the room!" Alexander announced in a hurried tone. "We're going to have Commander's Call in here in twenty minutes! Students! Scram!"

"Hell! He's a week early," Freed said in a stage whisper.

The flight scheduling officer, Captain Victorio Nuñez, glanced my way.

"Rob?" Vic said in his Texican accent around the heads of the exiting students and scrambling instructors. "Shall I hold you back tomorrow?"

I nodded my head affirmatively, feeling both dread and disgust. I then watched as the slim, angular-faced Chicano rubbed out a couple of aircraft numbers written in grease pencil on the clear, plastic board under my name. In its place Vic wrote the letters *DNIF,* which stood for Duty Not Including Flying. This was a new designation replacing NFDS, for Non-Flying Duty Status. Why the Air Force needed to change one term for another, none of us ever learned. Maybe it was their attempt to contribute to the inanely growing list of changes in the name of progress. But, whatever the acronym, it meant the same to me—*GROUNDED!*

Soon, instructors from other flights came in, a few bringing their own chairs. A majority simply brought their cigarettes and coffee. Before Colonel Meneur arrived, Ragtop Flight contained nearly seventy men. The room's air became increasingly stale. A single open door served as a vent for the cloud of man-sweat. Through this humid haze, I noticed someone had fortunately remembered to unhook the telephone receiver. The telephone would dare not ring while the colonel was present. Staff Sergeant Cervantes, our squadron's First Sergeant, stood at the door awaiting Meneur's arrival. The sergeant was a short man with a heavy physique and a pencil-thin mustache who had successfully managed to remain in Laredo throughout his entire Air Force career. A man of both efficiency and cunning, he not only ran the Colonel's business, but worked late hours most nights as a bartender at the Officer's Club. The colonel ran his own show. He could probably have run the squadron by himself. He was that dynamic. Yet, his first sergeant was worth his weight in gold.

When the last few officers scurried into the A-Flight room, we knew the commander was on his way. Many personnel began madly pulling out their smoking materials.

"Squadron! Ten-*hut!*" Major Cooke barked to the group assembled.

We quickly stood as Colonel Meneur entered. He seemed to part the stale air as he strode to the lectern facing the assembled officers. He jauntily scanned the room of pilots with a toothy smile.

"Sit down, gentlemen," the colonel ordered through the haze. With no pause, we all did what he said. The First Sergeant shut the Ragtop flight room door securely behind him, thus, trapping all the remaining stale air for the rest of us to breathe.

The short, curt, sandy-haired commander glanced smilingly once more around the room with a self confidence that left no doubt who was in charge. The man could strike terror in the heart of anyone, yet, strangely enough, because of his outlandish honesty, everybody greatly respected him and liked him as a person. He had seen war and was battle-toughened, but he also exhibited a compassion that we knew was honest. Meneur could be trusted at his word.

"I'm glad you all could make it," the colonel began. "I also realize you had no choice. Today is a weather day. We like to take advantage of such things."

Colonel Meneur reached into his flightsuit breast pocket to pull out his pack of cigarettes. Taking one out, he tapped it filter down on the podium and put it in his mouth. Captain Military stepped forward with his flaming lighter. To his other titles I added, "Ass Kisser." I could almost see the brown ring around the C-Fight commander's neck. The real misfortune was that Meneur's cigarette was the catalyst for over half of the officers to light their own. The room's door was still closed. No venting was possible as the colonel began his ramble. The smoke became increasingly thick, obscuring his view of us through the haze. I was totally IFR.

The main function of a commander's call was not to give out new information but to reassure the personnel that nothing had really changed. These meetings accomplished very little, except to enable the colonel to give his rambling, sometimes enjoyable and humorous, slow-paced discourses on nothing of any consequence. The squadron may not have enjoyed it, but the commander reveled in it.

"One bit of news I want to share with you, in case you men are not aware of it, yet. There is a promotion board list coming out soon. I expect many of you senior captains should be interested. So, if you are going to screw up, now is not the time."

Muffled laughter amplified the room. Pilots turned their heads to each other, checking their fellow airmen for captain's bars. There was less than a handful of captains eligible for promotion to major in the room. Perhaps someone would get a below the zone promotion, an earlier than eligible step up. I was sure someone in the room was first to realize that Captain Military could be among the aspirants. The laughter in the room soon turned to the universal body language for *WHAT?* No one said anything, but a pall of gloom joined the tobacco smoke to envelop me.

Oh, what a depressing day it would be.

It was a great honor to be promoted before the normal date for eligibility.

Colonel Meneur had experienced such an honor himself when he received two promotions in less than a year and a half to become a full bird colonel. But this? The system was definitely flawed if my greatest fear was realized.

The commander, maybe sharing our anxiety, quickly rambled on to other subjects. In the corner a pilot bent down to pick up a slip of paper that Sergeant Cervantes was slowly sliding under the door. He looked at it, then cautiously carried it over to our commander. Colonel Meneur took the paper with some irritation, then read it and smiled.

"Captain Alexander!" he said in a louder tone. "I just got a note here that says your wife is at the hospital. She's gone into labor. If you'd like, you can go down there now. I normally would not allow this, but I see that it's getting near the time slot I picked out for your baby pool. I'm sure you'll honestly report the exact time of birth, so I can collect my money. Okay, John. Get out of here. *Now!*"

John snapped to attention at that order, saluting smartly.

"Thank you, sir. I'll give everyone a full report."

"Not all the gory details, John." Colonel Meneur returned the salute. "Just the time."

The group laughed boisterously as John left the room trailing a cloud of smoke. It was the first time to my knowledge that anyone had ever been excused from a Commander's Call. One thing I liked about Colonel Meneur. He knew the rules. He knew when to break them. Above all, common sense prevailed over military logic.

As Meneur continued to discuss something else of minor significance, the cigarette smoke continued to grow thicker. With my eyes watering, the commander stood veiled in a thick, dirty, white cloud. My own breathing became labored. I dwelled on the realization that a smoke-filled room was the equivalent of smoking several cigarettes myself. I grew more hopeful each time a smoker inhaled, hoping somehow, if they took more drags, they would filter the filth first through their own lungs before it reached mine. Already the pain in my sinuses began to throb behind both eyes and my upper jaw teeth. The sensation was certainly not new to me. I experienced similar pain after each flight. Whether it was a rapid change in air pressure or some minute object floating through the air, it never failed to attack my sinuses. For sure, I would not be flying tomorrow. It would have been so nice if I could have routinely taken some sinus medication, but rules banned the mixing of medicine of any kind with flight operations. It was common practice for pilots to fly with a hangover but never with an aspirin.

When Colonel Meneur finally ended his monologue and exited the flight room, I got my chance to gasp my way out into the hallway for a breath of fresh air. I headed for the snack bar, glancing over my shoulder to see the thick cloud of smoke slowly oozing out of Ragtop Flight. It was madness to subject a person to such a torture, yet, it seemed I was the only one who was ever affected.

"Damn this smoke," I said to Vic Nuñez as we entered the snack bar. "I don't understand why they don't ban that. The colonel doesn't realize what he's doing to me."

"It's still not as bad as the thought of Military as a major," Nuñez said, confirming my own thoughts of the C-Fight commander. "Can't Meneur prevent that?"

"True...." I agreed before being interrupted from over my shoulder.

"Prevent *what?*"

Turning around, I met face to face with the infamous Captain Military with a smile on his face, a cigarette in his mouth, and a coffee cup in his hand.

"Cigarette smoke." Nuñez knew the routine for me and cigarette smoke before I could say anything.

"Amity, are you bitching about that again?" Military gave me a gritted-teeth smile. "Smoker or not, you're a damn wimp if you can't take that for an hour."

"Well, what are your odds of promotion, Captain Military?" I tried to divert his insult. "I know you want to be promoted in the worst way."

There was a brief icy stare before he added, "I'd like to get hold of you someday. What I could do to you if you were in my flight instead of your buddy, Alexander's?"

"You might get the chance, I guess, if John gets a major slot. You could take his place."

Captain Military glared at me without saying another word. It was like he was playing the game called, *He who speaks next loses.* What silly games we played. Finally, he took a fresh cigarette, a full cup of coffee, and his obnoxious self into the hallway.

13

I PICKED UP A DR. Pepper and a bag of Fritos then headed back to A-Flight where I still had to take advantage of the spare time the weather had afforded me. I milled about in the hall as long as I could to let the last traces of cigarette smoke clear out of Ragtop Flight.

As the Ragtop gradebooks officer, it was my duty to check all gradebooks filled out by the other instructors. I made sure that they graded their students, not according to how well they performed, but according to how well instructors followed the Air Force mandates for each stage of training. For the next two hours I sat down with my bottle of Clorox, bleaching out grades of fair or better where the regulations said an unsatisfactory should be. The only local regulation we instituted was a requirement that all gradebooks had to be marked in water soluble felt-tip pens. Otherwise, the bleach would not work. If everybody played the game correctly, I could obliterate any hint that the grades were tampered with. On a few occasions, a grade would be altered so many times that I would burn a hole through the grade sheet. If that happened, or if the instructor failed to use non-water-soluble ink, the IP got to redo the entire sheet. It never mattered if the student could fly the T-37 or not if his gradebook looked correct. No wonder Lieutenant Ark was totally ignorant of handling runaway trim.

I completed that absurd job and cleared off my table to end the day. Freed walked past me to the door to get a note that Sergeant Cervantes held out from the hallway. The First Sergeant had a grin as big as his head. That always meant bad news for one of us. Freed read the note, frowned, then called two names.

"Wise! Amity! Front and center! You each have an important mission to perform."

My heart sank. Skinny, hyperactive Wise turned with apprehension.

"What?" We both asked at the same time.

"Captain Wise," Freed said. "Report to the gym for a no-notice piss eval!"

"Bullcrap!" Wise said in disgust. "This is *twice* now!"

The dreaded no notice piss eval. The greatest fear I had in my military career. This was even worse than my fear of crashing or of getting lost VFR and calling for radar vectors to get home. This was serious. I did not worry about drugs in my urine. I had never done any of that stuff. It was the personal humiliation of someone watching me while I tried to pee. It would be like a reenactment of a scene out of the movie, Alice's Restaurant, where Arlo Guthrie walked around asking other draft recruits for some extra urine.

"Robert Amity!" Freed said. My stomach came up to my throat. "Report to the Officer's Club for a drink."

Boy, was I a changed man? My life had just passed before my eyes. All because some poor bastard, other than me, had to go piss for his country.

"You're a lucky bastard," Wise said. "I outrank you. You go in my place."

"Hey, I'm sorry, man, but Captain Freed ordered my ass to the bar."

Being late in the afternoon, I debated whether to go straight to the bar or to proceed directly to the hospital to see if John and Suzy were parents yet. I watched poor Wise shuffle out into the hallway to go donate to his country's cause.

"Hal, I'm going to stop by to see the Alexanders first," I said, feeling awkward talking about going to see someone else's wife deliver a baby. "Why don't I meet you there in the club in about an hour?"

"I'll be there if there are any women left."

I knew he was not kidding. I put on a lightweight flight jacket over my flightsuit, stepped outside to my ten-speed bicycle, then peddled the few short blocks to the base hospital. I expected a delivery to occur any moment. Following the cement path to the hospital front entrance, the date palms lined my way. It was a too familiar journey. For a southwestern desert region, palm trees still seemed out of place to me. For that matter, so did the fog.

Passing through the lobby, I headed to the far waiting room of the OB-GYN ward where I found my friend, John, calmly sitting, immersed in a novel, unaware of my arrival. I tapped the back of the large paperback, sending my flight commander stiff with a startled jerk.

"Oh, Rob." He sighed, then chuckled. "It's you. You caught me in deep concentration here."

"How's Suzy?"

"She's dilated to four—whatever *that* means. The doctor thinks it will be an hour or two longer before the big push."

"So how can you sit reading so cool, calm, and collected at a time like this?" I took the book from his hand, being careful not to lose his place. "*A Farewell to Arms* by Hemingway, eh?"

"Yeah, and I just finished reading the part where the heroine bleeds to death while giving birth." Amazingly, there was amusement in his voice.

"Good grief. You've got great timing. You need to read *Bambi*."

"Even Bambi's mother got killed in that one."

"You're just a damned pessimist. If you don't come up with bad thoughts, the bad thoughts come to you. This book... bleeding to death? Come on!"

"Oh, I'm not really a pessimist." Alexander took his book back from me. "I figure, if you expect the worst at all times, you can feel good about being disappointed."

"I think this childbirth thing has affected your brain, Alexander."

"Quite possibly so. As it is, I feel lucky today!"

"Good."

"By the way... what time slots did you pick for the baby pool?"

"How about 0130 and 1700 hours?" Then it hit me. "I hope the morning slot is no good, but 1700 hours is pretty damned close."

John looked at his watch. "That's an hour from now. Hell, I'll go tell Suzy to hold up!"

"What?" I was in disbelief. "You're going to do *what?*"

"Nothing special. You just wait here."

Before I could protest, Alexander was off down the hall. As I cautiously looked where he headed, John met the obstetrician, Dr. Collins, as he stepped out of the labor room. He was a bit overweight, probably a former clumsy, six-foot, football lineman for some losing high school team. Though he slouched, even from a distance I could tell he was thoroughly enjoying his work. They talked a moment, then both entered a room together. For the first time I realized there were several women in various stages of labor if the different quality of moans was any measure. John came out of the room by himself and motioned to me. I reluctantly walked straight ahead down the hallway, afraid I would make eye contact with a woman in labor. Rumor had it that all women briefly hated men in these circumstances.

"Come here." John gave a come-hither motion of his hand. "It's all set."

"What's all set?" I approached him with a sick and suspicious feeling in the pit of my stomach.

"Suzy's not going to drop her load until after five o'clock. Doc Collins said he'll guarantee it for a share of the pot!"

"What? A share of the pot?" Then I started thinking about this prospect. "How *much* of the pot?"

"A bottle of good bourbon. Wild Turkey, maybe."

"I can't believe this. What's Suzy say?"

"Doc Collins said it's quite easy to do, the way her labor is progressing. Also, right now, I think this is the only part of this whole event Suzy has viewed with amusement."

"What if she holds back too long?"

"I asked Doc the same thing. He said to me, they didn't board certify him in OB-GYN for nothing!"

"This is just crazy enough to work."

"Our criminal minds at work, just like back in college." John squirmed with anticipation. "Well, I'm going back in there with Suzy. Stick around, okay?"

I walked back to the waiting room, hoping no one would ask what an unmarried pilot was doing by the delivery room. I was out of place, embarrassed but greedy.

So, I stayed.

The minutes dragged coming up to five o'clock. Suzy and John were still in the labor room. That meant, I learned later, that birth was not eminent. The pace of my heart and the passing minutes accelerated as one after 1631 hours came into my baby pool time block. Finally, ten minutes into the block, Suzy's gurney rolled out with an entourage of green-clad personnel in tow heading for the delivery room.

John spoke through his mask to me. "Doc said we've got plenty of time."

As they pushed through the silver swinging doors, John gave me a thumbs up, then stopped abruptly.

"Hey, Doc," Alexander said, looking alternately at me, Doc Collins, and something I couldn't see inside the delivery room. "That clock is twelve minutes slow. Don't go by that or we might miss the slot."

"Ah, no sweat," Doc Collins said calmly, pointing inside at the wall clock. "If we miss the real time, we'll make that our official clock."

The doors shut me off from their conversation. I stood uncomfortably in the hall as near to the delivery room as I could without arousing the ire of some battle-hardened nurse. Occasionally, there was laughter or the doctor's order to push. In five minutes, it was all over. A nurse stuck her head outside, dropping her face mask under her chin.

"Doc Collins says he would like Wild Turkey." She smiled. "It's a boy."

"Thanks," I said, then mustered my courage to ask. "Do you have an official time?"

"Are you a relative?"

"No, just a co-conspirator."

She stepped back into the delivery room. "What's the official time of birth?"

Doc Collins cheerfully called through the silver doors. "Fourteen minutes before five!"

"Sean Robert Alexander!" John said to me from inside.

They had named the baby with my name in the middle. The little squirt had just made his Uncle Rob some bucks. Wanting to be honest, though, I checked my own watch. Even by using their "official" clock, this was a legitimate win.

I turned to the nurse. "Everything okay, then?"

"He has all his fingers and toes and nothing extra that shouldn't be there."

"Tell the parents I'm leaving them alone now."

She nodded, then slipped back inside. I walked back through the hospital lobby and out into the now dark night's fog. Mounting my bicycle, I peddled toward the Officer's Club to join Freed, until my head, jarred by the tires on the pavement, could take it no longer. I concluded this was not a night to hit the sauce. Instead, I got off and walked my bike in a new direction the rest of the way home to my quarters. The combination of the fog and the cigarette smoke from Commander's Call had joined to make my eyes ache and my teeth throb in discomfort. From experience I knew that my painful sinus condition would only abate after a night of sleep.

14

I SLEPT FITFULLY DURING THE night. When the alarm clock went off the next morning, my head was still painful as I raised it off the pillow. A steamy shower helped relieve most of the discomfort, yet it would never completely go away. I moved a bit slower getting dressed. The increased sinus pressure from bending over to tie my flight boots was an acute reminder I was not well. Soon I was outside unlocking the chain anchoring my ten-speed.

Peddling in the dark to the flightline, I was strictly on instruments, again because of fog. I knew already we would not fly this Friday either. The jarring tires on the pavement reminded me that my sinuses were still painfully sensitive from yesterday afternoon's smoke-filled Commander's Call. The first thing I did when I arrived was write *"SICK CALL"* on the flight scheduling board by my name for the 8:00 a.m. flying slot.

I hoped I could claim my baby pool winnings from Freed before anyone was caffeinated enough to ask questions. It was futile. Upon entering the small private instructor's room adjacent to the A-Flight room, I interrupted a tall tale our resident hippie was telling. All the IPs met me with jeers and boos. John, sitting at the head of the conference table, had already told them.

"Here you go partner," Freed said, slapping the money into my hand. "Thirty-six for you. Twelve for the baby." He stretched across the table to Alexander to give him the cash.

"Thanks."

"That's just enough to buy us a keg of beer," Jim Starchweather said, interrupting one of his endless stories.

Captain Jim Starchweather would probably have preferred drugs. At least that is what he wanted us to think. As the squadron hippie, Starch relished the notoriety of being odd. His blond hair never was regulation length. No one ever asked him to get a haircut, while Colonel Meneur was forever asking me, "Rob, when does the barbershop close?"

I never understood why Starch was lucky enough to escape such scrutiny.

One would think Starch was on some chemical downer to hear him talk. He slurred his words. His brain seemed scrambled. Even when Starch was comprehensible, his ideas were demented.

"When I was in Nam flying C-7s, I did a barrel roll on initial. It scared the hell out of my passengers." He sat laughing, slouched in a chair, his long bangs nearly hiding his blue eyes.

"You're lucky you still have your wings," Wise said.

"Who gives a damn? In Nam, nobody else gives a damn. You know, I really wish I was back there now. It'd be a hell of a lot more lax than this place."

"At least you don't get shot at here," Freed said.

"Who really cares about bullets? At least you shoot back at 'em in Nam."

This was a new side of him. "You seem more like the peace and love type to me, Starch. Not the shoot 'em up type."

"I found out I liked to hunt," Starch said. "That's what our government wants. Wipe out those gook bastards."

There was a chuckle around the conference table as Starch went on.

"Gooks, man, ain't human. And they let you shoot 'em. But back here, you can't shoot the enemy. They won't let you. I can't shoot Gooks. I can't shoot Beaners. I can't shoot draft dodgers. Hell, I'll go back anytime they want to send me."

"Don't send me back," Freed said quietly, almost to himself.

Starch went on, "I used to give the wheel to my copilot, while we were down low, and I'd pump rounds from my thirty-eight at anything below. Now that was *real* hunting."

It shocked me to imagine that Starch the Hippie relished such sentiments. Or had I figured out how his mind really worked? Barrel rolls with passengers, bullets for Gooks, beer, and drugs were like many topics of returning Vietnam veterans. Many stories were simply variations of the same plot. Often the stories were identical with only the characters changing. Somebody's brother did this. Another's instructor's roommate did that. A student's fraternity brother's sister whose husband had done both this and that. It was always secondhand information or a personal testament to an unwitnessed event.

Only Wise could back up his claims to a true and exciting story. Captain Wise was a Vietnam survivor, not once, but twice ejecting from his F-4 Phantoms. Both times his co-pilots died. Both times Wise should have, too. The first month of his Vietnam tour, after sustaining battle damage, he punched out on his landing approach at less than 200 feet. Wise's parachute nearly got sucked into the resulting fire ball with a magnetic pull reminiscent of a moth's fatal attraction to a campfire. He suffered no serious injuries, except for a little heat burn and the heart-felt loss of a close friend. Nine months later Wise's fighter jet took another hit. It was night. Cockpit lights were inoperable. There was no horizon. He felt the Phantom hit, then ejected after the aircraft bounced off the treetops. He never talked about his two dead buddies. He kept his feelings in his own private world, cloaked in a swagger of words about cheating death. Both times his life hung on a split-second decision to pull the curtain down to rocket him out of the cockpit, just before certain death. Hyperactive Wise owed his own life to his light weight and a nervous twitch. As best as I could tell, what he said was true. To back up his claim, Wise put pictures of the events on his living room wall behind a converted armchair—his F-4 Phantom ejection seat. Nobody else ever quite bested his story.

But Starch tried. He rambled on.

"I once had a monkey that...."

"That's BS!" I interrupted Starch, while other IPs groaned. "Fred Picks told me that same thing happened to his brother."

"No. It's true, man! I was there, I tell you. Who you gonna believe? A student or an IP? Picks is just some damn tobacco spitting Okie!"

"Well, go on, Starch. Tell us again for the tenth time. I want to compare these versions."

"This is *true,* man. I was *there!*" Starch continued in his slurred delivery. He wasn't half through the story setup before we cut him off.

"Same story," Freed said. "Remember McKee two classes back? Same bull."

"You don't believe me? Get me a monkey. We'll do it here."

Freed never bothered getting him a monkey. I never got Starch a keg of beer, either. Maybe I would buy that keg at my promotion party when I made captain next week. The keg was a promotion tradition. With that in mind I just quietly pocketed my baby pool money and left early for sick call.

The tree-lined walk to the base hospital looked the same as the night before. The fog still enveloped the base, although a brighter, warm sun threatened to burn away its last vestiges in short order. It might become a fine day for flight. Damn those cigarettes.

I passed through the hospital entrance into a massive crush of military dependents packed together on benches like sardines in a can. Those men, women, and children without a place to sit milled around or stood in random, silent clusters. I walked out of sight of their expressionless gazes, stepped through the door of the nearly empty Flight Surgeon's office, and stopped at a small desk.

"Lieutenant Amity, to see Doctor Terra," I said to the sergeant at the front desk. He knew me well. He did not even ask for my first name before pulling out my chart, which thickened exponentially with each visit.

This was a place where no one wandered aimlessly, and no one had to wait. Pilots got right in.

Doc Terra stuck his head out of his office doorway. "Well, Lieutenant? What's your pleasure today?"

The doctor and I were like old friends. He was somewhat older with prematurely gray hair around the edges. He had practiced as a civilian physician for several years before joining the Air Force. Medicine set well with him. He enjoyed every aspect of his job, except for flying the Tweet. By his own admission he spent most of his flying hours with his face green, his stomach tumbling, and his barf bag full. What made him exceptional was his skill flying the T-37, after retching his guts for the first five to ten minutes. Always game for another try at it, he slowly improved until most pilots gave him respect no other flight surgeons shared. It was Doc Terra who busted his butt trying to learn all there was to know about flying a jet. Except for his routine air sickness, he would have fully qualified to fly solo. I found him very easy to approach.

I stood. "I've got another sinus block."

"Come on in here." The doctor motioned me inside with his whole arm. "Is it hurting you now?"

"Every time I move."

Terra shut the door behind me and pointed to a chair. Without another word he took his thumbs and pressed them firmly against the brow above each eye. I flinched at the first surge of dull, nauseating pain that ran from my forehead down to the center of my stomach.

"That hurts," he stated frankly.

"Yes!" I groaned.

"Both sides?"

"Yep."

"Do your teeth hurt?" He pressed on my cheek bones.

"Just the top ones do now. Sometimes the lower teeth hurt, too."

He pressed harder on the bones just above my upper teeth. I flinched again. The pain radiated through my upper teeth becoming nausea in the pit of my guts.

"Bingo!" I groaned again.

"Hurts?"

"Uh-huh."

"Let's get some X-rays on you, then come back here, okay?" He filled out a triplicate form and handed me the slip to present to the technician.

"I've probably had fifteen or twenty of these done in the past year. Is this necessary?"

"I want to see one that is current. So, yes. I need one."

"But they take three or four different views each time. That's maybe sixty shots of me last year. What's that doing to my brain?"

"Nothing worth worrying about. Today's X-rays are a small fraction of the radiation they used to be."

Not exactly reassuring, but I went grudgingly. They shot three pictures of my head. They never took the same number of x-rays as the time before. When I returned to his office, Doc Terra was already viewing the films on a florescent screen. He looked at me, then glanced at the films for an uncomfortable moment, as if sizing me up.

"Have you ever considered quitting?"

The question took me by complete surprise. A myriad of imponderables rushed through my mind.

"What?" I could not think to say more.

"Your sinuses are in terrible shape. I think you should consider that you'll have to quit flying soon. At the most, in six months, you'll have no choice."

I was a bit stunned by the sudden turn of events. The shock was a mix of sadness, yet elation. I had flown in constant pain for so long that the discomfort had since become dull and unnoticeable. But I knew that it had gotten progressively worse. I was surprised by my own conflicted feelings. I was relieved by the prospect of having the burden lifted from my life. But I had learned to enjoy flying. I was comfortable with my fellow instructors and students. I would miss that.

"Can I do anything to stop it?"

"Let me show you why not." Terra slapped on the screen the one and only view of the three or four X-rays I posed for each time that any doctor ever showed me.

"Doc, I've already had nearly a hundred X-rays on my head. Could you get them to take only the one picture that you show me each time?"

"I know you get a lot of exposure to X-ray, but today's machines are only one percent of what it used to be. You will be fine."

"I don't like it. Can I tell them that you only need this one?"

"It's our protocol. You'll be fine. Now, let me show you where we stand on your sinuses."

Pointing to the frontal sinus above each eye socket, he then directed another finger to each maxillary sinus above my upper jaw.

"See these? Your frontals probably don't bother you as much, but your teeth must hurt all the time by the looks of this. Look close here." He pointed at the maxillary sinus in more detail. "See the line of crud there. Those cavities are half full. They're just slowly filling up with a tarry substance that won't ever come out."

"Is there any way to fix me back up?"

"How badly do you want to fly?"

"Well, how much would I have to go through?"

"They can put windows in there. They go inside your nose with a hammer and chisel and knock out a hole the size of a quarter on each side."

"Damn, Doc." I shuddered. "What does that do?"

"You'll never have a sinus block there ever again."

"Any drawbacks?"

"Several. I don't recommend it." Terra made his point with emphasis. "There's a chance you'll have pain from it the rest of your life, due to exposed raw nerves. Your voice might become more nasal."

"Do I have a choice on this?"

"How badly do you want to fly?"

"Are we speaking in confidence, Doc?"

"Sure. Nothing leaves here."

"My only career goal in the Air Force has been to get out at the first available opportunity. I certainly don't want to do anything else to my body, but I had hoped I could get at least a thousand flying hours before I got out."

Doc Terra leaned forward to give me my options.

"I can probably ground you now by sending you to Wilford Hall, or you can fly until you're ready to quit."

"Will you back me up?"

"Whatever you decide, I'll back you up." He held up my X-rays. "Anyone seeing these films would wonder how you have flown as long as you have."

"Well, let me think this over. I want to fly a little bit longer if I can."

"Okay. Get these prescriptions filled. Come back on Monday. I'll put you back on flying status if you're doing better."

"Thanks, Doc."

"Just don't fly when you shouldn't, okay?"

"Don't worry. I'm no dummy."

"Who knows?" Terra said. "You might make it past six months and get those thousand hours."

"Six months. I'll give it that."

I walked out through the door, happier about my health than I had been in over a year. I made a monumental decision. There was a way out if I chose to take it.

15

I ARRIVED BACK AT THE flightline with a smile on my face that caught the attention of my flight commander.

"So, are you going to fly anymore, or is this it?"

Alexander's question startled me. He was already speaking in terms of finality. Getting my career wish to get out at the first available opportunity did not seem so exhilarating. It would mean leaving my friends forever. I surprised myself by making my decision the split second after John asked me.

"Sure I'm going to fly some more. The doctor said I've got six months, yet. Don't rush me. Besides, I want to make captain first. No telling where they might send me if I got grounded. Probably Greenland."

"Or worse, Vietnam."

"Yeah, right. Keep me flying a while longer here. Ground me from flying. Then send me to Vietnam. That would never happen."

"Good then." He banged his hand on my shoulder. "You can join the flight gaggle to Laugh In the Friday after New Year's."

"They approved it?" I was a bit surprised.

"Yeah! If you can get your ass ungrounded!"

"How many Tweets are going?"

"Colonel Meneur said at least eight, maybe twelve." Alexander had a wide grin of anticipation. "We should get all the painted birds to take along for the show."

The Tweet instructor pilots at Laughlin Air Force Base in Del Rio, Texas, just 150 miles to our north, had invited our T-37 IPs to visit. To us it was Laugh In Air Force Base in Diarrhea, Texas. To them we were Lardo Air Force Base instructors. Colonel Meneur accepted the Laugh In commander's invitation after surmounting a sea of red tape and a score of reasons given him not to go. Our plan was simple. We would impress them with antics on our arrival that they could not hope to top. That one-upmanship began with our painted airplanes.

The year before, Laredo Air Force Base was chosen to test different paints and colors on T-37s as a means of reducing the corrosion of the aluminum outer surfaces. It was a way to extend the service life of the Tweets for several more years. My personal favorite Tweet was painted blue and white with accents under the wings, making it look like a mockingbird in flight with its white markings prominently displayed as it streaked overhead. Another T-37 was nearly solid red with only a few accents of black and white to break up its monochromatic image. I doubted if red aircraft paint would fare any better than the sunbaked oxidized red finish on cars I had seen in town. The remainder were painted in myriad styles of black and white or blue and white. Wherever we went, they always brought comments. This would put us one-up on our Diarrhea, Texas, counterparts from the very beginning. They were great new toys.

"Anyone going to get to fly today?" I was breaking out of my daydream.

"Not us." There was disgust in John's voice. "A whole week shot."

"I might go to the O-Club early to get a good seat for the show."

"I'll be with Suzy and the baby tonight. Give me a report."

It seemed like I left with the whole squadron in tow. I kept thinking about the card my student, Ted Ark, had showed me of his girlfriend, Honey, and her friend, Boopsie, from San Antonio. They were indeed women of spectacular profiles. I could only conjure up one coed from my Oklahoma State days who came close to being quite like Boopsie or Honey—horny, uninhibited, liberated Jane. With her on my mind, I walked outside absent-mindedly into the still cool hazy afternoon air. I unchained my bicycle from the rack, where four others awaited their owners, like so many horses hitched to a rail. Bicycles were just now becoming the rage on college campuses, so my green ten-speed was my one link with the campus life I looked back on so fondly.

It was nearly three and one-half years since I had joined the Air Force. I had missed Jane for a while, until I realized she had not cried over my departure more than the time it took me to pack my bags. It had only been a year since I had given up writing her letters. She would never come to see me in Texas. My visits back home to see her provided strong hints that we were worlds apart without a word being spoken. It was a hard decision for me to join into the Vietnam war effort, especially on the level of a pilot. The pilots portrayed in the press were getting a lot of flak, both from the enemy and the American public. After two years of my military service and two years of Jane's continued college antiwar protests, the extremes of our lives broke us apart. Ironically, Jane and I believed the same about the war. It was insane. But I joined the Air Force because I was about to be drafted. I was a patriot, for sure, but only my parents, John, and Suzy were happy about that. There was nothing I could do to please everyone else in my dilemma, so I did what would please me. Being a pilot intrigued me. Jane's shameful idea for my being a Canadian refugee did not appeal to me. Jane and I never said goodbye. We just quit writing.

I waved to my other flight mates, both students and instructors, who were heading directly to the Officer's Club. Their cars roared past me as I mounted my bike's thin seat and pedaled home to my BOQ for a short nap. I was one of only a few instructors who lived in the Bachelor Officers Quarters. Climbing the stairs to the second story, I stepped inside to a room as barren as they come. The floor was a brown short pile carpeting. The empty walls in the incandescent light of the ceiling fixture glowed a dirty off-white. Two square-backed green vinyl chairs shared the room with an inexpensive cowboy style wooden coffee table, a matching nightstand, and a single bed with headboard and footboard. I hung my flight cap on the wall thermostat by the closet, then threw myself on my bed with the orange Oklahoma State bedspread I had brought from college. I closed my eyes and drifted again to dreams of my days in college with Jane, and before that, with Suzy.

Suzy was beautiful, intelligent, compassionate, and steadfast. Jane was spectacularly gorgeous, less intelligent, self-centered, and irresponsible. Suzy I would bring home to Mom and Dad. Jane I would take to any public gathering where men could eat their hearts out. Jane turned heads. While Suzy might turn heads, she also turned their minds. Jane was more physical. Suzy had a body and brains. Jane had a greater body and fewer brains, but oh that fiery red hair was a lure. Testosterone in college dictated that there was not much priority set aside for brains. A body was all that mattered. I learned the error of that thinking too late. Alexander had lucked out at the expense of my hormone-induced stupidity.

I closed my eyes and tried to nap. I dreamed of Suzy—brains and opportunities lost. I dreamed of Jane and remembered her uninhibited, unremitting, aggressive, beg-for-mercy libido. Since my animal nature still reigned supreme, I opened my eyes, got off my bed, and headed for the Officers' Club. Watching Honey and Boopsie would have to do, but I still missed the erotic narcotic that Jane had to offer.

16

I GROUNDED MY TEN-SPEED at my quarters, instead taking my red Datsun 240Z to the Officers' Club. This called for a different image if I were going after women. Settling in my car seat, the engine came to life, with a few extra roaring revs just to make me feel good, before I expertly left the parking blocks like Stirling Moss at Le Mans. Even the simple act of driving that car made me horny. The Doors, performing one of their drug-inspired tunes from the *Morrison Hotel* record, blasted in my ears to set the mood. They had always given me such a rush in college. With the volume cranked up, Jim Morrison sang "Waiting for the Sun," which shook the car windows each time the band's notes blasted those low octaves, the same way an F-4 in afterburner rattled the ground. They made me feel non-establishment. I felt down and dirty hearing that singer's angry voice. Jim Morrison was about as far from what I was as one could be. He was the rebel. I was establishment. Being a rebel sounded pretty good.

I parked my Z on the far end of the parking lot in a socially acceptable manner rather than the two-parking-spaces routine so many jerks tried with their own cars. Limiting the door dents was my only goal without incurring the wrath of people trying to park in a crowded lot. A few irate car owners were known to go out of their way to ding a jerk's car. I wanted no part of jerks.

It surprised me to see Freed and Alexander running up to greet me, both sporting excited grins. Hal was first to speak.

"Rob, we're pretty certain that Military's promotion is not with this cycle."

"There appears to be some pushback way up the line." John chuckled. "He may even get bumped down to first lieutenant if what I hear is true."

"Don't set me up like that, guys," I said. "I'm on to your games."

"No! It's true," John said. "We can't tell you who told us, but if he ever had a chance, Military's not on the review board list."

Freed said, "It's a great day to celebrate and get lucky."

Before I could say more, the two captains were off—Hal to give the news to others and John to check on Suzy and the baby. What a joyous evening to go to the show inside.

I walked rapidly up the entry of the Officers' Club, through the lobby, and quickly inside to the back room. A mob of officers of all ranks and types grabbed madly at a huge plate of chicken wings still being carried by a moon-lighting sergeant to the front table. As a kid back home, I had seen my dog attack table scraps the same way. So, I joined in the frenzy. My animal instincts took over, ignoring the horror of so many dead chickens sacrificed for our pleasure.

The room was quite large, reminiscent of the school auditoriums I knew from grade school. There was a large, raised stage at one end that extended out into an open arena of folding chairs, which rimmed the elevated platform five rows deep. My trek to the bartender brought me past at least two hundred flight-suited officers and another fifteen or twenty non-flying lieutenants and captains. At least a hundred little MacArthurs stood around posing and posturing, strutting and staring. Drinks in hand, they had all developed the skill of holding their drinks with hands held out like little airplanes to illustrate how they "slipped the surly bonds of earth." Flight suits were great. If we spilled our drink—who cared?

I found several of my friends. There were other instructors, some from the T-38 Talon squadron. There were some of my former students. There were all three of my current students. I enjoyed seeing everyone in a place where rank was dropped, and nobody gave orders. And then there was the duo of Honey and Boopsie.

Years ago, my conclusion was that men needed these fantasy outings because women in the real world failed to perceive about our needs. To men, sex is a devout religion, with all its lifetime commitments and trappings. By contrast, a woman views her own libido with the same caution as a reluctant convert. They do not get that godly thrill until we male missionaries drag them hesitatingly to the alter of worship. While women may feel the fire of worship on these metaphorical Sundays, they disavow this god for the rest of the week. But men pray to their goddess hourly.

I am always amazed that the most outwardly idiotic gyrations of a talented female can elicit such extreme sexual feelings. Honey and her equally buxom friend had just begun dancing to songs on the jukebox as the beer and booze flowed heavily. Honey writhed to the first song fully dressed. She was a tall, reddish-blonde woman in her late twenties, whose face was a pleasure to watch. She enjoyed her work. Boopsie—as Ark called Honey's friend—danced the second number, like Honey, with her clothes intact. Unlike Honey, she had a rough, angular, weathered face, though with a better body. She had a nasty twinkle in her eye, a bouffant, brunette wig, and a desire to turn me on. Honey returned for the next record to tantalize me further by undulating and unbuttoning her blouse agonizingly slow. On the typical six-button blouse, she always got behind and had four buttons to go and both cuffs fastened with thirty seconds remaining in the song. There was always a young pilot willing to help her hurry.

The striptease went on for over an hour before the crowd of officers began to thin out. One more quarter for the jukebox landed at her feet. She stepped back off the stage to the jukebox with the quarter in hand.

"This is our special routine, which we're real proud of and we've worked up just for you," Honey announced. "I hope you all enjoy it… and remember us in your dreams."

She turned to the muscular forty-year-old Officers' Club manager, Major O'Brian, and nodded. The red-headed Irishman, who had appeared for the first time that day, took her quarter and dropped it in the jukebox, programming three songs for twenty-five cents. He selected Honey's trademark record three times in a row. She always played it to open her act and to close it. It carried a rhythm roughly twice the tempo of a regular heartbeat. The loud electric bass guitar pounded the beat to the pit of my stomach. A brass section blared out the melody. A tenor sax added a slightly erotic flavor.

Honey and Boopsie began a slow and subdued response to the music, leaning forward, swaying from side to side. I found their motions both erotic and artistic. A sort of bare-assed ballet. They began to increase the tempo of their movements with every other beat. It had an instant effect on all of us. A few animal groans and boyish cheers mixed with the music as this ballet evolved in a quickening pace. Now they were gyrating at full speed, choreographed hips and arms moving rapidly about. They put both hands down on their thighs and slowly moved them up. Their pelvic moves continued at a rapid rate, then increased in intensity as their hands got closer to the *V* of their torsos. It was now the artistry of pure sex. The music seemed to evoke as much as did the women themselves. They spun around to face the crowd, then faced each other, never missing a beat, penetratingly staring into each other's eyes. Artistry continued as intensely and rapidly as the music allowed. It was then that I realized that the music volume was slowly increasing as Major O'Brian attempted to overcome the roar coming from all of us. I imagined myself up there with them. The musical beat pounded deeply into my most primitive soul. There was a natural urge to step closer. They continued to move rapidly, sweat dripping steadily from both women. They kept their eyes fixed upon each other and smiled happily.

Unexpectedly, the two naked women turned around and dropped to the stage floor. The first row of men moved forward in unison, putting their elbows onto the edge of the stage for a closer look. This served to block the view of all the others. Many stood up to see the women. Their cries of *"Move!"* ignored, and a chain reaction followed as everyone began climbing forward over chairs. The heated mob then began climbing over each other. The more forward the throng crawled, the more impossible it became to see the two women, who by now could not escape. The nearest pilots were so close, Honey and Boopsie could feel the heat of their bodies, the warmth of their breath. The volume of male voices reached a crescendo as more than a hundred officers ringed the stage three and four bodies deep. More desperate men began to pile on to get a view. The music abruptly stopped as the enforcer stormed on stage.

Major O'Brian fought his way in from the jukebox, his wild Irish eyes blazing. He stepped up to the first two student pilots, grabbed them by their flight suits, and hurled them off the stage onto the pile of writhing, struggling officers tangled up at the foot of the platform.

"Get down!" he bellowed in a voice so forceful that it rivaled the strength of his arms as he continued heaving men out of his path to rescue Honey and Boopsie. *"Now move!"*

The officers began to move back one layer at a time until the women were once more in full view of everyone. The two were sitting up, gazing about with nervous glances at the gentlemen surrounding them from a greater distance than before.

"Get backstage and put your clothes on," the major ordered.

He stood there angrily pointing a finger dramatically at every one of us while Honey and Boopsie made a hasty departure.

"You men blew it!" he called out. "I just hope none of the top brass saw this! If the Old Man knew this happened, all your asses would be canned!"

He placed his hands on his hips, staring threateningly at us even more.

"One more chance is all you get. If you blow it next time, I promise you there will never be another floor show as long as I'm here!"

Then the major looked at the mob of gentlemen. In a last statement which must have swelled the hearts of all those young MacArthurian hopefuls, Major O'Brian said, "These proceedings are closed."

Without another word, Major O'Brian turned and walked backstage. All the men quietly left the room, many going home to their poor, innocent, waiting wives. War was Hell.

17

UPON FLEEING THE OFFICERS' CLUB and leaving Honey and Boopsie, Freed met me outside. This man of absolute self-confidence liked me for some reason that I never quite understood. He had precisely the right mix of cocky swaggering and supreme intelligence I admired in a man. There was no bluff in him. With brilliant ideas of his own, he also wanted to listen to other opinions. He would stand up for someone's views, even when they were not popular. When I announced the month before that I was voting for George McGovern, who opposed the Vietnam War, it was Freed who had defended my decision to the men in our squadron. It was a very unpopular stand. He relished the controversy. Freed was the kind of pilot who would hang his ass out for you—a good man to have on your wing in combat.

As a highly decorated fighter pilot, Freed seemed blind to the fact that our common interests were separated by gaps of age, experience, and social sophistication. The only thing we shared in common was a hatred of the war and an abhorrence of conformity. He was a real war hero. I was a stateside rear-echelon type. He seldom talked about his combat experiences. On those rare occasions when he did briefly talk about it, as I learned later, his hesitance meant that it was the truth. Only liars and braggarts willingly told war stories to the uninitiated.

"Let's go find some friendlies," Freed said, using the name he coined to describe the local townswomen. "What do you say?"

"Let's go."

"How about Golding's?" Freed referred to a Mexican restaurant and cocktail lounge with open air tables and a higher class of clients.

"Sounds good. Let's get the hell outta Dodge. Take my car?"

We got in my 240Z, buckled up, and roared out of the parking lot, staying in second gear. Any other gear would have meant a speeding ticket on base. Freed fumbled through my stack of cassette tapes, replacing *Morrison Hotel* with *Led Zeppelin II,* the ultimate in depravity set to music. Freed, without asking, stepped the volume up to near ear damaging levels. Having never tried LSD, I could only imagine that this was the sensation that the chemical induced.

The opening rhythm of "Whole Lotta Love" pounded into my chest followed by Jimmy Page screaming the lyrics. The instrumentalists took over, driving their psychedelic sexual message to the core of my crotch. The electric guitars, and who knows what else, swirled left-right, left-right from the car speakers in a dizzyingly shrill volume. Then the voice of Jimmy Page returned. I had no clue what the last line meant, but it had to be something bad.

Everything I had learned at home about morality was the antithesis of these lyrics. I had learned about the other side from Jane back in college, but even she was an amateur compared to the likes of Boopsie and Honey. They seemed to take the philosophy of Led Zeppelin to heart. I was still in the formative stage, unlike Freed. The Air Force had been a quick lesson in life. People really lived lyrics like this. What an eye opener that had been.

We stopped at our quarters to change out of our flight suits into bell bottoms and colorful mod shirts. I could not quite stomach leisure suits yet. Then, hopping back into my car, we headed to Golding's Cocktail Lounge, accompanied by the bodily function lyrics of "The Lemon Song."

Captain Hal Freed had come directly from Southeast Asia to Laredo, quietly and without leave. The Air Force had assigned him here as punishment for his antics out at Kadena, the big airbase on Okinawa. A graduate of the Air Force Academy, Freed had flown over a hundred combat missions in North Vietnam from Korat Air Base, Thailand, in the F-105D Thunderchief as a Wild Weasel. The Thunderchief—known colloquially as the "Thud"— carried a two-man crew of a pilot and a backseat electronic warfare officer

—an EWO in aviator lingo—with the backseater charged with operating the systems meant to identify enemy fighters, antiaircraft artillery, and surface to air missiles, or SAMs. The crew's primary goal was to destroy the SAM missile control complexes. Targets of opportunity were secondary options. The tactic used was one perfected from the early days of aerial warfare. Thuds never flew alone. They always flew as two aircraft in formation. Freed had lost buddies to SAMs, AAA flak, and to enemy MiG fighters. Those men were now classified as either Missing In Action or Prisoners Of War. No one knew for sure.

Flying in formation as lead or wingman, Freed's most haunting memory was of the sporadic blip on the small rear cockpit scope indicating the bearing and distance of a North Vietnamese SAM site's scanning radar. To destroy the enemy's radar facility, Freed had to wait for the audible steady chirping of lock-on just before a SAM launched at his aircraft. The lock-on of the enemy's radar allowed the Wild Weasel's EWO to fire his own automatic homing AGM-78 Standard ARM or the shorter range but cheaper AGM-45 Shrike missile right down the radar beam of the enemy. If the radar sight were knocked out, so was the enemy's SAM air defense. With the radar site destroyed, the two-ship could circle around and bomb the other facilities one mile away without risk of being hit by their missiles. Destroying the SAMs was the next objective, but blasting the radar by baiting them with their own aircraft always came first.

Not every mission Freed and his two-ship crew flew drew a response from the enemy. Weather, target assignments, or bad luck was more frequent than actual enemy contact. But with every mission flown, Freed had to assume it would be a struggle of cat and mouse. Without warning it might happen. Being on alert saved lives. If the chirping lock-on sound of the enemy's radar entered his headset, he began the desperate search below for the orange glow of one or more SAMs, climbing closer and glaring brighter. His split-second decision had to be correct—a hard turn that his Thud could make, but the SAM could not. SAMs often broke apart trying to match such turns. He had made the right choice each time it happened, always returning with his backseater and wingman healthy and safe. The painful memory of seeing his friends in other formations bailing out of their doomed jet fighters still tormented him. Oddly enough, the curious sound of their emergency beepers wailing on the GUARD, the emergency radio channel, put Freed at ease. It meant a parachute had opened and that another buddy might still be alive to await rescue. Still, he wondered if he would ever see his friends again.

With each return to safety, Freed had to go back through the same obstacles he encountered going into harm's way. The beauty of his F-105 was its speed at low level. Often, he returned home on the deck at full military power—or in afterburner, if necessary—flying faster than any enemy MiG could match. Speed was salvation.

He was returning to the states with that worry when he stopped over at the air base in Okinawa. This was the home of a wing of B-52s. Called the Buff—Big Ugly Fat Fella if you're being polite, and something else if you're not—the B-52 was the most terrible and the least vulnerable weapon in the Air Force inventory. Nobody got shot down. Nobody got shot at. The biggest hazard aircrews had was the danger of falling asleep from boredom while they flew the thousands of miles and a dozen hours to reach the target and return safely. At 30,000 feet, no enemy could see them, much less defend against them. They never flew in harm's way, where SAMs or MiGs might lurk. Freed likened the Buffs to farts—silent but deadly. Compared to Freed's Wild Weasel missions, B-52 missions were milk runs.

That did not stop the Buff wing commander on Okinawa from issuing a decree, which revived an old World War Two tradition. Upon returning from their stratospheric missions south of the twentieth parallel, called Operation Arclight, all non-bomber personnel had to clear out of the Officers' Club bar so the returning bomber heroes could celebrate their bravery without any "wimps" around. This was the circumstance when Freed met his first B-52 pilots. A colonel with his squadron aircrews came into the bar and ordered Freed out. He was justifiably upset, since the heavy bomber missions were not in the same class as those bomber raids of World War Two, where each crewman had had a one in six chance of not returning from the mission. These guys always returned. They expected to return. He could not remember a single B-52 airman ever taken prisoner by the enemy.

It was the classic confrontation of fighter jock versus bomber pilot. It was Freed's Thud against the colonel's Buff. Rather than leave graciously, Hal decked the colonel with a right hook to the nose.

This was all rumor, of course. Freed would, in those classic words, neither confirm nor deny.

So, here I was helping Freed serve out his sentence in Laredo, Texas, driving at high speed outside the base and blasting my ears with drugged out erotic tunes while planning to drink myself a bit silly and learning how to pick up women from a pro. Not a bad sentence.

We turned off the paved main drag and took a gravel shortcut down a few side streets and pulled into Golding's parking lot very slowly. Most of the streets of Laredo were unpaved. Sizable gravel and rock, called caliche, was everywhere in town. Kicking up rocks was a bad way to keep my 240Z looking good. We got out of my car, kicked a few small boulders out of the way, and went inside. We were still not hungry after all those chicken wings earlier, so we went into the lounge to sate our other appetites for wine and women. I had had it with song. The booze was more expensive off base, which bothered me some, but Hal reassured me that "you get what you pay for." Indeed, there were several couples and unaccompanied young women in the area. It was a warm night for December. Several were outside eating in the open air.

"Let's stay inside for now," Freed said. "It's warmer in here. They wear less."

We sat down and started with two Carta Blancas. While waiting for our order, I scouted out in more detail the particularly attractive ladies who lurked in the shadows. My eyes caught a glimpse of a beautiful Chicano señorita at the next table. Her chair faced our table, but she seemed preoccupied talking to her young friend, who fortunately seemed more appealing to Freed's taste for thinner ladies. My discovery was no stroke of luck. It was evident that our hostess had steered us over near their turf. My señorita had ravishing dark eyes, long straight dark brown hair, light complexion, ruby red lipstick, and a most captivating laugh. Her smile was comfortable.

"Well, we're not in Boys Town, anymore, Rob. They have all their teeth," Hal whispered.

"You take the stick woman," I whispered. "I'll take the Natalie Wood type."

"It's a deal." He looked very focused.

They still would not look at us, but I knew they must be aware of our attentions. The Air Force seemed totally opposite to my fears of what military service was going to be. It was not all combat and saluting twenty-four hours a day. Here I was with Freed, who for a few more days outranked me. But rank was immaterial. We were on equal ground as friends. I was still surprised by the informality of officers of different ranks and ages.

"Well, Freed, I didn't know what to expect when I joined the Air Force," I began, glancing once more at my señorita's full ruby lips. "I thought it was going to be all bombs and bullets. Now I know that this is the real Air Force, right here in Laredo."

"The *real* Air Force!? Bull!" Hal said. I had tripped a hot button. "There is no real Air Force! It doesn't exist!"

He looked awkward in his civilian shirt and bells with his short black hair that contradicted his military affiliation. Hal slumped in his seat, wiry in appearance, with a heavy, black, five o'clock shadow after an early morning shave.

"I guess you were in the real Air Force," I corrected. "Hunting down SAM sights probably qualifies."

"Hell, this is probably more the real thing than what I did."

"Come on, Hal. I'd say getting your ass shot at is more like the real Air Force. You're certainly more of a hot stick than I am."

"That's not true." Hal seemed to be a little embarrassed. "But if that was real, everybody would be bombing North Vietnam. They don't, though. The reality is that most are safe in their little hooches or—like those Buff assholes—they're at 30,000 feet and a hundred miles from the nearest enemy."

I was distracted momentarily by my girl looking up. She did not glance my way. Instead, she merely sipped on her drink and stared at everything else in the room except me.

Hal brought me back to reality. "Let me tell you a story. I took a joy ride once on an EC-121 over the DMZ into the North. This EWO said to me, 'Wait till you get to the real Air Force.' Hell! We were flying over North Vietnam at the time, for crying out loud! And that stupid bastard told me that! So, I finally concluded there is no real Air Force! The real Air Force only exists wherever you are not!"

Once more I glanced over to the dark-eyed beauty. She continued to ignore my rude gaze but suddenly looked up, seemingly aware of me for the first time. I started to look away in shyness but stopped myself. She watched me blankly, then slowly dropped her parted lips to her drink and began drawing on the plastic straw. To my great surprise, she returned my purposeful stare with a gloriously wicked smile.

18

IT WAS FREED WHO INVITED the two young ladies to join us for dinner. As it turned out they were sisters and rich to the gills, being members of one of those families granted enormous expanses of land in the early Nineteenth Century. I had flown over their ranch hundreds of times. It was the same area Captain Military and his father had been assigned the year before, when they got "all of east Texas." Like us, these ladies were out trolling and had hooked them some live ones. As the night wore on, Hal and I learned they were abundant with more than just their wealth.

Three days later on Monday morning, when I finally dragged myself home from the ranch, I stopped at a stand to get the Monday morning newspaper. I was working the afternoon shift at the flightline that week, which meant there was no need to report until about 11:00 a.m. The headlines declared that all hell had broken loose in Vietnam. I cleaned up in my quarters and got to the Ragtop Flight room. The place was buzzing with uneasiness. It remained so all that week.

America had recently re-elected President Richard Nixon, though I did not vote for him. Watergate was a word that meant little to most people, and most public attention focused on the prospects for peace in Southeast Asia. With the Paris Peace Talks again broken down, our commander in chief flexed his newly mandated muscles.

On Sunday, December 17, 1972, the fog in Laredo lifted, and the war clouds rolled in. The TV news reported that the Navy had dropped mines in the enemy's Haiphong Harbor. Monday's newspaper reported that the United States was renewing its bombing of North Vietnam north of the twentieth parallel. The real shocker came on the following day when the newspapers confirmed that America's monstrous B-52s, supported by Navy and Air Force tactical fighters, were in use over the Hanoi and Haiphong areas for the first time in the Vietnam War. Air Force and Navy unleashed aircraft in nearly total war over the North. The normally militant Nixon-for-president pilots at Laredo Air Force Base became nervous.

"I told you to vote for McGovern," I teased my friends in A-Flight on Tuesday. In truth, and to my surprise, I was happy. It was about time.

"Hell," Fred Picks said,, "the war will be over before I get a chance to get over there. My career is shot!"

Picks was not alone. Much to my shock, most of the pilots told me the same thing. They were nervous because their career advancement was on the line if they did not become battle-decorated officers. He and his chums wished for more years of conflict to satisfy their own selfish wants. What an insane world I was in!

The previous month I had stated to anyone who would listen that anything that would end this national insanity was worth a try, even having Senator George McGovern for President. Since we all knew the Democratic nominee did not stand a chance, most of my squadron mates said I was crazy to state my feelings publicly, especially within an Air Force building.

"Maybe I'll achieve my long-term military career goal when they kick me out. All I've ever wanted was to get out at the first available opportunity."

Now it looked like things were never going to end as Nixon continued to raise the stakes. By Wednesday, December 20th, the United States confirmed the loss of three Buffs and two other airplanes, along with four other B-52s damaged and fifteen airmen lost in air attacks over North Vietnam. Nixon was sacrificing our biggest warplane at the rate of one a day.

On the twenty-first, the first films of captured B-52 crewmen appeared on television. We lost another of those big bombers. Nixon came out verbally punching with a threat to both the North and South Vietnamese. If the two sides failed to sign a peace agreement, the President promised more bombs for Hanoi and a cut-off of aid to Saigon. By Christmas Eve it was clear these pilots were merely pawns in a bigger than life struggle with no clear end in sight. In a week's bombing, the United States confirmed the loss of fourteen aircraft, of which ten were the monstrous B-52s. Fifty-five men were listed as missing in action—almost as many as there were pilots in our T-37 squadron at Laredo.

Then the North Vietnamese paraded our captured American crewmen before television cameras. It was the most deeply depressing career event I had ever witnessed. I personalized the whole crisis. Those were my nameless buddies. They all got to walk up to microphones and state their wish that the war would end. What a contrast from only two years before. The peaceniks were coming out of the closet. These did not look like the hardcore career officers the news had portrayed before. They often looked very young, always appeared scared, and usually seemed tired—tired of this interminable war. Gone was the fear of giving in to the interrogator's questions. Many were so frightened and worked up that they would not shut up. Before our television eyes our own officers said in their muddled words that they did not care anymore.

"We have great sorrow... and... we hope and pray in negotiations, and Congress will see to it that the war was ended."

"I hope the war ends soon. I hope to be home soon."

"We were only told that all our targets are military targets and that these would be the only targets that would be hit. On that assumption is the reason that we did do the missions... for military targets only."

"I'd like to say to Mom and Dad, I'm okay."

"I would like to say that not only have innocent civilians been killed in these bombings, but some of the bombing has been very close to prisoner of war camps and has also exposed prisoners of war to the threat of death. And that it is my opinion that continued bombing of this sort will only stiffen the determination of the Vietnamese people to continue their fight."

"Merry Christmas to my family. Judy, I love you!"

Obviously, many were coached, but for most it was from the heart. The parade of frightened, disillusioned men was painful to watch. I knew why the enemy had allowed the prisoners' messages to be broadcast.

We looked defeated.

That night, for them, I broke down and cried. It became painfully clear to me now. My fellow airmen were breaking the code of silence. They forgot their training in the face of the enemy. I was disappointed to see it happen, no matter my personal feelings about the war. I could never say that to the face of America. What would Alexander or Freed think of me then?

That same day, Harry Truman died. Maybe because of that news, or possibly because the nation was simply tired of hearing about the war, a thirty-six-hour Christmas truce got little attention. The resumption of the bombing did not even make the front page. By December 30th, the United States admitted losing its fifteenth B-52. Those killed or missing rose to nearly one hundred. B-52 milk runs, if they ever were such, were a thing of the past. With SAMs, MiGs, and antiaircraft artillery fired at every Buff on every day, their crews were sitting ducks in the most frightening skies in the world. That Saturday I read an article in the paper quoting a B-52 mechanic on Okinawa.

"The flight crews are different. Before, when they came back, they were always clowning around. Now they're shaken. They just get out of the plane and into the bus and go to the debriefing."

The next day, New Year's Eve, the Hanoi government agreed to resume negotiations, and the American bombing of the Hanoi-Haiphong area ended forever.

With one hundred percent of their flights filled with stark terror, a total of 206 B-52 crews out of Guam and U-Tapao, Thailand, had gone through eleven days of Christmas Hell, certainly the most memorable of their lives.

Freed and I would never dismiss the B-52 and its crew in the same mocking way again.

19

IT HAD BEEN A GOOD time to have sinus problems. I was grounded a week, then Christmas and New Year's came. The base always shut down during the holidays, giving me the time I needed to fully recover. The break from flying turned out rather enjoyable. Captain Military's lack of promotion did wonders for my mood. Word had it that he went apoplectic at hearing the news. I savored the image of this tyrant's rant in disgrace. Now, three months later, it was the middle of spring in Laredo. The days were hot, and the evenings were warm. It was near the end of T-37s for Ark and Picks. They would soon be bumped up to the T-38 squadron. Few students ever came back to say hello to T-37 IPs once they went supersonic.

I did dwell on my flying job, though. Would my Iranian student ever solo? Would those guys, Ark and Picks, ever learn to descend at a suitable rate on their penetration turns? The fact that my students still would penetrate at only 3000 feet per minute really bugged me. It was almost like they had a conspiracy under way. They demonstrated the worst case of collective incompetence since the 1968 Democrat convention. I ended up yelling at them incessantly. I would force them to achieve a 6000 feet per minute drop by physically pushing the stick forward for them. As soon as I looked away the nose was back up, the descent had dropped to half the proper rate, and we were ten miles too far out from the VOR. It happened every time just like clockwork. My solution was to comply with the mandated grade guidelines, pencil whip them as skilled, and kick them upstairs to the other squadron. Let those T-38 jet jocks have a shot at them.

And then there was Cadet Mossare. It was time once again for him to solo. Oh, how I dreaded that. But then, coming back after my Christmas grounding, I needed to retrain myself. It had been a long, rusty time. Although Mossare was still not soloed, we hoped to achieve that before he got washed back, yet again, to another class. The flight gaggle we had cooked up for Laugh In Air Force Base was well timed for my need to unwind. I would be flying copilot with Alexander. Our college roommate days flashed by in my memory. What fun we were about to have on a much grander scale than we ever knew at Oklahoma State.

On that first Friday back at work, sixteen of us took off in eight Tweets, with only two of them the conventional bare aluminum color. The other six were the many colors of the corrosion control birds. Colonel Meneur led one flight of four in the red Tweet, while John and I led the second flight of four in my favorite mockingbird blue T-37.

"Easter Egg zero-one Flight, initial, full stop," Colonel Meneur called over the radio to Laughlin Tower as his colorful flight of four T-37s approached the runway at 1500 feet above the ground.

"Roger, Easter Egg zero-one Flight, you're cleared to land runway one-three. Report right break. Winds: one-six-zero at ten knots, gusting to fifteen. Altimeter: two-niner-niner-two."

Colonel Meneur soon called his right break, pitching out in a sixty-degree-banked turn, followed at four second intervals by his three wingmen. This placed the commander in a position downwind to lower his speed brake, landing gear, and flaps before starting a slow, descending turn to the runway for landing. Behind him Easter Egg zero-one numbers two, three, and four called their right breaks and gear checks on final approach before touchdown.

"Easter Egg two-one Flight, initial, full stop," Alexander radioed the tower as our own four-ship formation approached the runway in echelon formation.

Tower relayed the same clearance and wind.

"Easter Egg two-one lead, right break," I radioed to the tower after Alexan-

der banked our bird into the pitchout and reduced power to sixty percent on both engines.

We were an extra 500 feet more above the runway than students were used to flying in training. Attempting to land on cross country flights usually blew their minds. The landing gear warning beeper blared in our ears.

"Oops, I forgot my radio call, didn't I? I'm glad you remembered for me." He loosened up his turn to correct his spacing for the winds. "If it weren't for students, I'd forget to do a lot of things. Thank goodness, they never know when we make little mistakes."

"Stick with me," I said, "and you'll go far."

"Then take the stick and land this thing for me while I look around for our reception committee."

"I've got it." I shook the control stick out of habit to indicate I held the controls to the aircraft.

Slowing to 150 knots, I slammed down the landing gear handle, forcefully as always, and waited for the three-green gear-down lights to come on and the warning beeper to stop.

"Gears down and locked." I breathed an audible sigh. "And that's good because I'd rather land gear up than listen to that damned beep-beep-beep another minute."

"Why don't you turn early so number four won't have a two-mile final turn."

"Good idea," I said, dropping full flaps and beginning our descending final turn simultaneously. *"Easter Egg two-one lead, gear check, full stop.* Notice, John, that I remember my radio calls."

"Good, then why don't we drop the speed brake?" He laughed.

I had forgotten the blasted thing. At the time I took control of our aircraft, I was supposed to drop the drag inducing speed break before my final turn. Sure enough, by forgetting to add drag, by turning early and, by flying the pattern at a 500 feet higher altitude than students practiced their landings, my landing would be long. Instead of landing within the first 1000 feet of the runway, I would be lucky to put the bird down in less than 2000 feet.

"Holy Cow!" Alexander said. "Put this mother down as short as you can. They've got two fire trucks spraying water to taxi us in!"

Reducing the engines to idle, I searched for the object of Alexander's excitement. On the taxiway near the 4000 feet marker were two large, red, fire trucks, spraying their fire hoses much like the ships would do for the arrival of the *QE II* in New York's harbor. Colonel Meneur's four-ship was following one of the red fire trucks back to the parking ramp.

"Slow this mother down!" Alexander laughed again as I flared our Tweet for landing. "If we miss that turnoff, you'll be the laughingstock of this base!"

"My goodness! That fire truck has something worth stopping for. Look!"

Pointing to the back of the fire truck, Alexander finally realized why my braking was so effective after touching down just past the 2000-foot marker. Standing on the back of the enormous fire truck were two young ladies, wearing tiny bikinis and holding up a sign that said, *"FOLLOW ME."* We fortunately slowed down just enough to pull off the runway and follow. The ladies cleverly held their sign between them to enable an unobstructed view of their bodies, which our hosts undoubtedly selected for those anatomical features they so proudly hailed. They were probably two horny wives, married to pilots who most often got their rocks off flying airplanes. As the fire truck began the trip to our parking spot, the ladies waved enthusiastically, their bounty up top bouncing in cadence with the seams in the taxiway. I was warm all inside with a young man's ardor. Where but in South Texas could we see bikinis in the early spring?

"You're a lucky son of a gun." Alexander was praising my quick braking.

"Luck, my ass!"

"Look at that pair!" John raised the airplane canopy for a better look. "Good grief! I haven't seen a flat stomach in five months!"

The two women waved again and blew us a kiss before turning their attentions to the next Tweet pilots landing and lining up behind us.

"Keep your visor down so we can leer at them with our eyes, and they'll never know."

"Don't kid yourself, Amity. They know what we're doing."

"Look at her! Damn!" I pointed to the one in a yellow two-piece, which contrasted sharply with her tanned skin. Her bikini bottoms tied at the hip exposing a great deal of skin, leg, and her luscious navel. She filled out her yellow top well, especially as she leaned forward to wave. I had not seen a bathing suit like that worn so well since *Life* magazine's feature on California girls.

"Look at bouncing Betty!" Alexander pointed to the other more amply-endowed lady with a blue and red striped two-piece. Alexander seemed most impressed by her chest. I could see why. She was a bit overweight, but that could be forgiven after seeing how she swelled up and out of her tiny top. She had a habit, too, of leaning over to display them in all their gravitational glory. It was only after my gaze rose above the first lady's navel that I observed they were both auburn-haired with pleasantly attractive faces. I then went back to concentrating on that navel.

"I bet they see us doing this," Alexander said after realizing he pointed a finger straight at them.

"Yeah, and they love it. Just think, John. You only have three weeks to wait on Suzy before you can...."

"Hell, man. It's been nine weeks already. This isn't fun... it's torture."

We continued following the spraying fire truck with its sirens blaring. After checking us onto the Ground Control frequency, the controller gave us our taxi instructions.

"Roger Easter Egg Two-one Flight. You're cleared to the parking ramp. Just follow the enhanced Follow Me truck."

"Roger, Ground Control."

"Use pilot discretion," the ground controller said.

And we used less and less discretion as the evening wore on.

20

AFTER PARKING OUR BIRDS, WE noticed the base personnel had quickly skirted the bikini-clad nymphs out of sight. It was warm enough. They should have stayed. I comforted myself by rationalizing to my squadron mates that the ladies were married already and best left alone. Nobody would have wanted that complication. We unhooked our extra clothing from its perch on the ejection seat tracks and carried it to a waiting van. They took all sixteen of us to the Visiting Officers Quarters, where our official reception began.

Our crew from Laredo consisted of myself, Alexander, Colonel Meneur, our squadron hippie, Starch, the hyperactive Wise, the brawling Thud jock, Freed, as well as that S.O.B. and still Captain Military, and nine other Tweet instructors.

Laugh In's Tweet commander, a rather tall, large, and cocky light colonel, welcomed our colonel with an air of superiority and a smug, closed-mouth smile. I sensed that this balding commander held an ace up his sleeve but was only waiting for the right moment to call our Old Man's hand. It was the kind of game Colonel Meneur could masterfully play.

"Colonel Hurd, I hope your reception isn't over, yet. Those girls in bikinis you got gave us an appetite to see more!"

"I'm sure you'll be entertained," said the light colonel.

"With naked dancing women?" Colonel Meneur's expression was deadpan.

"Only maybe." Our host had an uneasy reply.

"Maybe?" Our colonel's bark was in his more customary delivery. "Uh-huh? We'll see about that!"

What our commander did not tell his host was that he had sent spies up the week before. We found out what preparations their squadron was making for our visit. Our squadron had practiced and prepared with our own marked deck. We knew every card in Laugh In's own hand. Colonel Meneur's unabashed goal was to annihilate their colonel's ego and to prove to them that there was only one "shit hot" Tweet squadron in south Texas. Our commander was a good leader to have on our side in the game of one-upmanship. Bikini girls? Yes. Dancing girls? No. We knew there would be no dancing girls at Laugh In. Their base commander had banned them from the Officers' Club after the night his wife took a wrong turn under the effect of one too many martinis and walked in on a naked performance.

"We're hungry!" Colonel Meneur stated before our host could bring it up. Then he turned to his officers. "You men check in here, then let's hit the bar! Okay with you, Colonel Hurd?"

The balding light colonel gave a closed mouth nod, still extremely confident in his little game. The grey fringe of hair on his head and the wreath and star over his pilot's wings were noticeable indications that the lower ranking Lieutenant Colonel Hurd had served several more years than Colonel Meneur. It was a point our commander had learned from his spies. It paid off rather well after our crew ate dinner at the Officers' Club.

At the conclusion of our meal one of the Laugh In captains approached our group.

"Colonel Meneur, sir?" He motioned toward the pass-through into the bar. "If you all will follow me to the bar, the men of Laughlin would like to present you with something."

We left the dimly lit dining room, took a few steps down the hallway, walked around a louvered partition, and entered the darkly carpeted area of the combination bar and ballroom. The floor was covered with chairs and tables facing a wooden dance floor and elevated stage. Typical of tradition, all of us headed straight for the bar, which with drinks at thirty-five to fifty cents apiece were cheap entertainment. Recessed in the high ceiling in the shape of a painter's palette was a massive array of indirect lights. Our hosts pointed to it with a high degree of pride and excitement calling it the "bat rack." I asked one of the locals what that meant, but he just grinned and said, "You'll see." Then he ignored me.

"What's the bat rack?" I turned to Freed who had spent his early pilot training days at Laugh In.

"You'll see."

"Whose side are you on, Freed?"

"You'll see that, too."

It was obvious he was deliberately trying to bug the hell out of me.

My aggravation was ended by Lieutenant Colonel Hurd's request for silence. As he motioned for Colonel Meneur to step onto the stage with him, Hurd pulled out a gift wrapped in old pilot navigational charts and tied in a bow of parachute cord.

"I present this to you as a token of thanks for bringing your fine aircraft and crew with you." The light colonel handed the cleverly-wrapped gift to our commander.

Colonel Meneur nodded his head then began opening the package but had difficulty untying the parachute cord. Captain Military, who already was hovering around the two commanders like a puppy dog, pulled out his knife used for cutting parachute cords after ejection, and handed it up to his commander. A nylon string connected the knife to Military's flightsuit, which made any use of the knife impossible until he moved closer. He climbed up onto the stage with the two commanders. Military instantly transitioned from the puppy dog to king of beasts—lording over, what were to him, the inferior masses before him. Colonel Meneur cut the cords on his package, closed the blade of the knife, then handed the instrument back to Military with disinterested thanks. Captain Military responded with a smile but continued to stand there in a posture that for him was At-Ease but looked to the hundred or so of us as Parade-Rest.

"Thank you," Colonel Meneur repeated as he and Colonel Hurd stood for an awkward few seconds staring at Military. The pompous ass remained. In fact, he had diverted his attention from the package to the pilots rimming the dance floor. His posture changed to a straight-ahead stance with arms folded.

Somebody yelled, *"Il Duce!"*

"I'll deny I know this moron!" Freed wisecracked.

Initially, the Laugh In group hooted while we Laredo types bowed our heads in shame. But then Wise started booing. The whole barroom reached a critical mass of more boos, catcalls, and even a few personal salutes.

"Boo-oo!"

"Il Duce!"

I was close enough to hear Captain Military tell our commander, "Sir, I can get names."

"Just get the hell off stage, Captain!" Colonel Meneur barked over the catcalls sending him flying onto the dance floor with a shove.

Military, with a surprised look on his face, began his descent in the middle of the mob. Two Laugh In officers caught him, while three of the Laredo officers nearby seemed content to watch him hit the floor.

"What a jerk," a local said to me after cushioning his fall. "You've got a real prick at Laredo, don't you?"

That prick put Laugh In one up on us.

Our commander began again to tear open the package, pulling out what looked like a box of candy. Boldly printed on the cellophane protected package were the words, "Road Apples."

"Horse turds!" Colonel Meneur shouted to the Laredo instructors, panning the box of horse manure across the width of the audience for all of us to see. "Are we going to accept that?"

"No!" we all said in unison.

Colonel Meneur continued to hold up the package displaying the eight neatly arranged horse droppings, each resting under cellophane in their own little compartments.

"Lieutenant Colonel Hurd." Meneur turned to his host. "I think you're having trouble pronouncing my name. You don't say *M-A-N-U-R-E, manure.* You say it like, *tenure.* *T-E-N-U-R-E!* That's what you've got more of than I do... and I still outrank you!"

The room exploded in whistles, cheers, and a few boos that even the light colonel found entertaining.

"Let me remind you, Lieutenant Colonel Hurd, that *Hurd* rhymes with *turd!* So here. You deserve them!"

He handed back the road apples to the laughing light colonel, who took them back without a sign of protest. There was another loud cheer as the two commanders stepped off the stage to head once more for the bar and to mix with the pilots who grew in number with each tick of the clock.

The group numbered nearly 200 men, all clad in their Nomex flight suits. Some fliers still wore their flight caps, affectionately called cunt caps. Those still wearing them were usually the captains and higher ranks while the lieutenants followed the rules and kept their flight caps in their pockets when indoors. It was usually the younger pilots who would talk loudly with hands up like little airplanes in formation, illustrating some boastful half-truth. It was a sight that to anyone but another pilot probably looked ridiculous. Many were incapable of any other conversation except flying and combat.

A voice started shouting. "Bat hanging time! Time for bat hanging!"

There was a rapid moving around before Laugh In officers in pairs picked up a dozen inverted airmen and lifted them boots first up to the palette-shaped recessed lights ringed above our heads. I now knew what they meant by "bat rack" as the locals hung by their toes to the massive, recessed light on the ceiling. It was an impressive display. As the seconds then minutes progressed, more pilots one by one fell to the ground.

"Two minutes, ten seconds!" announced a Laugh In student who had appointed himself the official timekeeper and program chairman. "Next! Step right up!"

Some jerk shoved me forward, along with Wise. Two men took my arms, showed me how to curl upside down, and hoisted me up. I could not even protest. The blood rushed to my head so fast I remembered why pilots avoided negative Gs in airplanes. As a kid this was easy. Now was a different story. My sinuses began to hurt badly, but pride kept me hanging determinedly by my toes to the recessed light. Wise hung next to me, seemingly relaxed, arms folded, and evidently in deep concentration. It was possible that his lighter weight made this test easier for him. I began to lose my composure when I noticed Wise's face. It was so red that his freckles were hidden, and his red hair was only slightly brighter. Two other batmen near me were laughing, causing one of them to fall to the floor just as someone shouted, "twenty seconds." I set a mental goal to hang on at least one minute. It was hard to do while suppressing my own urge to laugh.

"One minute!" the timekeeper said.

I hit the floor a second later.

Nobody caught me. What a stupid stunt. I risked a broken neck for the glory of Laredo Air Force Base, and my blasted buddies failed to catch me. Fortunately, I had looked up at my feet as they slipped off the ceiling, causing my impact to be evenly distributed over the back of my head and shoulders. Continuing the rapid roll, I ended up sitting on the floor.

"Way to go!" Freed said over the laughing crowd as he reached for my hands to pull me up.

Back on my feet, I checked my head for signs of blood. There was none.

"You didn't catch me, you son of a bitch." I laughed.

I continued to hold the back of my head. The throbbing pain was just beginning to get my attention.

"At least you know how to fall," Starch said.

"Fall, hell!" I shook my head at the shaggy pilot. "I nearly broke my damned neck!"

Starch pointed to the floor. "At least you're better off than he is."

I looked down on the floor where the first to fall at the twenty second mark was laid out flat. He was just now coming to. As he crawled off to a chair, I turned my attention to Wise, who was still hanging with his arms folded. The words of encouragement came loud and fast as the timekeeper called out each succeeding ten seconds.

"Two minutes!"

The crowd noise reached new high levels. It was an appropriate time to buy a gin and tonic. If Wise fell and hurt himself, it was of no concern to me because my head in its battered condition was my first worry. It still hurt.

Only a small bump had formed, which, judging by its size, meant the pain would not last but a few minutes.

"Three minutes!" the timekeeper said as I gave the bartender my order.

"Four minutes!" he announced as I gave the bartender my fifty cents and took my gin and tonic.

"Five minutes!" the timekeeper said as I discovered my head no longer hurt.

Splat! Wise hit the floor, and my headache passed to another man. Freed attempted to cushion Wise's fall but was inadvertently punished by the last man, a Laugh In instructor, who fell on him a moment after Wise dropped. The winner was unhurt. Wise had a headache. Freed got his bell rung.

"Five minutes, seven seconds!"

The crowd cheered its approval.

"My head is ringing." Freed groaned.

"That was our best hope," Colonel Meneur said. "I better halt this before we get somebody hurt."

Without wasting a second, he stepped to the center and called for the light colonel.

"Hurd! Get up here so we can settle this!" Meneur handed me his scotch and water. "Hold this for me, Amity. And stay close."

I held his scotch and water while the two commanders directed men to hoist them up to the bat rack in the ceiling. Starch and Alexander stayed under the light to catch Meneur while two local instructors stood by to catch Lieutenant Colonel Hurd.

"Move!" Meneur barked upside down. The whole group of four took a step back.

"One minute!" the timekeeper said.

The cheers grew so frenzied that I instinctively looked around for a stripper. The excitement was so familiar.

Two minutes. Three minutes. They still hung on with no hint of an end. Four minutes. These guys were good. Lieutenant Colonel Hurd, showing his age, began losing his toe grip. His face started emoting that expression of strain mixed with defeat. One foot came loose, causing the mob's cries to grow desperate for him to hang on. Two pilots moved under him and stood there for a least fifteen seconds watching his tormented, dangling, one-footed hold. Hurd attempted to put his other foot back in place, but the movement caused his whole body to rotate, resulting in an inevitable descent into the pilots' rescuing arms. Commanders do not hit the floor.

Everyone turned their gaze to Colonel Meneur, who continued to cling by his toes. The crowd's sudden silence went unnoticed as the timekeeper again called out *"Four minutes, thirty seconds! ...Forty! ...Fifty! ...Five minutes!"*

The fifteen of us Laredo pilots shouted words of encouragement at that milestone. Freed and Alexander moved closer to catch him, but the Laredo commander waved the two away again.

"Where's my scotch?" he ordered in a voice weak from the strain. "Bring me my scotch!"

"Five minutes, ten seconds!" said the student as I stepped closer to hand Colonel Meneur his drink.

"Thank you, Rob," he said, carefully taking the glass from me and holding it awkwardly against his chest.

"...twenty! ...thirty! ...."

The hush in the room broke only when they mumbled their muffled approval with each ten second interval.

"Five minutes, forty seconds," said the timekeeper.

Colonel Meneur took a deep breath then proceeded to pour the remaining contents of his scotch and water, ice and all, very slowly into his mouth. Then he folded his lips around the liquid contents and swallowed in one long squishing gulp. The scotch, water, and ice somehow managed to go uphill to his stomach, defying the laws of gravity, nature, and good sense. He gave a breathy, thirst-quenched sigh before giving me back his empty glass. The crowd in unison quietly mumbled its amazement. The timekeeper had stopped counting. We all just stood in awe as Meneur continued to hang.

"Okay. Get me down," he finally said in a strained whisper.

"Call the time," Alexander said.

"Six minutes and counting," the timekeeper announced. "Wow. That's a new record."

Alexander and Freed gingerly took the colonel by his shoulders and arms, bringing him down in triumph to plenty of shouts, whistles, stomps, and handshakes.

"Six minutes and fourteen seconds!" said the frantic timekeeper.

It just proved again that spies and practice did pay dividends. We were way up on Laugh In once more.

21

"CARRIER LANDINGS!"

I looked in the direction of the loud voice to find three long tables lined up end to end with a Laugh In captain pouring nearly a whole pitcher of beer down its entire length. Before I could fully comprehend the idea of long tables with beer sloshing down the sides, a student pilot running balls to the wall hit the first table belly first sending a spray of foam and sticky beer to each side. Two tables down from the impact point, two students stood, one on each side, holding a heavy dowel rod across the table as an arresting cable.

The first landing sprayed to a full stop a foot short of the human cables. The student rolled off the far side of the second table just before it was hit again with fresh beer and another student pilot. This person was considerably huskier. His impact put severe stress on the first table and the drag, due to his excess weight, put a stop to his landing roll almost immediately. His boots still dangled off the approach end of the makeshift aircraft carrier as the room of pilots began to laugh at this beer-soaked fatso. To my surprise, it was my own student. What is one of my students doing here? This is an IP only flight. More officers tried their luck. Only a couple ever slid into the makeshift arresting cable. With the cost of beer and the mammoth proportions of the cleanup rapidly rising, the game soon ended.

Colonel Meneur turned toward his host. "Are you going to have any dancing girls?"

"Oh, well... uh, I'm afraid not," Colonel Hurd said. "The base commander's wife, she raised hell about it, so any floor shows are in limbo right now."

"Well, we brought a present for your squadron from all of us at Laredo." Colonel Meneur turned toward the stage. "Lieutenant Ark!"

From a side door behind the bar, much to my surprise, my very own student stuck out his head.

"Yes, sir."

"Bring out the girls!"

A sudden hush enveloped the room. Men looked from side to side, trying to make sense of what was happening.

"Gentlemen," Ark said to the crowd, still dripping with beer. "Coming to you direct from Laredo Air Force Base, may I present... *Honey and Boopsie!*"

The two women appeared from behind the bar, pranced through the crowd, over the dance floor, and up on the stage, while a jukebox began blasting out the heavy bass beat of Honey's trademark tune. The area broke out in pandemonium as the sex-starved Laugh In pilots got a mental grasp of unauthorized dancing girls before their eyes. The Laredo crew seemed to enjoy watching their reactions as much as viewing the ladies. The women were dressed as usual in their six button blouses and blue jeans, slowly unbuttoning, but never stripping, until the second record on the program. They did it well. The excitement of the spectators built to a crescendo of noise—truly an unexpected student pilot's dream come true.

Ted Ark had spent all afternoon driving the two women from San Antonio to Del Rio to perform as a gift from Easter Egg Flight. Colonel Meneur had sent him on an unofficial temporary duty assignment for the whole week as a spy and social coordinator. The two big-breasted beauties were our ticket to fame and gratitude from all the officers of Laughlin Air Force Base.

Freed stepped back from the encircling crowd around Honey and Boopsie to get another drink. The former Thud pilot had a regular habit of stepping back to observe a group in action, seemingly anti-social at times. Maybe he had the right idea. There was just so much thrill anyone could get from seeing the same pair of naked women for at least the twentieth time. And certainly, their performances tonight would never approach the wild sexual fantasies performed at Laredo. Laugh In was simply not ready for something that intense. Freed laid an elbow on the bar, put his scotch on the rocks to his lips, and stared straight ahead. He cast a striking "shit hot" image, the "Marlboro Man" of fighter pilots. He wore his flight cap tipped forward over his eyebrows, carried his long frame in an erect, but relaxed, posture, and drank his scotch with authority. His flightsuit looked tailored on him. His River Rat patch signified credibility. He wore it with more pride than any medal he had won because it symbolized his more than 100 missions over North Vietnam and the frightful raids over Hanoi and Haiphong. He slowly downed his scotch, oblivious to the cheers and whistles of the other officers.

Soon other men joined Freed at the bar, though most still turned to enjoy the action on stage. Except for the students and a few young instructors, the more seasoned officers were bored. It occurred to me that I had gotten more enjoyment from observing the men's reactions to the girls themselves than I had gotten enjoyment from gazing at their bare asses. Deep inside I was embarrassed. Was I slipping? Was this what it meant to be mature? I stepped over to the bar to get another gin and tonic. I was more comfortable immediately.

"Hal," I said, breaking through his vacant stare at the wall. "What we need to do is step out on the town and get laid."

Freed turned slowly to glance at me but said nothing as he took another swallow of scotch. He knew I did not mean it.

"Let's call up some of your friends here and bug out of this joint. What do you say?"

He stood there a moment, staring deep into my face, as if trying to cast some dark spell on me.

"Bug out of this joint? Hell!" He laughed and gave me a sarcastic smile. "Let's bug out of this useless Air Force. It's too damn boring anymore, you know it? Hell! Starch was right. I miss the excitement and the guns. This place is just BS!"

"I'm with you, man. Let's bug out."

"Oh, how I wish I could." Freed took a last mouthful of his drink. "Let's go."

"Let's go," I echoed, and we walked briskly down the hall to the front door of the club. Stepping out from under the canopied entrance, we disappeared into the warm, dark Texas night air.

22

MY TREK WITH FREED INTO the town of Del Rio did not result in finding more sisters with a wealth of ranch land and other talents. Our night degenerated into a search for the Mexican transmitting tower of Wolfman Jack's radio station. We never found that, either. By morning Alexander was telling us what fools we had been. It seems that our visit had educated our hosts more than they planned. Honey and Boopsie had performed things on stage I had only dreamed of. We sat dejectedly on the stairwell of the Visiting Officers Quarters, not saying a word.

A *plink-plink* of quarters tumbling into the beer machine broke the mid-morning quiet as a can of Millers fell out of the vendor with a rattle of metal rolling against metal. We looked up to see Colonel Meneur bending down, grabbing the can, then inserting it in another contraption above. Pulling down a levered handle, he put two holes in the top of his beer can. Foam poured out both openings, but the commander took no notice. Instead, he quickly tipped the can to his mouth and chug-a-lugged the entire contents.

"There now." He caught his breath as he tossed the empty can into a nearby trash barrel. "Best cure for a hangover I know. Now let's go fly!"

Captain Military could not resist imitating his commander and dropped in his own quarters for a beer. He tried to chug, only choked, and we all chuckled to ourselves. The motive for such behavior was some FAA re-searchers who determined that flying with a hangover was considerably more dangerous than flying while inebriated, although sobriety was still the best method to ensure safety. Since hangovers seemed to be a status symbol for many Air Force flyers, several pilots were conspicuously holding their heads and looking bleary-eyed. Few, though, took the cure.

Two noticeable nonparticipants were Alexander and Freed, whom I had noticed before never took more than two or three drinks in a whole day of partying. I think that was why I liked them. They had no need to impress anyone and by their actions cast a positive influence on everyone near them. This was not the case with some other instructors who routinely taught the importance of drinking to their students.

In the case of Colonel Meneur, the commander never needed to show off for anyone. Anything he did was for his own needs, not for its effect on others, and he sincerely believed a hangover was dangerous.

"I sometimes wonder why I do this," he continued for those near enough to listen. "Do you realize how many million brain cells we killed last night?"

We all laughed because it was true. It was amazing how our bodies rebounded after drinking, bat racking, not to mention flying, with its physical and mental stresses. We were set again to see if our bodies could survive the 150-mile flight back to Laredo.

Alexander and I were planning to turn our return trip into a spin ride— an annual requirement for T-37 instructors. From experience the Air Force had learned that Tweets had frequently entered spins inadvertently. A continuing practice for instructors and students was to intentionally enter a full spin to learn the sure way to get out of it. Some pilots, even with experience, were known to have bought the farm, spinning to their deaths. I viewed spin practice as a fun and free ride in an amusement park.

This form of entertainment was completely safe if you stuck to following the prescribed procedures. All spins had to be entered at least 18,000 feet above the ground. The fuel had to be below 1400 pounds and be equally balanced in each wing. All fuel systems had to work to prevent fuel starvation and a flameout of the two jet engines. Alexander and I knew that the 150 miles back to Laredo would burn up the fuel to safe levels about the time we reached an area for spins.

Our group filed four flight plans, checked over our aircraft, and taxied the birds out to the runway in pairs. On our wing for takeoff was the Tweet piloted by Captains Freed and Wise, both ex-fighter pilots. I had a hunch about these two. I guessed right. As soon as we departed Laugh In and established our trip under VFR conditions, the dogfight began. It was all innocent enough at first as our wingmen kept moving into the trail position and making short bursts of noise over the radio simulating the sound of F-4C 20 mm Vulcan Gatling cannon fire.

"Say again?" Alexander radioed back over Maytime frequency.

"B-b-b-b-b-b-b-b-!" Our wingman shot back.

We flew a few more miles before Alexander called for an area.

"Maytime, Axon two-one Flight, Encinal, request high and low East area."

"Axon two-one Flight, assigned East one and two."

"Roger, Maytime," Alexander repeated, *"East one and East two."*

Bam! In the same breath Alexander put the engines at full power and pulled the stick back sharply, attempting to pull up, around, and behind our wingmen, Freed and Wise. The jet engines banged and popped as they wound up to full speed, but typical of T-37s, all the fuel converted into noise and very little thrust. No matter how hard John turned and pulled up or swooped down in gyrating turns, our wingmen stayed on our tail.

"Dang it! We're dead about twenty times over by now," John said as he leveled out and began a straight and level climb at the most efficient airspeed. We climbed past 20,000 feet when Alexander got an idea.

"I'll fix 'em," John said. "I'll send them spinning into the ground. Watch this. *Maytime, Axon two-one number two, departing East one and East two."*

Maytime confirmed that the area was no longer occupied. *"Axon two-one number two, departing East one and two."*

"Axon two-one number two, departing your frequency for Tower," Freed radioed from his aircraft, acknowledging the area departure Alexander had just given him.

Alexander then turned his attention to Freed and Wise, pointed his index finger downward, and moved it in an earthward, spiraling motion to indicate a spin. He wagged the tail of our Tweet with the rudder, signaling for more separation. They dutifully began to widen the space between our aircraft from three feet to about forty feet as Alexander waved goodbye. Our wingmen's spacing rapidly grew larger and farther behind us, so we turned to the left for a better look. Their Tweet was now 40 degrees nose high before the whole airplane seemed to pivot nose down on the imaginary hinge of its empennage. Freed and Wise began the unmistakable turn into a left-hand spin at one rotation every three seconds while falling at ten thousand feet per minute.

"B-b-b-b-b-b-b!" I radioed.

"Roger, copy that," Wise's response was now more cryptic since we were off the books of authorized procedures.

The plummet seemed quite graceful as they quickly fell out of our sight into the haze below us. Ironically, what seemed like such a rapid rotation inside the T-37 cockpit was gracefully slow when watching it from our own bird. They probably fell a mile and a half before they got the aircraft out of the spin and back to flying airspeed again.

"You ready to play?" John rolled the airplane level again. I was already checking the balance of fuel in the wing tips. He checked to ensure the fuel booster pump was working. We both stored away all our loose items that might fly unchecked in the cockpit.

"Let me try the first one," I said. He gave me control of the aircraft just as something hit our windscreen with a splat!

"What the hell?" I said, looking at a white mass of semisolid guano spreading out on the windscreen right at my eye level.

"I think we just scared the crap out of some bird," Alexander laughed. The altimeter read twenty-three thousand feet.

"I hope that bird brought his own oxygen supply." I pulled up the nose of the Tweet into a twenty-degree right bank and put the jet engines into idle.

"Hell, those geese don't need oxygen. They just open their mouths and breathe ram air."

The airspeed bled off rapidly and, as the aircraft entered a stall, I pulled the control stick all the way back and applied full right rudder to get the aircraft spinning. The nose sliced down across the horizon, rolling to the right, turning halfway around on itself, bobbing back up, then falling nose downward to stay for good, as we entered a stabilized spin. The nose pointed forty degrees down, forcing us to look up to find the horizon as it swirled rapidly past our view. The rush of wind over the wings created a loud roar not evident at other times.

"Throttles idle!" I said. "Rudder and ailerons neutral! Stick... abruptly full aft and hold!"

I made a double check of all my controls to check for any flight controls out of place. They were all good.

"Rudder... abruptly apply full rudder opposite the direction of spin and hold!" Slam! I stomped the left rudder pedal down as hard as I could. "One turn! Stick... abruptly full forward!" *BANG!* I jammed the stick fully forward as forcefully as I could. The nose pitched down to a near vertical attitude. We were now pointed straight at the ground as I continued to hold the stick full forward with full left rudder.

"Controls... neutral when the spinning stops... and recover from the ensuing dive!" I centered the rudder pedals and control stick, and the plane began to gain speed, at which time I started the pull out to halt my rapid descent. The Tweet began to shudder as I pulled the nose up just short of stalling the wings. When we finally got back to level flight, the altimeter indicated we had lost more than six thousand feet. It had taken only thirty-five to forty seconds to fall more than a mile and recover to level flight.

"Who needs a roller coaster?" Alexander said over the intercom. "Give me that stick."

"And we get paid, too." He took over control of our plane, added full power, and began the long slow climb back up to a safe spin entry altitude.

"What's on your social calendar tonight?" Alexander talked over the monotonous whine of the two jet engines.

"Nothing yet, unless you've got some hot date lined up for me."

"No. I just figured, if you got bored, you could come over and help cheer Suzy up... cook steaks or something."

"And change diapers?"

"Oh, I'll do that for you," John became more serious. "I called Suzy last night. She's really depressed... postpartum blues I guess."

"Oh, I might come over," I said cautiously, "but I was gonna call up that gal I met just before Christmas. She's kind of a sweet kid. If she's free, I'll drive by to see her this afternoon. If not, I might take you up on that... to cheer Suzy up."

"I'll stick around the house. Give me a call, why don't you?"

"I'll let you know, pronto!" I leaned over to check the balance of fuel still in the wing tanks. "We're seventy-five pounds heavy in the left wing."

The new father quickly switched to gravity feed on the wing fuel tanks and applied right rudder yaw to bleed fuel more quickly out of the heavy wing into the main fuselage fuel tank.

"How is it now?" We leveled off at twenty thousand feet.

"Okay. We're down to fifty pounds." Less than a seventy-pound wing fuel imbalance was considered safe for spins.

Alexander switched back on the fuel pumps, checked the fuel booster pump, made a clearing turn to check for any aircraft below him, and started his entry into a nose high left-hand spin, pulling the power to idle. As the Tweet entered a stall, it performed its normal shudder and left rotation into a nose low attitude. After one rotation the spin stabilized.

"Throttles... idle. Rudder and ailerons... neutral. Stick... abruptly full aft and hold." Alexander said calmly. "Rudder... abruptly opposite turn needle and hold." SLAM! went the rudder. "One turn... stick... abruptly full forward." Smash! went the stick. Smash went the glass on the CDI gauge. Down went the nose into a dive. "Controls neutral...."

He never got the words out before the nose passed the vertical position and continued back up toward the horizon, putting us inverted and still in a spin. Glass from the smashed CDI floated up to the canopy and stayed there as both of our heads hit the top of the glass canopy. We were suspended off the seats in an upside-down position but still held firmly by our seat and shoulder straps.

"Wow!" I yelled for joy as we spun inverted. "You really screwed that one up, partner!"

"Take the bird! *Take the bird!*" Alexander screamed over the intercom.

"What?" I laughed in disbelief.

"Look! I've lost controls! Take this—" His voice went silent just as I noticed the death grip he had on his control stick which had broken off inside the floor of the aircraft cockpit. Alexander held the stick to the side showing the broken end with its rough edge and loose wires dangling uselessly.

"I've got it!" I said, taking my own stick. The first rush of fear surged in my brain. "Throttles idle, rudder and ailerons neutral," I whispered to myself, not realizing that I had actually failed to recheck the controls. My fear let me say the words but not make the motions. "Stick abruptly full aft and hold." It was only then that I realized the stick was still full forward, which held it in its inverted spin attitude. When I attempted to pull the stick back, it resisted. I pulled harder. Harder! *Harder!* Nothing happened.

Oh God! I'm going to crash!

The Tweet continued its sickeningly dizzy spin toward the ground. We were getting ever closer to a decision point. The colors that disappear at altitude were growing brighter.

"Bailout!" I screamed and reached down to the arming handles. I turned again to John on my left. *"Bailout!"* I yelled again and again, but with the blood rushing to my head and the spin causing disorientation, I couldn't see him or hear him. I pulled the arming handles up and the canopy blew away. A rush of air added a fresh new sound. I barely remembered to tuck in my feet and chin and to straighten my back before pulling the ejection trigger, blasting me out of the cockpit head first toward the ground.

"John!" I looked up to discover that the aircraft was directly above me. It occurred to me that my parachute might open underneath the spinning jet. Then the butt snapper on my ejection seat pushed me tumbling away from my seat and clear to one side of the plummeting Tweet. One second later my parachute popped out, uncurled, and billowed open, snapping me violently back to an upright position. A wing came slicing past me, and the high scream of a jet engine at idle lowered its pitch like a passing train when it fell below me. Then there was silence.

I began to drift with the wind. I looked around me for John's parachute, but there was none. I threw open my face mask and lifted my dark visor to get a better view of our doomed aircraft below me. It fell for another half mile before I spotted John's chute opening below me, seconds before a ball of flame reached skyward after our Tweet impacted the earth below. Within seconds the roaring sound of the crash climbed up to shake the risers of my parachute as thunder would rattle a window.

"Thank God he's okay," I said aloud.

I quickly checked my own chute for tangled lines, tears, and secure lanyards. Everything seemed good, so I reached behind each rear lanyard and pulled the red tab attached, which cut the lines of four cords. The oscillation of my chute stopped, the descent rate decreased, and my drop developed some forward motion. I could now steer the contraption to a safe spot for landing. I looked down to pick a sight when horror filled my eyes.

"No, John! No! No!"

His parachute beneath me began a descending turn slowly into the magnetic attraction of the fireball below. He was trying to steer away but ended up spiraling into the hell below. The billows of black smoke swallowed up his canopy, and he was gone.

"God, oh, God, no! *God, no!*" I found myself screaming a prayer in the vast desert below me. The air was now silent once more, causing me to realize for the moment that I was all that remained. It had all happened so fast that I did not grasp its full impact until I found myself weeping. The tears began to fall below me. How I wished there were enough to kill the flames. But as the black smoke began to lift above me, I pulled the left rear riser down and started a slow turn away from the smoke and flame, opting instead for the desert floor and its grass, cactus, and mesquite. Then in a fit of stupidity I turned back toward the flaming wreckage and the body of my friend because, if he were still alive, I wanted to be nearby to help him. I was descending more rapidly now, remembering to look at the horizon and not the ground. I was too far over to be sucked into the flames as the wind carried me away from the direction I had tried to steer. My feet slammed into the ground before I expected it, which made my parachute landing fall almost perfect. My body was relaxed, absorbing the shock of the earth's impact quite well.

The parachute remained inflated by the wind, dragging me a few yards across the desert floor before I could pop loose the front risers from my harness, thus, deflating the canopy. I stood up and unsnapped my parachute straps from my legs and chest, then spotted Alexander lying face down very near the flames. My hopes grew as I ran the one hundred yards or so to his side. He had managed to walk out of the flames before he collapsed. His parachute was burned up, with only the lines still attached to his harness, and they were smoking, as was my friend and the small mesquite tree he lay against.

I knelt by his head. "John? John, are you awake?"

I was forced back by the unmistakable smell of burning flesh, his Nomex flightsuit and helmet having melted to his body. The heat was intense, so I rushed back to him and quickly dragged his lifeless body by the arms through the brush and cactus to a place of safety. He seemed dead, but when I rolled him over and removed the partially melted oxygen mask from his face, his lips moved ever so slightly.

"You're alive," I said softly as more tears filled my eyes. "Don't say anything, just lie still. Everything will be all right."

I knew that was not true. As I touched my fingers to his lips, I noticed for the first time that my hands were covered with bright red blood and bits of charred flesh. I stepped to one side and threw up just as another Tweet flew low overhead. I looked up to see the aircraft pull into a climbing turn and circle back to have another look. Freed and Wise were undoubtedly calling out our location to the H-43 rescue helicopter, which I hoped would come soon with medical aid. Alexander's breathing was weak and labored. As I looked at him, fear looked back. His burns covered him entirely, including inside where the heat and flame had fried his lungs. I took his singed helmet slowly off his head, exposing his wide open, frightened eyes staring wildly up at me. His lips moved now only in a struggle to get a breath, but it jarred my memory of what he had told me before about his own flying paranoia. His eyes were pleading for help. His most bizarre fears had come true.

I tried to feel his pulse but was interrupted by the approaching scream of jet engines once more overhead. I stood up and waved my arms as the Tweet approached in slow flight—gear, flaps, and speed brake down, with the thrust attenuators adding to the high-pitched whine of the engines at nearly full power. Wise, sitting in the right seat, waved back, passing by at fifty feet. They added full power and flew out of sight, leaving me again alone with my friend.

The silence gave me a chance once more to check his heartbeat, but blood covered his chest, and the skin around his wrists was fused to his melted flightsuit. I was afraid now to touch him for fear of injuring him further or causing him pain. Nausea swelled up within me again, but I managed to stop it by sheer force of will. I had to give him hope. He lay there gasping for air. I sat down beside him and spoke calmly over the softening sounds of our burning aircraft.

"We should hear a helicopter coming over any minute now. Funny thing when a control stick breaks off like that. We've been smashing those sticks forward like that for probably a million spins. Probably every bird in the whole fleet is broken. I bet they ground every damned Tweet we've got. You'll get a keg of beer out of this. I remember Colonel Meneur telling our class that anyone who broke the glass on the CDI would win a keg of beer. He wanted us to slam that stick hard, didn't he?"

Of course, John did not answer. I could not look at him as I talked. I ran out of words, stared at the ground a moment, before turning to see him again. His breathing had stabilized, which relieved my fears of what I would do if he started to convulse. I looked closely at his lips while in the distance I began to hear the distinct beat of rotor blades approaching. Alexander's lips moved, forming words.

"John!" I bent down to him. Realizing I still wore my helmet and could not hear him, I pulled it off and tossed it aside. "Tell me what you need!"

"Suzy," he struggled to say. I put my ear close to his lips hoping I could hear him before the helicopter rotors drowned him out. "Suzy." He began again his frightening struggle to breathe.

"We'll talk when you're well, pal."

I turned away in tears. Suzy and the new baby came to mind. How happy it always made me to see them as a family. I stood up facing the twin rotor H-43 as it slowly drew closer. The crew approached close enough to spot me and wave me down to the ground. The rush of the rotors and the blast of wind and dust overloaded my senses.

"God! Why John?" I screamed into the noise. Again, the rush of nausea overwhelmed me.

The chopper touched down. Instantly, two medics and Doc Terra jumped out on the run for us. They carried two stretchers with them, heading straight for me.

"Over there!" I said, pointing to Alexander, then vomited. "I'm okay. Help him, damn it!"

But Terra came to me first, while one of the medics rushed to my friend. The other medic stopped beside me and laid out a stretcher.

"Damn it, help John! Not me!" I sobbed at the medic, as the doctor looked at my face.

"Were you in the fire?"

"No, but I pulled Alexander away."

"Lucky you! You must have had your helmet on, or you would have burned your hair off." Doc Terra then looked at the medic. "This man is burned, too. Take care with his face."

With that, Doc Terra ran over to Alexander's side, and a great sense of relief swept over me as the first sense of my own pain became a reality.

I gazed up at the medic. "Did he say I was burned, too?"

"Just lie down on the stretcher for me, sir." His voice was calming and gentle but became more distant with each word. Someone held me under my arms while I floated and rotated in my own clouded dreams.

"Down we go, sir." Everything went blank.

23

MY EYES BEGAN TO SEE light glaring above me once again as the round form of a face slowly came into focus, eventually becoming that of Doc Collins, who had delivered little Sean Alexander so recently.

"There. You're coming to. Where's that bottle of booze you owe me?" His voice was happy, but the lines on his face reflected the agony of the situation. "You're a lucky man, Amity."

"What?" That was all I could think to say.

"You're gonna be okay after you recover from that bad case of sunburn to your face."

"I'm okay?"

"You could walk outta here right now, if you were allowed to, but we'll keep you overnight just the same... that's routine after any bailout."

"And John?"

He looked at me a moment, the pause telling all. He said nothing at first, but the flaring of his nostrils and the reaction in his eyes were enough.

"As soon as we can stabilize him, he's going to Brooke Army Medical Center." A deep sadness showed in his voice and eyes. "They have the best burn unit in the world. For now, we're doing all we can."

"I see."

"Let's get you to a room for now. Do you feel like riding in a wheelchair?"

"Sure."

I sat up off the table with help, rotated to plant my feet on the floor, and stood up. I was physically drained but stable. I sat down easily enough, then Doc Collins wheeled me out of the cold, white, sterile treatment room into the hospital hallway, where there was a great deal of activity associated with the adjoining room. I stopped the chair a moment to look in the doorway as a nurse came out. John lay on a table on his back, stripped naked, with bits of charred flesh and red blood stuck to the white sheets. A clear plastic respirator hose ran into his throat where they had performed a tracheotomy. His breathing appeared desperate as he heaved his whole body in his agony of death. His red and black form looked more like jelly than human as the organs in his abdomen swelled and receded in rhythm with his lungs. I turned my eyes away before the door closed again.

"Why don't they help him," I said weakly. "Why let him suffer? Can't they end his pain or something?"

"Let's get you to your room," Doc Collins urged.

But at the end of the hall stood Suzy Alexander, arms folded in a tight crisscross against her body, her eyes red from tears and worry. Before Doc Collins could stop me, I stepped out of the chair and walked rapidly to her. She ran to meet me.

"Rob, please!" She clutched my shoulders then rested her head on my arm. "Tell me he's alive, Rob—my Johnny's alive."

"He's alive, Suzy." A tear fell down my red face.

"Then I want to see him," she said more desperately, trying to go around me to where the nurse had just walked out.

"No!" I grasped her arms with all my strength.

"I want to see John."

"Suzy! He's dying!"

She shook her head back and forth several times. "No! That can't be!" She tried to pull away once more.

"I won't let you see him. It's not what he would want."

"But he's my... he's my...."

Her struggle ended, and she fell upon me with sobs of fear and the agony of not knowing how he suffered.

"He's my best friend," she said finally.

"He's my best friend, too." I sobbed and held her tight in my arms.

"He can't die. What could I do? The baby?"

I held her for a minute of silent tears.

"Let's go sit down, okay?" I said finally.

Doc Collins came with us, just as my flight surgeon, Doc Terra, wearing a bloodied surgical gown, stepped into the hallway and pulled off his surgical mask. He walked toward us—the message written on his face—relief.

"Missus Alexander?" he began as he sat down in the chair beside her. She nodded, yes. "I'm Doctor Terra. I've been treating your husband for his injuries—"

"Is he okay?"

"No, ma'am, I'm sorry," he said softly. "I'm afraid your husband is gone."

24

IT IS HARD TO ACCEPT the death of my friend in rational terms. One minute he is there speaking to me and next his soul is taken. He still lies there—he keeps his presence about him, but somehow, the loss is undeniable. When Alexander died, myriad memories we shared as friends died, too—those secret experiences we would have shared years from now in some raucous recollection. They were such innocent, decent, optimistic times in which we bonded our friendship. Now, remembrance of him would be stained forever with the painful knowledge of his agony. In John's case his death came as a great relief. He no longer suffered. That was good. What tore me apart with doubt, though, was my last view of him alive, not because he was suffering such tormenting misery, but that my friend struggled to hang onto life at all—to breathe—to stay with his charred remains.

And why did not fate select Captain Military or someone else no one liked?

IT WAS SEVEN IN THE evening when I woke from an all-afternoon slumber to find dinner and Freed positioned on opposite sides of my hospital bed. He looked at me with a calm expression and no tears or concern. He had been through this before—seeing his buddies die. A slight upward curve of his mouth suggested he was glad to see me awake—or was it to see me alive?

"Do you always grind your teeth when you sleep?".

I stared at him until I got mentally reoriented. Where was I? *Why* was I? The drab hospital room had two beds, the other empty.

"Oh, it's you," I said under the flagging effects of sedation.

"You don't look sick to me!"

"I'm not."

"Then let's get up! Let's take a walk. I don't like to see bodies that can only lie horizontal."

I pulled myself cautiously into a sitting up position. "How's Suzy?"

"She's okay for now. Some of the other wives are staying with her. They'll put her to bed early, I'm sure."

"It's probably good she has the baby to take care of. It'll give her less chance to think about John."

"That's bull. It'll make it worse."

Upon reflection, I knew he was right.

"Can I bring you anything?"

"No."

"Clothes or something?"

"My flightsuit survived. It's still good until tomorrow. I wish I could leave now. This place makes me depressed."

"Hell, it wouldn't stop me from taking a long walk."

"That's a good idea." I gave him nervous smile. "A quiet stroll a bit later. That would help."

"Why wait? Let's go now."

I swiveled my legs out of the bed covers and planted my feet firmly on the floor. I looked at my white, wrinkled hospital gown in the mirror. "I can't go walking the halls dressed like this."

"Get your flight suit and boots, and let's go then."

"Let me take a minute for a whiz." I stood, testing my stability.

I stepped into the small bathroom, closing the door before relieving myself. I wanted to be alone. I was fine—well rested and unimpaired mentally—only a bit depressed. I stepped back into the room, pulled off the tasteless hospital rags, stepped into my flightsuit, and laced on my black boots.

I quickly ate the tray of dinner by my bed and said, "Let's get the hell out of here for a while."

"After you." He gave an underhanded sweep of his arm out into the hall.

"Is anybody out there? Such as a doctor, an armed guard, or, heaven forbid, a nurse?"

"Not yet."

"Then let's go."

"Stay cool, Amity. Look official."

We walked as loose as we could down the hall, past the nurses' station, and out into the lobby.

"Hal, I'll give you a call in the morning," I said. "Right now, I've got to go see somebody."

"Be careful, Amity. Don't be gone too long, or they'll have both our asses for this."

I waved at Freed behind my back, passed through the glass hospital doors, and headed into the warm April night air.

The wind was moderately gusty, chilling my reddened face. My eyes began to let loose tears, sending rivulets of cold, salty water down the burned skin on my cheeks. To keep warm, I took up a brisk walking pace, tried to jog, but found it too exhausting. I was mentally alert, but the sedative had taken all my energy. I travelled one half mile before coming to the officer's quarters I had so frequently visited.

Suzy's base housing was a duplex which backed up to the golf course on the north. The other unit was presently unoccupied, the officer and his family having just moved out that same weekend. Two cars were parked in front. As I walked up the street to her house, I could see four women pacing around the kitchen and in the baby's room. Choosing to remain incognito for fear of being caught out of my hospital room, I walked to the unoccupied side of the duplex and behind onto the golf course. Finding a tree, I sat down to wait.

The grinding start of a car engine jostled me awake. It was about 9:30 at night. A second car started, and they both soon drove off together. As I quietly walked around to the front, Victorio Nuñez's wife, Ramona, was speaking in her distinctive Texican accent. She lived four houses down the block. Her voice was comforting.

"No, really, I'll be fine," Suzy said. "I think I could use some time alone for now."

"I understand completely," Ramona said. "I'm just down the block. I hope you will call me."

"If I need to, of course."

They put their arms around one another then parted for the night. When she passed the porch light, Ramona's face carried the grief she shared with her friend. She headed down the block to her own family. I waited a moment then stepped into the same light.

"Suzy." I talked softly.

She looked up into my eyes and smiled ever so gently. By the porch light, the puffiness of her eyes and the slump of exhaustion in her shoulders said it all.

"Rob. I'm so glad you came." She trembled, reaching out as if to pull me toward her with an invisible string. "Now it feels like my family is with me."

"Suzy." I repeated her name, reaching to take her in my arms like a child. We said nothing for a while, just held each other in our shared grief. "I miss him so."

"Me, too," she whispered, squeezing me tighter. "Me, too."

She walked me inside to the kitchen and offered me something to drink. She always had Dr. Pepper for me. I took a can out of the refrigerator and popped open the top. The hiss of escaping carbon dioxide made her jump ever so slightly.

"I'm sorry," I said.

She sat down, her chin resting in her left palm, her elbow on the breakfast table. Her fingers partially covered her face and its grief. I noticed for the first time that she was in a nightgown—one that John had just bought her as a coming home gift from the hospital.

"Hold me, John," she whispered too softly. I must have misunderstood.

"What, Suzy?"

"John? Hold me?"

I reached out and grabbed her right hand. She squeezed mine hard, then stood up and led me out of the kitchen.

"Hold me, please?"

I said nothing as she walked me down the short hallway into her bedroom, not bothering to turn on the lights. She stopped next to the bed and started unzipping my flightsuit. I didn't move but grabbed her hand. She pulled at my collar as if to pull the suit off my shoulders and down to the floor. In a whimper of desperation, she persisted in pulling at the material, oblivious to my efforts to stop her. She turned in frustration and peeled back the covers of her double bed. I watched in the darkness as she pulled the straps of her nightgown off her shoulders and let it fall to the floor. I quickly reached out and caught the silk lace. Suzy resisted my pulling the thin straps back to her shoulders.

"Just hold me, John." She pulled me to her and onto the bed. "Just hold me." She cupped my face in her two hands.

In the dim light Suzy studied me in puzzlement. She started to kiss me but moved back in surprise.

"John, what's happened to your face?" Her words were pitifully confused.

"Suzy." I spoke softly to her. "This is Rob you're talking to. John isn't here. Do you understand, Suzy?"

She looked at me again curiously, touching my red, uncomfortable face. Her eyes finally registered a return to reality when she glanced down in both shock and embarrassment. Choking with emotion, Suzy looked at me once more. Her gaze met mine in silent words of acceptance.

"Oh, Rob, I miss him so," she said in a stream of swelling sobs that peaked and fell in crescendos of weeping, as did my own waves of sorrow.

As we held each other, both raw of emotion in our moment of pain and comfort, we knew it would not last. For nearby came the suggestive sound that told both of us that life goes on. In the next room, ever faint, yet powerful, came a primal plea for comfort—the cry of a newborn baby.

25

THE MAJESTIC TOWERING CUMULONIMBUS, HERALDING the first turbulent signs of springtime in Oklahoma, grew slowly as I peered to my right along Interstate 35. The bulging cloud appeared bright, almost blinding, opposite the afternoon sun as Suzy and I entered the south edge of Oklahoma City. Little Sean Alexander lay sleeping in his mother's arms, oblivious to any of the emotion swirling around him.

Suzy should have flown home a day earlier, but she could not bear to leave her husband. Instead, she chose to accompany John with me as the military escort this Monday, bringing his casket home to Oklahoma.

Suzy's parents, with tears gushing, met us upon our arrival at the funeral home. Since John's real parents had died before I had ever met him, this father and mother of Suzy had been John's parents, as well. Strange how when I dated their daughter back in the Sixties, they had told me—practically *ordered* me—to join the military for my own good, not ever implying it was also for the country's good. A hell of a lot of good their advice had done for John Alexander, though I suppose he did some good for the nation.

I could not bear the emotional baggage that lingering with Suzy's parents would heap upon me. I excused myself rather quickly to go claim the casket inside. It was a welcome escape. I had dealt with enough of the World War II generation in my own parents, especially my mother. I did not want to compound the guilt trips and the patriotic lectures from an extra mom and dad. One pair of patriotic parents was plenty.

I turned over control of John's body, until the burial service in the morning, first making sure an American flag would drape the casket. Finding that my presence was unnecessary, I called my parents to tell them their son was almost home.

I was glad to see Mom and Dad again. It had been over a year. Considering the circumstances of my visit, I knew some mothering and father-son chats would do me good. Turning into my old neighborhood, John's early death and his infant son came to mind. I had a fear of growing old, not because I would die, but rather because my own parents would be gone, leaving me alone. How must they feel now? How must Suzy feel?

I pulled into the driveway of my boyhood home, feeling that sense of relief in knowing I was back where no one would expect much from me. I would be pampered. Everything I said would be new and interesting. I could be myself. Mom and Dad were both sitting on the porch watching for my car. As my mother rushed up to greet me with a hug while I climbed out of my car, I knew things were not going to be perfect. She laid a gentle hand upon my cheek.

"Thank the Lord your face doesn't look as bad as you described it over the phone. Oh, how nice you look in your fancy blue uniform. I'm so proud of what you do."

"Well, thanks, Mom." I kissed her on her cheek. "But I'd rather be dressed like Dad."

I looked up on the porch where my father sat, older than I had seen him in my memories, but still a fit man of sixty. His salt and pepper hair was longer than I was used to. He had grown sideburns. I laughed aloud.

"What did they do to you?" I was walking toward him.

"Hello, son." Dad held out both his hands to envelope me in his grasp. He whispered in my ear. "Sorry about John. He was a good boy."

He seemed smaller than I remembered. His head rested below my own chin.

"Good to see you, Dad." I looked over at Mom. "Doesn't she look great?"

"Pretty as a picture."

My mother was one of those who aged imperceptibly. If she had a grey hair, she never let anyone know. At fifty-eight, she could still wear a mini skirt, though I wished that she would quit. Thankfully, she wore plaid slacks and a wooly sweater that were at the top of the current fashion. It was almost too hot for sweaters. This year in Oklahoma, April was unusually warm.

"I'm afraid you might find things changed a little," Mom said as soon as I had stepped inside the house. "I'm sleeping in your bedroom. It's the first time I've gotten a good night's sleep in years. You know how your daddy snores."

Dad looked over at her with a perturbed expression and audibly sighed his resentment. True, his snoring was terrible. Listening to him sleep was like listening to early morning feeding time at the zoo. Nevertheless, I realized rather quickly that my arrival was creating complications.

"But I'll sleep with Daddy tonight," she continued. "I can lose a night's sleep to make my baby feel he's back home the way it used to be."

"Mom, I can sleep on the couch. You don't have to sacrifice for me."

"Yes, she does, Son," my dad said. "Mother wants you to feel at home, and I think that's important."

It was only then that I noticed the suppressed smile and the look of triumph on my father's face. He was getting to sleep with Mom all night long.

"It'll be like old times, huh, Dad?"

He smiled. We both knew I had guessed right.

"We have two visitors from Japan staying with us this week," my mother said as we walked into my home's familiar early American living room. I was not prepared for foreign visitors, though I was not really surprised. They always had visitors from foreign lands. Maybe they were serving Mom as surrogate sons. Two Japanese young men stood up to meet me. My chance for quiet escape at home was gone.

"Mister Himura. Mister Yamashita," Mom said, holding her hand toward each one as she said their names. "This is my son, Robert. He's an instructor pilot in the Air Force. He flies jet planes."

"So, this is the one you have told us so much about." Himura shook my hand and bowed slightly. I turned and shook the hand of Yamashita. He bowed and smiled nervously but did not say a word. They both looked very young, very thin, and very Japanese.

I bet Mom bored them to tears talking about her son. I hoped they weren't members of the Red Army Brigade in Tokyo.

"Mister Himura and Mister Yamashita? Is that how you pronounce it?"

"Very good." Himura smiled.

His English was quite passable. I concluded Yamashita's was not.

"I'll get dinner ready while you all talk." Mom then disappeared into the kitchen.

I looked for Dad. He was getting my bags out of the car.

Not this! Not now! I was stuck here with these strangers. *I don't think my dad likes the Japanese very much.*

"Well, what do you gentlemen do in Japan?"

"We are students," Himura said, "on a year's leave from school to learn American business practices."

And so, the conversation went on forever, until Mom finally called us to dinner. Only then did Dad emerge from the back hall and join us.

"Traitor," I whispered as he walked by.

"No. Veteran in the Pacific." He winked and skipped ahead to hold out the chair for Mom.

He never did that. But then, she never sat down, either. After three years of learning to do everything for myself, I was shocked to see my mother running back and forth to the dining table, as if she were trying to single-handedly show the Japanese at our table that she was even better than their own mothers. I should have known better than to expect her to change in my absence. They must have concluded that my mother was more exhausted than their mothers. But the food was the best. Mom was the greatest cook a son could have. Her roast beef tonight looked and smelled like home. Potatoes on the side with carrots. Brown gravy. This was living.

"Misters Himura and Yamashita are both students in Japan," my mother said, when she finally sat down for an instant. "It's so nice to see some serious students for a change. American students only know how to dress dirty and do their silly protests. And then the American press distorts things even more by only showing the bad parts. In fact, late last year they showed those protests and riots by Japanese students. Just a small communist group, I'm sure."

"We were there," Himura spoke up to politely correct my mother.

Here we go!

"As observers?" Mom tried her best to avoid conversational disaster.

"No, we were protesting the war in Vietnam."

My mother's eyes reacted in horror, but her poise remained intact. "I don't understand."

Dad's eyes just rolled up to the top of his forehead.

"We feel the war is a mistake and is ruining the American economy," Himura continued. "Without a strong American economy, we will not be able to sell our goods overseas. The world depends on a healthy economy in the United States."

"The war is very bad," Yamashita said. "We do everything we can to stop it."

So the little silent one could speak after all. Hell, I even liked some of what he said.

"I feel the same way, Mister Yamashita."

I think it was the first time in my life that I knew my parents had listened to what I said. My dad's eyes rolled back again, and Mom's face took on that unmistakable look of horror.

"You mean the war is bad on the economy, don't you dear?"

"Well, you're right that it's bad for the economy, but I am convinced the Vietnam War is a mistake." I looked straight into her eyes.

"You don't really mean that," she said to me but looked at Himura and Yamashita as if she were speaking on my behalf.

"Of course I mean it," I said, then to the two Japanese students. "What actions have you taken in Japan?"

Their eyes showed the excitement of meeting a fellow convert. It was probably doubly thrilling to hear it from an American military man.

"We protest," Himura said, eagerly. "We demonstrate at your American naval and air bases. We have even blocked roads in and out. It's time America ended the senseless bombing of innocent women and children."

"Well, we try not to do that."

"Do you protest?" Yamashita asked in his slow and nervous voice.

"No, I don't protest. I'm a loyal officer in the armed forces. We had students last month saying they didn't want the war over until they got to Vietnam and enhanced their careers. I challenged their goals by reminding them that our goal should be to achieve peace. They might listen to another jet pilot before they would a hippie."

"He doesn't mean this." My mother's eyes blazed in panic. "He's had a terrible tragedy this past week, and he's not feeling well."

"In America, we protest policy with our vote." I became angry. "I voted for McGovern in November. I was one of only two people to say so publicly. Two out of eighty people in my whole squadron."

"I'm sure there are many Democrats in the Air Force, dear." My mother was still trying to salvage her idea of a civil conversation.

"I voted for him as a protest of a war we are not willing to win." I repressed an urge to curse. "There are too many civilian leaders in government who remember winning a war once but who seem hellbent to sabotage our efforts with a thousand self-inflicted cuts."

"Robert, remember you're speaking to your father, also." Mom was speaking sweetly.

"I'm speaking to both of you. There is honor in opposing this war." I tried to calm myself. "I did it your way at first. I joined like a good boy. Never mind all the people who wanted me to do it their way. Run to Canada! Go to jail! I volunteered. More accurately, I was an involuntary volunteer. I decided to work for peace within the system. I'm proud of what I've said and what I've done."

"You'll have to forgive my son. He's very tired. He's not thinking very clearly. He's...."

"Excuse me." I was disrespectful to interrupt, but I needed to assert my independence. "I think I've been away too long for you to speak for me."

She looked lost for words as she mentally scrambled to salvage her dinner conversation. "But Robert, you've hardly touched your food. We need to move on to dessert."

"People are dying, but I'm not sure what for, and you only care about dessert.... If you will excuse me for just a moment."

I looked at my dad, who remained silent. As a veteran he had seen combat in the Pacific against Japan. He remembered the misery of war, not the glory. Most American women only knew about the glory. As I walked toward the hallway to my old room, my mother spoke. I turned around to listen.

Mom was still at it. "Would you like coffee with your dessert?"

She proceeded to prepare her apple pie with ice cream and to pour the coffee for her foreign guests, pretending nothing unusual had ever happened.

26

WE BURIED JOHN THE NEXT morning. Suzy was strong. I was not. John's friends were mostly absent—scattered to the four corners of earth. Most of those who attended were either family or parents of John's friends. Suzy, dressed in a cheerful polyester mini dress, stood proudly holding John's son, Sean Robert Alexander. With her free hand, she held mine close to her. Her parents, displaying profound grief, stood in the shade of a tree far away.

As the military escort officer, I kept my cool, but it angered me to hear all those parents say how proud they were of John. Proud of what? Breaking the control stick off his airplane? Or was it dying in the agony of his burns? Would they have said how proud they were of John had he walked in front of a truck? If he had committed suicide? If he had just died of old age? Why did he have to take an aircraft with him in a ball of flames to make them so proud of him? I think only my father understood my conflicted feelings.

I wasn't meant for military life. I do admit it had made a man out of me. I did not enjoy hearing a bunch of militant bastards tell me I should enjoy killing communists. The war seemed so justified at first, then it went to hell. Being a man meant not giving up my beliefs. Flying had never been a passion for me, just a temporary delay to my life's aspirations. I was obligated to active service for four more years. I was stuck. All I wanted was to have my hair long with sideburns down below my earlobes and a beard that I finally had enough whiskers to grow.

But, the night before, I had lost my cool. I insulted my mother and let myself get angry. She had the gall to try to speak for me of my own feelings. I did not have the guts to keep quiet. In the battle of gall versus guts, gall won. I lost. The generation gap could never be closed. Because of this under the surface clash of the generations, I decided to go back to my alma matter, where people would agree with me. I wanted to feel comfortable again.

"Dad, I want to go up to Oklahoma State and look up some of my old friends. Okay?" We stood in the cemetery at John's grave site. It was like I was back in high school again asking for permission.

"Sure, son."

"I mean for a couple of days."

Dad did not blink an eye.

"I think we'll do okay without you for a couple of days." He turned to take my mother's hand as she walked up to us with her two Japanese surrogate sons in tow.

"Oh, how handsome you look in that uniform," my mother said.

"Thanks, Mom. I know you're proud of your only son. I wanted to look my best for you."

"And you did. Missus Kinney came up afterwards and said she was so impressed by you. You remember Missus Kinney?"

"Sure, Mom, I remember her."

"The way you saluted and all. She was very impressed."

I looked away, unable to speak.

"Robert is going to drive up to Stillwater for a couple of days," Dad said. "He's going to... going... where are you going to be, son?"

"I'm not sure, yet. I'll be with some old friends," I said, still a bit defensive even after four years of being away from home.

"Leave us already? But we haven't had a chance to see you. You just got here."

"Just a couple of days, Mom. I'm here all week, so you'll have some time with me."

"Who's still there? You know it's been four years since you graduated."

"There are a lot of my friends there in graduate school. I called Jane. I hadn't talked to her in over a year, but she invited me to come up."

"I thought you gave up on Jane. She wasn't real keen on you, as I recall."

"Well, maybe my absence made her miss me, Mom." Maybe appealing to her sense of humor would lighten the mood. "You keep wanting me back. Maybe you two are alike more than you thought."

"Lord, I hope not."

"Mother!" Dad said. "Let the boy alone. If he wants to see Jane and she wants to see him, it's none of our business."

"But I hoped to see you a little more," Mom began to plead, tears now streaming down both cheeks. "A mother almost loses her only baby in a plane crash, and now he wants to leave."

How the tears can work on me.

"Okay, Mom, I'll stay until Friday. Then I'll have to leave for Laredo as soon as I get back from Stillwater."

And so, I stayed. I spent most of the week trying to do anything but relive John's death. Instead, I conjured memories of Oklahoma State and of the two women I met there who occupied my time for four years.

27

BY THURSDAY EVEN MY MOTHER recognized that I needed to get away for a while. She watched me daydreaming and came into my room. Sitting down on my bed, she placed a loving hand on my head and scratched it gently. It reminded me of why I so loved a woman's touch.

She spoke softly. "Go to Stillwater, dear. You need to leave your grief behind, at least for a couple of days."

And so, I left. I zoomed up I-35 to the Stillwater exit. Highway 51 was no longer a two-lane road going into Stillwater. The state was working on another pair of lanes with a center median. That was good to see, since once a year it seemed one student killed himself on this road trying to get home on Fridays. That was a change I was glad to see. As far as everything else went, I was hoping to see my old familiar college hangouts still pretty much intact.

The Oklahoma State University campus was always a gardener's dream—thousands of flowers to marvel at in the spring and summer, hundreds of randy ducks and frogs at Theta Pond, and hundreds of bushes in which couples could make out and pet to their bodies' content. The Library dominated the skyline. Its lawn in front was the focus of many social and political gatherings. The campus grounds had a compactness about them that I found satisfying. All the buildings for class work or socializing were brought close together.

Washington Street dominated off campus life. Also called The Strip, the street ran straight south from the Student Union and Theta Pond. The Strip was the real social center of the university. When OSU beat the University of Oklahoma in football for the first time in nineteen years, the students built a bonfire on The Strip that they pretended would set the town on fire. When friends came to campus, we took them to The Strip. When parents came to campus, we took them to the Student Union. The Strip was the center for youthful wickedness. We could risk getting in trouble but not get hurt. It was open season on beer sales, even though the law said 21 years old. If you were in college, you could buy it. The typical Friday night activity was often going down to The Strip to eat at The Coachman, stepping out and strolling down Washington Street, saying hello to everyone you had ever met in your life, standing on the corner in front of Bill's Italian Restaurant and swigging a can of beer, getting chewed out by a cop for drinking on the corner, or just watching everybody else get drunk on the corner after being chewed out by a cop. There was safety in numbers well into the early morning on weekends.

On the way home I would always walk or stagger back on campus through the banks of Theta Pond. There was always a bench to sit on or a bare stretch of grass to lie on. Someone told me in my freshman year that Theta Pond would never dry up because it was rubber-lined and the water could not seep out. I told Mom and Dad that interesting bit of trivia. I feared Dad was choking on his bite of steak. Then he added to the trivia by suggesting the rubber probably got thicker as you neared the shore.

"Why would the engineers do that?" I had to ask.

"It's a project the male students have been working on since sex was discovered at Theta Pond."

I finally understood. I guess the reason for my naïveté was the discretion of all the lovers. It was always dark. There were plenty of bushes. Besides, we were always too busy making out ourselves to notice what really went on in any detail. More likely it was simply a case, like all rumors, that it never happened quite like I remembered.

Until my senior year the single women on campus had to live in the dormitories in the university's attempt to save them from whatever their imaginations could contrive. Because of this, Theta Pond was the last place we could kiss before walking our dates to the front door of the dorm. The weekend curfew was 1:00 a.m., and no PDA was allowed.

It was Jane who always got us in trouble. Suzy always kissed me at Theta Pond then insisted we get to the dormitory fifteen minutes before curfew. Jane would take me to Theta Pond, find our favorite bush, and show me a myriad of simulated ways to make love before we hurried over to my pad. When we returned to the dormitory, she constantly got PDA slips from the counselor, which eventually led to her being grounded for the next weekend nights. These public displays of affection and violations of the curfew were so unremitting that Jane was finally called before the dormitory counsel. It was hard to explain to the dorm counsel why sucking my whole face between her lips every night of the week must go on at all, not to mention past 1:00 a.m.

I never had a car until my senior year. I was the only one. Chevrolet Malibu Super Sports, Corvettes, Oldsmobile 442s, and Pontiac GTOs were everywhere. How those students afforded them, I never did know. There were plenty of Volkswagens around to mix with the muscle cars and worn-out heaps like the Sunbeams, MGB's, and Ford Falcons. Nobody walked, except for me. Suzy never minded, but with Jane it was our first source of disagreement.

Now as I drove toward the campus, I wondered what cars were in style currently. In the Air Force all the Zoomies had Corvettes, all the nerds had AMX's, and all the rest had Datsun 240Zs, Mustangs, Grand Prix's, or Volkswagens.

Crossing the trestle bridge, where 6th Street began and the highway ended, a coed thumbed a ride out of town. Her hair was long and stringy. Her jeans were torn and soiled. Wooden beads hung from her neck onto a wrinkled peasant tunic. I was not sure what to call the style—perhaps barefoot and ugly.

Jane had given me directions to her apartment on the east side of town off Perkins Road. Driving through the main drag, everything looked much like I had left it. I glanced down The Strip as I drove by seeing the tree-shrouded campus at the distant end. The names of the bars and shops were different at my end of The Strip, but I expected a few changes. At the corner of Main and 6th, it was like I was back home again. The same silly left turn light was there, which came on last not first, unlike everywhere else in the world. The same old car dealerships appeared along my route. I turned on Perkins Road. It was nice to be home again.

My directions said to find the Monticello Apartments. There were lots of such dwellings. Things had really changed on Perkins Road. The apartment boom corresponded with the change in dormitory rules for women. Coming up on my right was a native red brick complex of apartments with high mansard roofs. I turned in the parking lot and followed Jane's directions to her dwelling. It was unusually hot for April, as I reminded myself, when I stepped out of the car. It had been warm like this for over a week. I read a note on her apartment door. Jane was by the covered pool. I knew with my first glance that I had been born four years too early.

"Jane.... Oh! Excuse me... I...." I stuttered as I walked up to her lying on her back, eyes closed, sunbathing.

One richly dark brown eye opened before she bounded out of her lounge chair. Grabbing me around my waist, she planted one of her potent popsicle kisses on my lips.

"*Rob!*" she said, jumping up and down with excitement, then extending a hand to my face. "Oh, Rob. Your face looks awful. How are you doin'?"

"You're... topless!" I stammered in amazement. And her boobs were truly amazing.

"This isn't the Sixties anymore, Rob. It's the Seventies, and I'm doin' my own thing!" She had the same tone of excitement she'd had when we first met. "Let me look at you!"

"I'd rather look at you." I was blushing. "You still look as luscious as ever."

"Thank you." Her voice was oddly formal. "Your hair's too short, but other than that, I'm still lookin' at a handsome man."

"Well, thank you."

I didn't like being reminded that my hair made me stand out like a sore thumb on campus.

"Any trouble findin' me?"

"No. Not at all."

"Got any bags to bring in?"

"Just one."

My heart was beginning to pound as I looked at her all over. She wore only one thing—a yellow bandanna bikini bottom tied at each hip. I had never seen a bikini bottom so skimpy in real life before—only in pictures.

"Let's bring your bag in, what do ya say? Here, help me with this top."

She turned around and bent over to pick up the yellow bikini top and placed the cups over her breasts. The view of her backside aimed at me was breathtaking. Straightening upright, she then handed me the straps behind her back.

"Tie this for me, please," she said, tying another pair of strings around her neck. I was only too happy to do so.

She took my hand and led me toward the parking lot, but as we passed her apartment door, she stopped.

"Oh, to hell with your bag." Opening her apartment door, she dragged me inside.

Jane shoved me against the closed front door and began a ritual best described as a menagerie of frenzied sexual behavior. Her tiger came out with claws that commenced tearing off my clothes. My seemingly shredded garments quickly lay at my feet. I reached for her bikini, but there was no need. Without pause Jane morphed into her inner piranha. Her lips and teeth began searching and probing me from head to toe until I was on my knees as protection from her frenzy. Jane was breathing hard now, as she knelt, bathing me with her full lips and moist muscular tongue. She was hard to hold because of the frantic rhythms of her desire. Putting my own lips next to hers, the force of her kisses took on a life of their own as she banged my head against her front door.

"Quick!" she said between breaths. "It's safer in bed." She took my hand once more.

She ran me into her bedroom at top speed with the urgency of a ravenous cheetah. Throwing me down, she pounced. Jane moved her whole body rhythmically until a first shudder of animal pleasure flowed in her quivering loins.

She paused briefly to recharge, rolled me over again, pulled me up to her lips, and kissed my mouth with vacuum efficiency. I didn't know whether to be excited or frightened. Except for the entertainment value, it so far had been a one-way street. There seemed no end to it.

Only briefly did she like the attention I gave her before she left me for another narcissistic pleasure quest. It was obvious I was only her vessel, not her lover. She continued in her inexhaustible undulating rhapsody, then without warning let out a carnal scream and shuddered like a wildcat in her death throes.

It was only after the wildcat died that she invited me into her world of passion and became human again. Mercifully, with time we collapsed in a well-earned moment of exhaustion. The whole session had taken no longer than three minutes. Some things about my college days had not changed. It was great to be back home again.

28

THREE HOURS LATER I WATCHED a naked Jane get up from her bed, climb nimbly over my prostrate and sated body, and glide energetically out of her bedroom. She had spent the time since I had arrived performing her hourly ritual of draining my life source, then bringing back the dead. I found it hard to move, much less to put on clothes.

"Why don't we eat dinner at The Coachman?" I asked Jane between panting breaths.

"We can't." She answered from the bathroom.

"Why not?"

"It's no longer there."

"Well, let's eat where it used to be. Is there another eatery in its place?"

"You'll have to drink your dinner if you do." She stepped into the short hall in her attire for the evening. "It's a bar."

My lower jaw nearly hit the floor. She was in a pair of bib overalls.

That was all.

No shirt. No underwear. No bra. Not even shoes.

The bib barely covered her ample assets. The galluses stretched taught, while a breast oozed out against each open side. The sides of the denim were snapped up, but gaps exposed the flesh where her panties should have been.

"Holy cow!"

"Rob!" She cooed then spun herself around. "Welcome to the Seventies."

"Well, is Bill's Italian open in the Seventies?" I was thinking of the awkwardness I was about to suffer. With Jane's equipment on display, I stopped worrying that my short hair would stick out like a sore thumb. No one would even notice me.

"Yes! It's still open. We'll go Italian tonight."

After I dressed, we stepped out of her apartment into a warm spring evening. The sun was already down, and I guessed the April air would soon get cooler, so I threw a jacket and a sweater in the back seat of my car.

"Oh, Rob, you know I never get cold."

She was sitting in my car's bucket seat now, the galluses loose because of her sitting position. There they were—all two of them—open for the world to see.

God! What was going to happen when we sat down at Bill's? They'd throw us out!

I drove apprehensively to The Strip but was amazed to find a parking place right in front. Four years before no one would ever find a parking place within four blocks of the place. What luck.

"We must be here early. The crowds are late to gather tonight."

"I don't think so." Her voice held a clear *"boy are you dumb"* inflection.

When she stepped out of my car and onto the sidewalk, I decided I was glad no one was there to see her. It was at this moment while looking at her that I decided—*What the hell?*—and chose to enjoy it. Nobody would ever see me again after tonight, so what did I care? And mercy! She was a turn-on!

Around the corner from where we parked was a new phenomenon—a bicycle rack, loaded full of every style of bike one could name. Few rode bicycles when I went to OSU. Now, when I turned around to look, bike racks were everywhere along The Strip.

"Where's your bike?"

"Oh, I don't really have one. If I ever need one, I just borrow it. There's always one that nobody seems to own."

"You just sort of steal it?" I opened the door into Bill's for her.

"No, no. Not steal. They're community property. We share them."

Had the students turned into a bunch of communists?

"Why does everybody have to own everything?" she continued. "That's why the world's always at war. They want to own somebody else or something else."

Communists! What was I thinking? I sounded like Captain Military!

"Two for dinner," I said to the bug-eyed, middle-aged waiter. Then to Jane, "Community bikes. That sounds like something a pilot I know would say we're fighting to defend against. Save the world from community bicycles!"

"You military people share your bombers where you work, don't you?" I held her chair, and she sat down. There they went again, falling out both sides of her denim bib.

"Well, first they're trainers, not bombers. You're right, though, we share our aircraft."

"Well, I like to call them bombers. They're all the same to me. No damn good. They all help to kill people."

There was a prolonged, tense silence. *What did she say that for? Aren't we on the same side?*

"What do you want to order?" I tried breaking an uncomfortable lull in our discussion. "I'd like a hamburger pizza and garlic spaghetti on the side."

"Let's order one with everything on it. And a pitcher of beer... make it a large."

"You better order something with garlic, or there will be unilateral chemical warfare."

Oh-no! Why did I have to say that?

"You mean like Agent Garlic? I'd hate for you to defoliate the trees alone." She was smiling as she said it. "Order me some garlic bread, and we'll pollute the world together."

"It will only defoliate our clothes."

"Oo-oo." Jane purred. "Now I like that."

At least sex was something we agreed on. I was beginning to revive, listening to her feline vocalizations. But I ate fast, once our order came, primarily because I was so uneasy talking to her. She had changed. She now had that way of jabbing at my military status, as if I alone were the sole cause of everything happening in Vietnam. Her jabs gathered steam as we ate dinner until it was as relentless as her sex drive.

"I hope your face gets to looking better. I might be embarrassed if it looked like that very long," Jane said, sounding not the least bit concerned with my own scrape with near death.

"I got it because I saved a man's life," I said, not at all happy even discussing it with her now.

"You didn't save John's life. All you did was make your face ugly."

For an instant, the swell of pain came back. The pain of seeing my best friend in agony, the flesh falling off in bits and pieces. Strange. John had never screamed in pain.

"I'm glad I don't have to depend on you to save my life," I stared at her spiteful, sybaritic grin.

She knew exactly what she was doing.

"I do only what is worth doing. I just wouldn't have burned my face for a dead man."

"Jane, that dead man happened to be a friend of yours!" I said in a raised voice. "Don't you care!?"

She stood hurriedly. "Let me tell you, Rob. I just don't... oh, never mind."

"You just don't *what?*" I was angrily standing up beside her.

"Never mind." Jane stepped toward the door. "Let's just pay and get out of here."

"What you said just now hurts." I was fighting back tears.

"I'm sorry, Rob," she said, unexpectedly changing her attitude at the same time as she reached for the door. "I get carried away sometimes. I don't really mean that."

"Thanks." But the adrenalin was still pumping wildly into my nerve centers.

"There are some friends of mine I'd like you to meet."

I asked for our check at the register, our waiter still stealing glances at Jane's chosen attire.

"Let's start this evening all over."

"Okay."

"Of course, I care about John." For the first time an expression of sympathy came into her face. "The crash must have been terrible on you. And poor Suzy."

Another first. She hadn't even mentioned Suzy since I had talked to her on the telephone.

"Yes. It was terrible, and I don't feel like talking about it."

"I understand." She seemed earnest. "We'll go up the street here, meet some really neat people, and talk about something less serious. We'll get your mind off things."

Good. I'll look at you and talk to them.

"Great." I smiled with a sigh. "Anybody I would remember?"

"I think so. Let's go find out who's there."

I paid our waiter cash with an overly generous tip, rather than wait for change. She took my hand and led me energetically across the street to what used to be a dry cleaner. I couldn't figure out what it was now. Nobody seemed to be near it. Then I realized something more. There was nobody near anything. Except for an occasional pedestrian or cyclist, The Strip was deserted. Dead.

"Hey! Where is everybody, Jane?"

"Inside."

"Inside what? It looks dead out here!"

"Inside houses, like where we're going."

"Why?"

"Hiding."

I was embarrassed and uncomfortable, like the kid who comes to a party dressed differently because he does not know how to be part of the in-crowd.

"What would they hide for?"

"Man, you can be so dense, Rob. They're doing drugs. Everybody is. And a lot of sex... if you get lucky."

I was dumbfounded. Drugs? This was the heartland of America. The center of conservatism. The Bible Belt. It was just four years since my own experience on campus. Could things have changed so much in so few years? A little underage beer drinking I had seen and experienced before, but not even hard liquor was consumed in my day. Heck! My day was only four years before. Could it have all come to this so quickly? Was I a fish out of water? Drugs? It was a foreign word in my vocabulary. Anyone admitting they had used any type of illegal drug was automatically grounded in the Air Force. One pilot, it was rumored, had run his Tweet into the ground within one degree of straight vertical. It was a feat considered impossible unless the pilot held the controls on purpose. The rumor had it that he had experienced a flashback from LSD. They had found drugs in his quarters. Drugs scared us to death. It was a dirty word. We didn't touch them.

"What did you say? Drugs?" Once more I scanned the empty street. "Is that where they all are?"

"Yes!" she said cheerfully. "You look shocked, Rob."

"Yes, I'm shocked! I can't believe this. Don't people get caught?"

"No."

"No? You mean it's okay now to do drugs?"

"Nobody cares anymore, Rob. Relax. It feels good. Just a little grass. Some hash, maybe. We don't usually do acid, but...."

"Don't *usually!* What has happened here, Jane?"

Jane turned around to face me, took my hand, and paced briskly down a side street to a white-frame house.

"What has happened? Vietnam. That's what."

29

JANE AND I WALKED UP to a dirty, white-frame house with a big, covered, wooden porch, leading to a large dark oak front door. To the right on the porch was another door, which led upstairs to a separate group of dormer rooms. A large, mature American elm towered gracefully over the porch and the front yard, its limbs just now springing forth with new leaves. Jane's bare feet shuffled through a flattened covering of last autumn's fallen leaves. The ground was absent of a lawn of grass, being too well shaded for that. A Harley Hog, its engine partly dismantled, leaned against the tree. A sweet smell seemed to cascade from the porch.

"This is it?" I hesitated to proceed any farther inside.

"My home away from home."

I didn't like that at all. "Who lives here?"

"Oh, just some guys. I only know four of them. The rest seem to come and go."

I took a deep sniff of the air. "What stinks so bad?"

"Oh, you silly...." She took my hand and laughed aloud. "You poor baby! You're so dumb."

Before I could ask any more questions, she led me to the steps and onto the porch where three men and a woman sat leaning against the house. They were passing among them the first marijuana joint I had ever seen or smelled for real, not just on the television news.

"So that's what it smells like." I sounded like some country hick on his first trip to town.

"Who's the ROTC guy?" The new male voice pronounced ROTC like *rot-see.*

He looked vaguely familiar, but his long stringy hair past his shoulders was a new twist. I had seen long hair on television, not in person. So, this was a hippie. At first, I might like hippies. Briefly, I might want to be one. I liked the idea of not worrying about anything and doing my own thing.

"You know Rob?" Jane was facing the hippie.

He was also barefoot, wearing bell bottom jeans and a black T-shirt. "Rob who?"

"Rob Amity!"

"Robert Amity? *That* son of a bitch!"

I tried not to react to his unexpected comment. "The one and only."

"You don't know who I am, do you?"

"Don't make me guess."

"Does Robert ring a bell?"

"Well, it's my name."

"Okay. How about The Reverend Robert, then?"

"Holy Cow!" I stammered. "You mean *The-e-e* Reverend Bob?"

Bob was one of the myriad students at Oklahoma State whose main goal was to graduate then go into some graduate school that offered further college draft deferment. Usually that was either medical school or the seminary. The closer Bob had come to graduation, the more pious he feigned his calling by God. Everyone knew he was full of bull. He even admitted it us unabashedly. He was always truthful to us.

"Unfortunately for me," Bob would say during his senior year, "I have no medical problems. I would be raw meat for the draft. General Hershey is not about to get ahold of me. I have decided to have God call me into the ministry... or not... if the war ends."

I looked at him, standing there with his smug smile. He looked anything but pious.

"Reverend Bob. That's what we called you, isn't it. So, you really did become a preacher?"

"Oh, to hell with God." Bob extended his hand, palm pointed up, in a shake I had seen only in the movies. "I quit the seminary when I got a good lottery number in seventy-one. How are you doing?"

"Fine, I guess." I was exceedingly uncomfortable talking to a guy in between sparks popping from the end of his joint. "You look a bit different than the last time I saw you."

"Different? *S-h-i-i-t!* Look at you! You look like a damn Nazi with that GI haircut. You a Marine or what?" To everybody but me, Reverend Bob was really funny. Jane's laugh was especially protracted.

"This is the way I've always looked." My reply brought more laughter.

"Get a bag, man," the dopehead next to Bob said. "You're too much."

In the light from the window I could see that all three men had beards, though only one was burly enough to have a heavy growth. The other two faces, including The Reverend Bob's, looked like patchy unwatered lawns.

Reverend Bob told me five years before that he was going into the seminary after graduation. It was one of the few ways left at that time to extend a college deferment from the draft.

The Vietnam War contributed more to making my own college degree less valuable than any other single thing that could have been devised intentionally. Men who would never have considered going into college quickly applied. Men who would never have dreamed of going to graduate school enrolled in abundance. A master's degree gained less and less prestige because of the sheer numbers of new postgraduates. A doctorate became commonplace. Then the rules changed. Graduate degrees became useless pursuits to avoid the draft. Soon fatherhood remained the only way to continue in civilian life, after getting a bachelor's degree. Finally, a man could only avoid military service if he entered the seminary or went for a medical or dental degree. I often wonder. How many former ministers or unhappy doctors are there who had post graduate degrees and at least one child before they even knew what they wanted to be when they grew up? I still look at a minister or a doctor from the Sixties and wonder if they miss getting to do what they really wanted. Every time I see an ad for a menial position requiring a college degree, I am reminded just how low the value of my own education has fallen. In my parents' day it was a position of status to have even been to college. Now a college degree got you a job making coffee.

I took another look at The Reverend Bob. Back then he had been clean shaven and clean cut, like I was. I so much wanted to dress and look like him now. With his beard and long hair and weird clothes, I wanted what he had. Perhaps for the first time, I was missing out on life. I hated the uniform I had to wear. Reverend Bob interrupted my daydream and spoke.

"I see you took the hawk's route and joined up. Do you ever think about those people in Nam you help kill?"

I decided a retreat was immediately called for. Had I just taken offense at that comment? My military buddies didn't deserve those insults. Maybe I didn't want what he had. That was a surprise.

"Are there any veterans around here?" I said, turning to Jane.

"Hey, good idea." She pulled on my arm. "Let's go inside. I know just who you should meet."

"Did you see that guy's face?" The Reverend Bob spoke to his buddies as Jane and I walked away. "Looks like somebody must have fried him."

We stepped inside to the weak smell of incense—or was that marijuana? There must have been environmentalists in there. Nobody was smoking inside. Several dim lamps illuminated the living room, which reminded me of a beatnik coffee house called the Black Brick back in The City. There was no furniture, only different-sized pillows—some glowing from a blacklight. The bigger ones tended to be scattered near the corners of the room. Each corner had at least one couple in embrace. A psychedelic poster called *Light My Fire* was pinned to the far wall. Instead of hanging vertically with the nude couple in a standing embrace, it lay horizontal with the man on top. Quite clever.

"You'll like it better in here," Jane said, still uneasy about my encounter on the porch. "People don't talk. They just experience the moment."

"It looks more interesting. Who's this you want me to meet?"

"Let me see. It's rather dim in here." Jane pointed to a couple in another room. "Here we are. Over there."

She pulled me by the hand into what should have been a dining room.

Instead, a pool table stood under an antiquated chandelier. No one else occupied the room except this one couple.

"Ralphie, baby!" Jane looked excited, dropping my hand to hug this strange man. "Hi!"

I disliked the way he kissed her on the lips then patted her on the butt.

"Is this Rob? Hi, how are you, Rob?" Ralphie extended his hand conventionally. "Jane told me all about you. Sorry about your buddy. Your face looks terrible. I'm Ralph Stafford."

His handshake was limp and clammy. "Robert Amity. You're who Jane wanted me to meet?"

"Probably not." Ralphie gave a nervous laugh.

"Ralphie was in the Army in Vietnam," Jane said with feigned enthusiasm.

"Is that right? My sympathies."

"Why do you say that?" Jane said.

"Just a joke." I turned to the girl who stood quietly against the wall behind Ralphie. "And who is this with you, Ralph?"

"This is the person I wanted you to meet, Rob," Jane said for Ralphie. "Rob, this is a new member of the house, Carla. Carla, Rob."

I took her hand to shake, but her whole body literally ended up pressed against me.

"I'm pleased to meet you, Rob," Carla purred.

I knew it right away. This was a set-up. I knew, also, that Jane and Ralphie were tight with each other. Was I a threat to Ralphie? It seemed so.

Carla was not unattractive, though at the moment it did not matter to me. I was not interested in this strange person—this little girl. Carla looked too young to be here. She still had that cute baby face, randomly pimpled, that reminded me of a girl currently learning to drive a car. The girl looked soft, well rounded, and potentially voluptuous. Her straight brown hair cascaded to each side from a part in the middle of her head. She had these brown doe eyes, which added immensely to her appeal.

Carla was jailbait.

"There's wine or beer over in the kitchen if you want some," Ralphie said. "Care for a joint?"

"No thank you." I was unnerved by what was happening around me. "I'll take a beer."

"Help yourself."

"Jane, do you want anything?"

Jane stood still. She looked at me with disappointment, holding Ralphie's arm.

"No, Rob. I'm going to smoke a joint." She put her lips against Ralphie's shoulder and smiled at him, squeezing his elbow.

"I'd like some wine," Carla said.

"Come on then," I said. "You better get it yourself."

She followed me like some teenage groupie into the kitchen. I was not about to pour the wine for her and get nailed for contributing to the delinquency of a minor. Not everyone had the same moral judgment as this straight-arrow military pilot. I could tell from her stares that she wanted to get nailed. She kept glancing at my crotch as if it were my face.

"I like pilots." She brought her gaze slowly up to my face. "I think they are *so* right on."

She poured herself a paper cup full of Chianti out of its distinctive straw-covered bottle. I peeled off the throw away tab on a Miller beer and took a sip. How come girls were never like this when I was in high school? How come they weren't like this when I was in college? They never had that carefree quality I saw here. Then again, Jane was like that.

A wave of depression swelled up in my conscience. I remembered how straight everything used to be on campus compared to now. Here all my undergraduate fantasies were becoming reality, and I was no longer the same person. Was growing more mature always this melancholy? I missed the freedom of college. No money, of course, but no real responsibility either. And no knowledge of what was really out there. There was a war now that I was forced to support, but these people could see nothing past the end of their joints or the fronts of their groin. How I wished to be one of them. But my time had passed. I knew too much.

"Let's go back to your buddy, Ralphie. What do you say?" Carla was visibly disappointed.

She did have a body worth admiring, with a flat stomach to go with her hiphugger bell bottoms and crop top—another style that did not become popular before I left college. So much had changed. So much fun it would have been.

"Rob, we could go sit down over there." She pointed to a corner pillow that was temporarily unoccupied. "I'm so tired, I feel like lying down a minute."

"I would rather...." She took my hand and led me the ten more feet to the corner and sat down.

Still holding my hand, she nearly pulled me off balance before I managed to break her grip. Chianti wine lightly sloshed on her belly.

"I would rather go talk to our friends over there."

"But, Rob, I would be so good to you." She moaned. "Let me make you, right here."

She held out her arms in an invitation to embrace me and began a rhythmic invitation with her hips.

"Come lick this wine off me. You'll be sorry if you don't."

"I know I will, kiddo, but, sorry." I turned and joined Jane and Ralphie.

"*What!* Are you crazy?" Ralphie was visibly dismayed. "That's prime stuff there, man."

"Yes, I know."

"Who has sapped this man's sexual source? Could it possibly be the U.S. Air Force?" Ralphie laughed at his little joke.

I was considerably tee'd off. "No, I already have a date."

"Oh, cool it, Rob," Jane said. "Just because you didn't have the brains to stay on campus with the rest of us is no reason for your prudish ideas to dampen our party."

"What's this about brains?" I was dumbfounded by this sudden outburst.

"I'm not your date now any more than anyone else is here. When you sold out your convictions to join the establishment, my loyalty left you."

"I don't get it. What set you off?"

"If you were a *real* man, you wouldn't have joined up."

"Did you want me to go to jail or run to Canada?"

"How should I know?" Jane sounded angry. "It wasn't my problem!"

"It should have been your problem." I spoke between clenched teeth. "There are enough of your friends or mine now killed or missing to make it a problem to me!"

"If that's true, why aren't you over there with them? No balls?"

"Jane? Please. I saw John die this week. Cut me some slack!"

"I think anyone who joins the military deserves what he gets. I don't care if John died."

"Would you care if I died?" My voice now trembled.

Jane gave me a long, awkward silent stony stare before answering. "I have no sympathy for your precious friends who are shot at or crash because they can't do their jobs right! They never got to see combat like Ralph did. Hell, he was on the ground. He has balls!"

I was trying hard not to lose control. I turned to Ralphie.

"Tell this woman she doesn't know what she's saying."

"I have no sympathy for you jet jockey types," Ralphie began. "You don't really see combat. You're just a bunch of REMFs! If you haven't been on the ground in Vietnam, you're nothing but a damn coward."

He sounded like Captain Military, calling me names. I remembered Military's own career gaps. I knew to ask the fatal question. This was too easy.

"Did you see combat?"

There was a long, angry silence from Jane and Ralphie.

"No."

"What were you?"

"I was a PFC."

"No, I mean, where in Nam did you serve?"

"In Saigon."

"What Division?"

"I was on General Abram's staff."

"What were you?"

"Clerk-typist."

"A clerk-typist!" I laughed. I looked around to see if anyone caught the irony. "Your biggest risk, then, was getting caught too long at the coffee pot, huh? Or was it getting your starched khakis dirty on a typewriter ribbon?"

"No."

"What made you a hero?"

He chuckled uneasily. "I'm no hero."

"You were a REMF, too, weren't you?"

"I guess I was." Ralphie spoke softly now.

"You're quite a hypocritical bastard!"

Ralphie stood still, red-faced, and speechless. I turned to Jane.

"I'm leaving, Jane. Are you coming?"

"I told you I wanted to smoke a joint."

"Suit yourself." I turned to leave. Underage Carla lay on the corner pillow, her low-cut bell-bottom hip huggers loosened. A young man's hand rubbed the lower region of her flat belly as she writhed to the beat of acid rock coming from the front room.

"Goodbye, Jane."

Jane mouthed the words back and lowered her eyes to the ground. She stood pressed tightly to Ralphie's side with his arm held behind her back. His hand now rubbed the side of her breast where it bulged out of the side of her bib overalls. The two looked at me with a "who me?" expression, like two dogs that just ate the Sunday ham. Jane did not look attractive to me anymore. I walked toward the front door.

"Hey, man." Ralphie held up two fingers into a V-shape. "Peace."

I continued to the front door then turned to reply.

"Hell, Ralphie," I said, holding up my own two fingers in a peace sign. Then I dropped my index finger. "I'll meet you halfway."

My middle finger flashed in his direction before I disappeared outside into the dark.

30

"THE WORLD HAS GONE ALL to hell," I muttered to myself, walking past the Harley Hog leaning against the elm tree. *"Everything's* gone to hell."

Smelling the pungent odor of cannabis everywhere, I could not bear to look back. Somehow, I knew that Jane would not be watching. She had other interests to make her forget all about me. I was hit by the realization that I was very depressed. Jane and college were out of my life forever.

God, my head hurt. How it hurt. I never wanted this. I felt like a fool. I hadn't wanted to join the military. I'd wanted to go to school. Now, both sides laughed and scorned me.

I had tried to go back to the familiar and the comfortable only to find myself alone. Thomas Wolfe was right. I could not go home again. I should have paid attention.

I shuffled back toward my car, my head down in grief. My tears welled up. I was completely abandoned by everyone. The music, which I had overlooked before, continued to roar along the walkway before me, its lyrics indistinguishable, but its message clear. "The whole world is going to hell. All is deceit." I agreed, yet the music seemed to force the point violently into my conscience. Whether the music was the cause or a symptom, the world was surely going to hell.

Nobody had seen the real *war. Nobody had experienced the* real *Air Force. We were all REMFs—all part of the support for this insane war. Nobody ever saw the* worst. It was always somebody else. The real enemy was your own men—your own commander—the MFWIC.

The ways our country and its people practiced deceit kept pounding in my head. Futile tears dropped unnoticed on the sidewalk before my feet.

I was forced to a higher standard by everyone. To be on display for everybody's amusement was hell. Even my most basic needs I must do in quiet and solitude for fear they would laugh at me. Why was something that simple so complex? So difficult? So much like facing down the barrel of a gun? John was the only one who had seen the real Air Force, faced death, and lost. It was always the good ones who died first. Why not the assholes?

Why John?

Across the street as I walked, two young men stood together under the streetlight laughing, seemingly without a care in the world. I was sure they had their own quiet worries, just that no one else would ever know of them. It was possible they were not aware of them either. Chalk that up to the powers of drugs.

Now, God, look across the street at those two students so smug, so cocky, so sure—defiant as they smoked dope before my very eyes. They didn't even notice me. They didn't care. This place was so blasted quiet. It wasn't like this when I left. In just four short years, what in the hell had happened to this place? This war made the world go down the toilet. And I was part of it. I didn't want to be part of it. I wanted to be part of them. I didn't want to see the real Air Force. Nobody did. Nobody ever had. But there was sin everywhere. There was sin here. There was sin where I played a part. Nobody was immune. And I couldn't even face them to do the most basic necessities. I wanted to be cocky and self-assured and respected, but I couldn't be. Instead, I wandered here, short hair, standing out like a beacon. All those around me had long hair. They fit in. Beards. I never had whiskers until now. And I couldn't let them grow. What had happened? Nothing was working out as it should be. God, how I hurt.

My head, too. It hurt so bad. My sinuses hurt, and I hadn't even flown. I felt like my eyes were popping out. My teeth were starting to ache. Hell! It was not from flying! It was from the cursed smoke! The choking marijuana smoke! It swelled up my head again. I was a basket case, and nothing seemed to help me. I had war wounds without the war. *Nobody thinks you're a hero if you don't get hurt in the war.* There was no place to go now. I looked around. There was nobody. My parents thought I was somebody else. I couldn't go home to Mom. She didn't understand me now. Maybe Dad? Maybe not. I wanted to go back to college. All I wanted to do was go to graduate school and teach. And now, this was all I had. *When I finally have whiskers to grow and everybody has a beard, I can't.* My thinning hair stood out so painfully short. Just when I had a chance to grow long hair. Now I stuck out so badly. They all thought I was an outcast. They didn't identify me as part of them. I couldn't go back to college. I was too old and too experienced. I'd seen so much. The sin. The sin of this newly discovered sex that I didn't know existed. And now, everybody had discovered it, and it was all around me, and I'd missed it. Instead, all I'd seen is the cruel use, the military's cruel use, of sex. And I couldn't go home.

God, the only home I have now, the only people who understood me, are those in the military. I am frightened. God, that can't be. I want to go back in time so bad. I want those times of love and hope and the sense of pride in looking forward to the future. Now, in the eyes of everybody, I am scum. I was a wimp to some, a killer to others. Nobody thought I was doing the right thing. All I want to do is escape and go home. God, my head hurts.

And my teeth ached. I didn't know if I could stand this feeling any longer. Where was everybody? The streets were empty. The only thing filling the streets was that sweet, horrible smell of dope. *Get me out of here. Get me out of here. Oh, God, help.*

I lifted my head to look once more at the abandoned dark streets. That sweet pot smell seemed to cling to my clothes. The pre-spring smells of flowers and sap were absent. Now the warm night was a wasteland of dope and anger and defiance.

Maybe draft dodging was the way to go. The real heroes had gone to jail, standing on their convictions. The dishonest dodgers had their fathers influence the draft board or they cut into the waiting list for entrance into some National Guard unit, saber rattling from behind the safety of their daddy's pinstripe suit. They were a collection of Barney Fifes. When Andy let them have their bullets, Mayberry became Kent State. I couldn't condemn those who joined the Guard honestly or still spoke out against this stupid war. The chickenhawks I despised.

I reached my car but decided I needed more time to clear my mind before driving back to the city. I left it parked in front of Bill's Restaurant and headed up Washington Street to the campus.

I didn't know anyone from Oklahoma State who went to Canada. I only knew those who went to jail. How I admired them. Those who fled to Canada made their own prison out of life. They may have been chickens, but at least they weren't hypocrites. Being away from friends and family in a strange land was punishment enough. It was like being sent on military duty to a foreign land, being pursued by the military police, but without being paid.

I reached the end of The Strip, stared a moment at the emptiness of the Wesley Foundation building on the opposite corner, then stepped across the street to Theta Pond.

This is where I got my first lesson in heavy necking as a freshman. Lush landscaping, darkened pathways, towering bald cypresses, magnolias, numerous park benches, semiprivate alcoves—a make-out paradise. I have fond memories of this place. It's dark enough to cop a feel but public enough to prevent the temptation of going too far with a girl. It's the best combination. Secrecy. Security. Serenity. It limited my passion. No public displays of affection.

I reached Theta Pond. Eyeing the dark pathway at my feet, I wandered down the familiar trail, wondering if couples still made out here. I discretely peered to each side, thinking perhaps I would see some of those young lovers. The dark form of an entwined couple grabbed my attention while I strolled slowly along under the massive, bare branches of a bald cypress. I did not see their legs before I tripped. Quickly regaining my balance, I looked to see what was at my feet. From behind the stump of a felled bald cypress, on the grass next to the path, a naked couple lay as one. They hardly acknowledged me.

"Excuse me," I said to them in the dark, feeling embarrassed.

They did not miss a beat. I walked away hurriedly, a little mystified by their boldness. The distant anger of an acid rock band carried discordant notes from one of the frat houses to yet another couple I spied sprawled partially unclad on the lawn farther up the fine gravel pathway. This second couple, I now realized, was no accident. This was a new trend.

God! How long had I been away? Not too many years, maybe? Had it changed this *much? Was this how the world was planning to go to hell?*

All I could think to myself were the same words. *Vietnam. Vietnam. Vietnam.*

I proceeded along the path to a thick stand of juniper where a blend of strong, sweet marijuana combined with the subtle scent of pine and cedar. From within came the soft moan, then the quiet giggles, of a young woman. The world had changed without me. I was born four years too early. My insulated Air Force life. I was missing out on actual life. Was I really this out of touch?

The whole scene reminded me of my last view of Jane next to her REMF boyfriend, Ralphie. My memory conjured up Alexander, laid out in agony on sterile white sheets. I kept flashing back to the naked couple that I just tripped over, sprawled on the dark lawn. Then I pictured the naked Alexander, struggling to live under those bright lights.

Both images made me feel sick to my stomach. Neither memory should be there. I had to get out of there. I had to get back where I felt comfortable at home. I was frightened. Tranquility was no longer here. You can't go back. Wolfe was right.

I walked, almost jogged, up the path to the open green of the mall. The tower of the stately library shown brilliantly to the north. To the east the Student Union faintly illuminated my path. A commotion ahead gratefully broke through my gloomy thoughts. Three campus policemen were holding onto a couple, handcuffed together. Their long stringy hair gave one of the cops a good handle by which to hold them. The girl was crying. The boy was defiant. I expected violence within seconds. One pot-bellied officer held up, I presumed, a bag of grass in one hand and a joint in the other.

"What do you call this, boy? You think you're something, don't you, you little hippie?"

Another sway-backed policeman laughed. "He's a jailbird now."

His laugh and silhouette were familiar. He had tried to arrest me and others in the late sixties for drawing psychedelic chalk designs on campus sidewalks. This era must be the best years of his life. His laugh was an outburst of joy. He had just caught another fish at Theta Pond.

I slowed my pace and turned to avoid the arrest for fear of getting taken into custody myself on some overzealous pretense. Now I feared the unknown. I had to get away. I got back to University Street and crossed to the residential area once more. Music from another local band screamed down the street at me from a nearby party. That sweet smell followed me for blocks. The barking of several large dogs startled me out of my gloom. Soon from bass to soprano, more dogs joined in the chorus of replies. Surprisingly, it comforted me by reminding me of home—back in those more innocent days. A young teenage girl began laughing from the open front porch of a ramshackle house. In the faint light she looked beautiful, womanly, innocent. The form of an older man appeared from behind her. She screamed when he took hold of her shoulders and pulled her back from the porch steps. The man, his voice angry, cursed at her. Then came the first frantic faint cries of pain from the girl. It was probably some argument that happened simultaneously in every city in the world. So why would I care, just because I was near?

I turned another corner onto 4th Street, avoiding the white-framed house where Jane was. One block later I gratefully reached my car. Now I could take myself home, except, I no longer knew where home was.

Could I go to my parents for comfort? Never again. They'd continue to press me into a mold of expectation that didn't fit me anymore. Was the Air Force my home?

That idea sent a fog of depression though my brain—a feeling I did not know if I could face one more second.

Why couldn't I die?

I was terrified of this feeling. I begged God to take this feeling away! I could not think of a single place I could go and find peace. John's death left me completely devastated and empty. While I grasped my car door in meditation, the truth of my feelings finally hit me hard.

I don't have a home. Help me, God! Don't make this happen to me!

At that moment, a familiar comforting voice called my name from the sidewalk entrance to Bill's Italian Restaurant.

"Rob, I've been hoping you would come back to your car."

I looked up to meet compassionate eyes and a comforting, concerned smile.

"How did you find me here?" I looked into this face that told me so much.

"You always come to Bill's."

I turned from my car, tears returning in unabashed relief. She met me at the curb, her arms extended to envelope me in comfort as only a woman can. I began to cry in heaving waves of release, her hair sopping up the stream of pain that left my heart.

"We're going to be all right," she said to me over and over. "We are going to be just fine. We're in this together. I need you, too."

In the safety of her enveloping arms, I escaped my fears. I could not conquer this alone. I ended all reluctance to share my grief and my misgivings with this woman. She was rescuing me from the melancholy depths of my own mind, with all its primitive fears and childhood insecurities.

I choked on the words as I tried to speak. Memories of childhood and of my mother holding me as an insecure toddler rose up to still my voice. I recalled once being lost and the long-forgotten plea I had cried to her when she found me. My nurturing, soft, secure life giver held me tight to her breast, as I was held now. The same tearful words returned to me in blessed relief.

In her loving, comforting arms I said, "Suzy, I don't know where to go."

31

SUZY AND I TEARFULLY SPED away together in my 240Z, leaving the campus area behind. We made it out of Stillwater in minutes. When the lights of town grew smaller in my rear-view mirror, I was relieved. Once on Highway 51, I pushed the car above a hundred miles an hour, senselessly thinking that speed would diminish my anger and depression. I held that speed for over ten miles, until I reached Interstate 35. From there I sped south with my Datsun at full throttle, savoring the rush of relief at escaping my phantom past. The exhilaration of speed approaching one hundred and twenty miles an hour gave me the feeling of being in control of my life again. My speed made it seem doubly certain that I would never return to that campus. For me, my history was dead, a book never again to be opened. Now, I only lived for today. I headed home with a sense of relief, still unable to say where that home really was. But with Suzy beside me, it seemed irrelevant. With her, I sensed I was home.

She leaned back in the seat, listening to the engine, in a visibly sensual trance. Her momentary serenity spoke volumes to me. Moving along at breakneck speed, she seemed energized with her own thoughts—that life for both of us would go on. Speed was our temporary escape to better futures. I unexpectedly realized that I missed flying. I missed the speed, the force against the seat, the adrenalin, the things I soon could not have.

We uttered no words for the half-hour back to the city. All had been said already. Our friendship was based on a comfort in silence. We were at ease in this serenity. We were home.

I slowed to a more reasonable speed as we approached the city limits near Edmond. It was then that Suzy laid her hand on the center console in open invitation. I took her hand in my own. A thousand words spoke to us in our touch.

They said, *I'm sorry we hurt. I miss John. Thank you for being near.*

I love you.

32

THE DATE PALMS AND A desert now in bloom came into view, thrilling me like seeing an old friend. The trees in Laredo lined the center median of I-35 for several miles before the interstate highway terminated a few blocks from the Rio Grande. It was late Monday afternoon. The air for a change was cold. Dark clouds began to roll in at the outskirts of the city. Within two miles of the city limits, a steady, gentle rain began to fall. Little children still ran barefoot down the gravel streets. I worried for those cold little *niños* who did not know they were supposed to wear shoes. I was always grateful that the city of Laredo was so far south and never got that cold. The children seemed oblivious to the cold rain. My own feet would have been in agony. I guess everybody has their problems.

I drove directly to my squadron building to check in from leave and to pick up a few of the most important mementos Suzy wanted to remove quickly from her husband's office. There were items in there, she said, that would last little Sean a lifetime. Outside, the roar of a T-38 in afterburner at takeoff thrilled me for the first time in days. I wanted to get back up in the air to face that demon who had killed my friend. Stepping out of my car, the scream of Tweets at idle pierced my ears. The dense, rain-soaked air was carrying the sound in unusually high volume to the front of the flat-roofed cinder block building. The flying status must be IFR. This looked like real instrument training today.

Once inside the squadron building, I walked the long hallway to the opposite end to check in officially with First Sergeant Cervantes. He seemed genuinely glad to see me.

"Good afternoon, Captain Amity," the sergeant said in his heavy Chicano accent. "It's good to have you back, sir."

"*Muchas gracias,* Sarge. Am I a captain now?" I was in genuine surprise.

"Yes, sir." Cervantes kept track of everything.

I had forgotten my own promotion. Even when I was in mufti, the first sergeant knew these things. *Captain* Amity. It sounded good. Promotion to captain was one of these automatic advances that you got, like getting the "good guy" ribbon. If you did not get court-martialed or receive an Article 15, you got captain's tracks at the third anniversary of commissioning as an officer. Since, relatively speaking, I had stayed out of trouble, I had reached the same rank as Captain Military. It was impossible to know when he would get his own advancement to major. I only hoped to see him on the streets before that happened, so I could walk past him without having to salute—just once. But first, I needed to ditch my old rank and sew on captain's tracks.

"How were things at home?" Sergeant Cervantes always asked about our families.

"Oh, just fine." I was wondering if he could detect a lie.

I signed the log, then turned to go the short distance to my Ragtop Flight. The flight room at first glance looked no different than before my last flight. The place was empty. The crew must have been on the morning shift this week. I had lost track of the schedule already. Ragtop Flight was dark except for a light someone had left on in John's office. A spread of light crept under the closed door and through the briefing room to the spot where I stood. I turned on the flight room lights. Looking around, all the old poems and sketches that had endured for weeks were erased from the green chalk boards. Gone was the drawing of pregnant Suzy with the word *"AIR"* pointing to her enlarged belly. The blank boards cast a Spartan, sterile spell over the room. I got a sense of a void of humanity—a continuing aloneness. I was still severely depressed over John's death. This flight room was supposed to serve as my safe haven from the cares of the world. Instead, returning here did not seem right. Could I not come back here either? Was this no longer home? Was Thomas Wolfe playing tricks on me still?

My knees were wobbly. I had an urgent need to sit down. I stumbled to my own briefing table and pulled out my comfortable chair to sit on. My desktop with its personal mementoes might comfort me. The class patches and family pictures, plus a few *Playboy* centerfolds that students had placed with my permission, added a more human touch. My eye first caught Boopsie's and Honey's business card that Lieutenant Ark had given me earlier. Next to it was my 5 x 7 picture of Jane. She looked gorgeous as ever. I had taken it just before leaving for the Air Force. The full-body shot of her was erotic by itself, but for me, I knew there was much more meaning in it. She was all body, no compassion. I lifted the plexiglass up off the table, pulled out Jane's picture, and tore it in two. Destroying it was not satisfying, but it was about time.

I glanced once more at my mementoes under the glass. The two centerfolds were gone. I looked across at Starchweather's table. The spaced-out captain always had a dynamite gallery of centerfolds. His desk was blank under the glass. Starchweather had been a one-track decorator. Take his centerfolds, and he was left with nothing.

Nothing would ever be the same again. I had a rush of sickening gloom. Where could I find comfort now?

I stood up from my table and headed directly to the instructor briefing room toward the light which fanned out from the closed door of Alexander's office. I stopped at the threshold, rubbed my eyes to fight the depression that was filling my brain, then walked over to open the door of John's office.

On the wall to my left was that familiar picture that had so recently made me laugh by its absurdity. It glared at me now, and my hopes sank that things could ever be the same again. There, looking me in the eye from that picture on the wall, with the American Flag as a backdrop, was the tyrannical stare of Captain Military. I opened the door further and found the real thing. Eyes glaring, mustache off center, jaw set in a rigid clamp, and topped with that perfectly manicured head of hair just a tad too long, the beast awaited.

"Yes?" Military looked up from his desk. "What do you want, Amity?"

Startled, I could not get the words out. I stammered for a split second too long. It was as if the dark clouds outside had just rolled into my sanctuary to loom over my head.

"Don't ever come in my office like this again!" He ordered.

"Sorry, sir," I responded. "I came to pick up some of John's things for Suzy."

"Never mind being somebody's gopher." A queer smile stretched the corners of his mouth ever so slightly. "You best think about this instead. *I'm your commander now, Lieutenant Amity, and your ass is mine!*"

33

IT WAS ROUTINE POLICY AFTER an aircraft accident to be grounded from flying. Once back on base it took only a couple of days to get cleared for flying status. After a brief checkup by Doc Terra and a quick check ride by a squadron Check Flight pilot, I was ready for work. Mercifully, Captain Military was too busy to give me too much hell. He had been flying with Cadet Mossare. My new flight commander had declared the Iranian student prepared to make another solo try. Miracles do happen, so I did not think much of the fact as the Iranian cadet and I walked out to our aircraft. After all, it had been many weeks since our air sickness accident in the cockpit. With an April morning overcast, the air was cool and calm. Perhaps flight-induced nausea was a thing of the past for Mossare.

Our mid-morning pre-flight check went smoothly. His spoken English even seemed more understandable. His thick Iranian accent in these few weeks had gained just a mere hint of a Texas drawl. Mossare's walk around the Tweet had that swagger of new self-confidence. I was picturing that bottle of booze in my quarters already. Mossare climbed into the cockpit eagerly, letting the crew chief help strap him in. I liked how it was going. As we went through the in-flight checklist, my cadet seemed unhurried yet sparing of time. He used no wasted motions. I relaxed a little.

Mossare started the engines, called Ground Control, and taxied out like a pro. As we approached the glass-enclosed Runway Supervisory Unit for the T-37 active runway, Mossare called *"number one for the active."* The RSU immediately cleared us onto the runway for takeoff. The cadet powered up the engines with brakes applied. There was no strain in his voice as he checked off the jet engine gauges, which all indicated in the green. That only came from lots of practice and strong legs. He released the brakes and smoothly started the takeoff roll. At 65 knots the nose came up. At 90 knots the aircraft lifted off the runway. After acknowledging a positive rate of climb, landing gear came up. Flaps came up. Mossare made his call to Maytime. We leveled off at 3500 feet and headed to the auxiliary landing field at Barfly.

"Okay, Mossare," I said jubilantly. "Three practice landings here, and I get out. You're doing great."

"Yes, sir." Mossare responded robot-like.

He really needed to say something else for a change. But it was then that a miracle happened.

"Captain Amity," he said with gusto. "I feel good today! Today I do it!"

"You bet you do it today. You're looking good. A real shit hot pilot today."

"Yes," he said with an excited laugh. "Today I'm shit hot. Shit hot, yes. Shit hot! Yes!"

I was afraid that in his enthusiasm he would forget his radio calls and landing checklist, but I was wrong. Mossare began his descent to 1000 feet above the ground on cue. He checked off each item like a pro, and his confidence swelled.

"Barfly, Axon two-two, initial," Mossare radioed as he leveled off at pattern altitude. As I had anticipated from our weather briefing, a thin layer of clouds hung more than 2000 feet above us. It was not a problem. In fact, it helped to keep the air smooth. This was an ideal day for soloing students. The clouds were an added bonus.

Mossare flew directly over the runway at 200 knots, executed his pitchout into a left sixty-degree bank turn, and rolled out downwind flawlessly. At sixty percent power with speed break down, he waited until the airspeed bled to 150 knots and slammed down the landing gear lever, then called, *"Gear down, sir. Three green."* At 135 knots he lowered flaps, adjusted his power to hold a good turning airspeed, and quickly said something to further surprise me.

"Sir, this is a calm day. I think the final turn should be delayed slightly, since the wind is not blowing us out farther."

I was amazed. He thought of everything.

"Axon two-two, gear check," he radioed soon after he began his left descending turn to the runway.

My Iranian student approached the numbers on the approach end as well as I could have. He pulled power, rounded out, and touched wheels within the first 500 feet. The landing was a bit firm, but I had done worse myself. Firmly on the ground, he reapplied power, achieved takeoff speed, and began the climb back out toward pattern airspeed and altitude.

In the military, to enhance the economy of time and fuel, pilots can request a "closed pull up," which avoids the need to go downwind and circle back to get on initial again. Requesting "Closed" cuts the time in the pattern by three-fourths. When the traffic pattern is saturated, it is sometimes impossible, but at this hour we were the only aircraft at Barfly.

"Barfly," Mossare radioed. *"Axon two-two, request closed."*

The supervisor's reply was instant. *"Closed approved."*

The cadet pulled the nose up in a left ascending turn back to downwind at 1000 feet above the runway. The climb was rapid and the turn exhilarating. Mossare did it perfectly. Downwind he applied the speed brake to bleed off airspeed, dropped gear and flaps, and executed another near perfect approach and landing. Two down, one to go.

He repeated the closed pull up, configured the Tweet for landing, and, as he started his descending final turn, he called his gear check to Barfly.

"Axon two-two, gear check."

"Full stop," I added to his radio call. He was ready.

I turned to my student, jokingly. "You're too shit hot for me. Get me outta this airplane."

We landed smoothly and slowed to turn off the runway. I shut off the right jet engine so the intake would not suck me in when I jumped out. As we taxied back to the takeoff end of the runway, I gave Cadet Mossare a few last-minute pointers.

"Perform three takeoffs, two touch-and-goes, and one full stop landing to pick me up. Turn off the right engine before you get to me. I will fly us back to the base. I can practice my own landing when we get there. Do *not* forget my booze!"

He was ready. I parked just short of the takeoff end of the runway. While Mossare stepped on the brakes, I climbed out. When I stood in front of the aircraft, he gave the signal to restart the number two engine. Within the minute Mossare was on his own. I left my helmet hanging on a peg near the taxiway and ran the short distance to the RSU.

Climbing up the stairs of the trailered vehicle, I found my buddy, Johnny Wise, a second instructor from C-Fight, and two student assistants.

"Howdy, gentlemen," I greeted them. "How does it look?"

"Come on in here, Captain," Wise said. "Those clouds have gotten a bit thicker. A PIREP reported the ceiling at about 2500 feet, but it may be getting heavier."

"It looked okay from the pattern," I said with a gaze through the glass roof to the clouds overhead. "This is a piece of cake."

On the runway Mossare closed the canopy of his aircraft and taxied forward slightly before radioing.

"Axon two-two, number one for the active."

"That's a negative!" Wise said over the radio. *"Your solo call sign is now Map three-one."*

"Roger. Map three-one, number one for the active."

"Map three-one, you're cleared for takeoff, runway one-seven, winds are calm."

"Map three-one, cleared for takeoff."

His voice was less understandable over the radio. He was speaking more rapidly. But he taxied out onto the active runway, set his brakes, and revved up his engines like a pro. The scream of the jet intakes penetrated inside our little glass unit as Mossare released his brakes. The takeoff roll of a new solo student was always exciting. I enjoyed this one especially because today he had been almost flawless. Not with all students on their first solos had I been this confident. His rotation and takeoff were perfectly controlled. Landing gear came up. Flaps came up right on cue. Then he made his first radio call.

"*Axon... er... Map three-one, request closed,*" Mossare radioed. His voice was much higher and rapid. It was almost incoherent, except for the word "closed."

"*Closed approved,*" Wise said.

I laughed. "He sounds a little nervous."

"*You* sound a little nervous," Wise said. We all laughed.

Mossare begin his closed pull up, just a bit farther out than the usual spot. His airspeed would be higher, but the longer downwind would help bleed that off. His nose came up in the familiar climbing turn. This time it stayed up as he climbed higher and higher, until he punched through the base of the clouds. He was gone—in the soup.

"*Damn it!*" Wise keyed his mike. "*Map three-one, state your position.*"

There was an endless pause. Wise called again.

"*Map three-one, state your position.*"

We waited again several more seconds before Mossare replied.

"*Axon two-two, gear check.*"

"That stupid idiot!" I growled in frustration. "Where in hell is he!"

"Well, at least we know that he's not going to hit the ground anytime soon," Wise said.

"*Map three-one, this is Barfly,*" Wise radioed. "*Can you see the runway?*"

"*Yes, sir.*"

"Oh, please," I moaned, knowing that his tired old phase meant trouble.

"*Map three-one, this is Barfly.*" Wise radioed very slowly and distinctly. "*What is your altitude?*"

Again, the pause seemed interminable.

"*Axon two-two, on the go.*" Mossare, we presumed, was adding full power, accelerating his airspeed, and raising his landing gear and flaps.

"Okay," Wise said, turning to all of us. "Everybody keep an eye out for this camel-jocking son of a bitch!"

"Johnny, I don't think he has looked outside the cockpit, yet. There's a chance he doesn't even know we can't see him."

"Here." Wise handed me the microphone. "You talk to the dumbass."

I took the microphone, exhaled deeply, and pushed the mic button.

"Map three-one, this is Lieu... Captain Amity. State your position."

"Yes, sir."

"If he starts this 'yes sir' routine," I said to Wise, "we're in for a long day."

"Barfly," Mossare called. "Axon two-two, request closed."

Wise and I looked at each other. Our instructor minds were thinking of the same Catch-22. The two students behind us began to chuckle.

"At least that might keep him in the vicinity of the pattern," the C-Fight instructor said.

Wise grabbed the microphone from me and radioed. "Closed approved."

We waited for a couple of minutes, hoping the silence would help collect Mossare's senses.

"Axon two-two, gear check."

"Okay," I said, taking the microphone back from Wise. "Here comes the real test. Map three-one, this is Captain Amity. I want you to look outside. Tell me what you see."

"Yes, sir."

"Tell me what you see outside."

"Yes, sir."

"Did you copy, Map three-one? I want a weather report."

The silence in the RSU was agonizing as we waited.

Finally, after half a minute, Mossare responded. "Axon two-two, on the Go!" He then screamed over the radio. "Mayday! Mayday! Mayday!"

"He's using my call sign!"

That was all. He said no more. He refused to answer our radio calls. I counted the minutes—one—two—three. Still no response. Then directly in front of the center of the runway, the missing aircraft reappeared.

From out of the clouds, Mossare's Tweet came screaming into the clear air in a nosedive at near maximum airspeed. His gear and flaps were down.

"It looks like a Stuka!" Wise said. "Map three-one, full stop! Do you copy?"

"Yes, sir," came his moronic reply. "Axon two-two, full stop."

I grabbed the binoculars to check the configuration of his aircraft as he rapidly pulled the nose up. He managed to bring his airspeed down, then slowly circled once more over the traffic pattern. Thankfully, there was nothing I could see hanging loose. Mossare lined up on final and came in for his landing.

"He over-sped his damn landing gear by about a hundred knots," I said to the gathering.

"We can't afford to let him check it out now," Wise exclaimed. "Just get this mother down."

"*Axon two-two, gear check,*" called Mossare.

"Tell him to go around!" I screamed. "He just raised his landing gear!"

"*Map three-one, go around, go around! Do you copy?*" Wise radioed.

"He's got his gear sequence backwards," I said. "Watch this. He's going to lower this gear and go around."

"*Axon two-two, going around,*" Mossare called. "*Departing traffic.*"

"What?" My voice was in a high pitch of panic.

"*Map three-one, negative,*" Wise radioed. "*You're cleared for closed and a full stop at this runway. That's an order!*"

"*Yes, sir, Axon two-two, departing traffic for a full stop,*" Mossare called, then lowered his landing gear, raised his flaps, dropped his speed brake, and slowly climbed above traffic pattern altitude and out of sight—once more in the clouds.

Our group sat there for a moment in silence. The clouds were thicker. They seemed to have come right into the RSU.

"Well I'll be damned," Wise finally said.

"Crap! He's going home." I said. "How in hell am I going to get back?"

It was three hours later that I arrived at the squadron building with my four other RSU buddies. Colonel Meneur and Captain Military were already in an intense discussion. Since no one met me with a report of a crash or of missing T-37s, I consciously decided not to ask how Cadet Mossare managed to make it back to the base alive. As I walked into the Ragtop flight room directly over to where Mossare sat, his swarthy face as white as a newly painted Tweet, I glimpsed his tyrannical Iranian lieutenant sitting stern-faced beside him. A replica of a class patch hung on the wall behind him. It portrayed Olympic Rings with a jet overlaid. The caption read "Laredo Air Games." Mossare looked as if he had already been sent back home for his execution.

Technically, to be soloed, the student was to make three successful landings. I knew we could not cook the books for him, but there were important things that I had to do. I had to try saving him from his lieutenant, which might take some time. There was one other important thing I selfishly could do right away.

"Congratulations, Cadet Mossare." I extended my hand as he stood up. "You're now a jet pilot. So since you've soloed, where in hell is my booze?"

34

COMING BACK TO MY BASE full of optimism had become a cruel hoax. In two short weeks my world had been ripped from me. The campus I had left was hopelessly mutated. In less than a month my familiar Air Force job had turned a shambles. Only the counsel taken from friends kept me sane. I knew I was falling in love again with Suzy, but I recognized that this was not the time for public affection. I spent every evening with her, helping her to pack. She had thirty days to leave base housing. It had not been easy to box up someone else's memories. Thankfully, other officers' wives were there to help. Mrs. Military was especially helpful and kind—a real gem.

With those images rolling through my head, I sat at my table grading Mossare's first solo flight. Simple job. He lived. He flunked. It was another bright red "Unsatisfactory" in his gradebook. I sensed the presence, even the hellfire body heat, of the person standing behind me. I turned around to see Captain Military.

"Captain Amity." Military smiled mysteriously.

"Yes, chief," I said from my chair.

He looked not at all irritated by my lack of military courtesy. Instead, he continued to smile—a bitter, angry, hateful smile.

He handed me a paper. "Congratulations. Go right now and report for a no-notice piss eval."

"Not me!" My stomach rising to my throat.

"I hear you visited your old campus," he continued viciously. "I hope they pick up all the funny stuff you probably doped up on."

"No problem." I just hoped I hadn't absorbed any pot smoke from that hippie house.

The rules for a no-notice piss eval were simple. I had to go immediately to the designated area, report to a sergeant medic, step behind a curtain, and pee for my country. It sounded simple—degrading but a piece of cake.

I headed by foot to the Phys Ed building with trepidation. I had been in a house with Jane, where students were smoking marijuana. Had I inhaled enough to make it detectable in my system? Would I get in trouble for something innocent like that? I was only in the house where smoke was. I hadn't smoked it myself. Would they understand that excuse? Hell, I might not be able to pee anyway. Would that make them suspicious that I'm trying to hide something? I'd be crucified for no justification.

These issues tumbled though my mind over and over as I paced toward my rendezvous with humiliation. As I entered the gymnasium, I handed to the sergeant the slip that Military gave me.

"Captain Amity, sir." The sergeant read my name off the slip of paper. "Are you carrying any articles on you which could alter the outcome of these tests?"

"No." I said.

What did he expect me to say? That I left my bottle of spare urine at home. Sorry?

"Sir, have you ever used any drugs not prescribed by a physician?" He dutifully wrote down my answers on a federal form.

"No."

"Sir, have you been on any prescription medications in the last 30 days?"

"Just some medication to treat a flash burn I had. I don't remember what it was."

"That's okay." He was in a hurry.

"Also, I took some Sudafed for a few days about two weeks ago for a sinus condition I had."

He noted all my comments, then handed me a clear plastic cup. His finger pointed to a curtained area.

"Take this over there, sir, and put a urine sample in this cup. When you are through, give it to the sergeant at the back table."

It was with a sense of awkwardness that I took my cup over to one of the curtains and stepped inside. I realized my worst fears when I looked up to see another medic staring down upon me to ensure that I donated my urine and not someone else's. He sat on a revolving stool atop an elevated platform. From his perch the medic could see at least four different airmen peeing for their country. He nodded to me as I looked up. I whipped out my pride and joy, pointed it at the plastic cup, and waited. Taking one more glance at the medic towering over me—that clinched it. What if I couldn't pee? I would never be able to provide a urine specimen as long as he was looking. I could not explain it. I found comfort in knowing I was not alone in my problem. There were three other curtained areas where other airmen were also gazed at. But that was the problem at this moment. I was not alone. If I had been, the stream would be instant. With my gawking medic above me, the dam was not about to break.

"Sarge," I said to the medic on his high perch. "I can't do this. I'm just telling you ahead of time. It just won't come out."

"No rush, sir, take your time. A lot of men take five or ten minutes."

He had no idea of the problem. I had decided most men did not understand. How about five or ten hours? I'd probably faint before I could pee.

I stood there with the cup at the ready, my flight suit unzipped from the bottom, miserable, embarrassed, and ready to crawl away with shame. Real men did not have problems like this. Maybe wimps did but not officers. Not *pilots*. They were afraid of nothing. Here I was, standing with my penis at the ready, humiliated in the presence of a twenty-year-old, three-striped sergeant. Even being metamorphosed into a cockroach seemed better. Then I could crawl away to hide in a crack somewhere. Maybe Franz Kafka had my problem.

I looked at my watch for the ten-minute mark. My watch seemed to slow to a snail's pace. At seven and a half minutes, I could wait no longer.

"Sarge, this won't work. I can't do it this way."

"There's no rush, sir. I can bring you some water. That always works."

"I'll tell you up front, that's not going to work."

"Here, sir, I'll get you some water. Drink all you need." He motioned to another medic.

The second medic handed me a full glass of water through the curtain. The gesture of help only made me angry.

"Sarge, I already feel the need to pee. It just won't come out. And it's not going to."

My plea fell on uncomprehending ears. I stood and drank most of the water. The minutes turned to two hours. All the airmen summoned to donate urine to the cause had gone and left, leaving me with six or seven sergeants and airmen, all standing around, in effect, watching me not pee. That made it even worse. Now I had a multiple audience of lower ranking enlisted men, talking about the allegedly shit hot pilot who was too much of a wimp to pee. I could imagine the jokes they must be telling.

Then I remembered the scene from the movie, *Alice's Restaurant.* Arlo Guthrie was taking his Army draft physical. He could not pee enough. He asked the other miserable inductees for some spare urine. I had deep sympathy for him then. He inspired me now.

I waited for the perched medic to look away. It was easy to do. By this time, he was both bored and pissed off. I quickly grabbed the glass of drinking water. With the small amount remaining, I poured it into my specimen cup. Setting the drinking glass silently down, I raised the other cup up and yelled at the top of my lungs.

"Done!"

The sergeants burst out in cheers and applause. I handed my clear liquid specimen to the medic at the back table, then exited in a mix of shame and relief. I glanced back briefly as several medics looked at my urine in puzzlement. I turned my gaze away just as the ranking NCO shrugged his shoulders and placed it with all the other yellow urine specimens. I had beat the system again.

I walked rapidly back to the squadron building, cheerfully singing a favorite Loudon Wainwright tune about stinking skunks.

35

"WHERE HAVE YOU BEEN?" CAPTAIN Military was in prime behavior.

"I was taking my no-notice piss eval."

"I'm your commander, Amity," Captain Military spit out geyser-like. "You may address me as '*sir*.'"

"Sir, okay, Captain, *sir*."

"That's better." His bellicose smirk returned. "So?"

I was puzzled by his last query.

"So what... Captain, *sir*?"

"Where have you been?"

"Well, Captain, *sir*, I was in a curtained area, waiting to pee for my country. For quite a while, I wasn't properly *inspired* to pee for my country. But then, I thought you might be wanting me back. I found it much easier to pee based on thoughts of you."

Military's face turned an instant bright red with rage. I had been through enough crap in the last few weeks to last me a lifetime. I had paid my dues.

I continued, "I just looked in the bottom of the specimen cup, saw your face down there, and it was very easy then to piss the cup full... almost to overflowing, Captain, *sir*."

Military began to hyperventilate—the sounds of air whistling between his teeth in angry forced breaths. When he did speak, he sounded as winded as an out of shape long distance runner.

"Your problem, Amity, is that you're a smart ass." He paused. "First, you killed your friend, now you're turning on me."

He grabbed the throat of my flight suit and forced me back against the wall of the flight room. By now, he had an audience of several instructors.

"Your promotion to Captain is only temporary, Amity. You just got busted to back to lieutenant."

"Captain, *sir*," I was becoming angry, so I paced my words to remain calm. "This time, I call your bluff. You wouldn't dare bust me. You're taking John's place to get at me, but now you're finding out that I'll hold you by your balls until you get the hell out of my life. You got it?"

"You can consider yourself grounded as of this minute, Amity."

"Try explaining that to Colonel Meneur."

"It's just between you and me now. You can't hide behind John Alexander anymore."

"And now, you don't have to hide from John Alexander. You're not afraid anymore he's going to deck you because he's dead? Is that it?"

I waited a few more seconds for Military to get enough air to continue.

"Alexander deserved to die," Military hissed. "He was screwing around up in the air. You were, too. And in the meantime, you've been screwing his wife."

Before I could respond, friends came to my rescue. Freed, backed by Starch, carefully ambled over to us.

"Alexander deserved to die," Freed said calmly. "Is that what you just said?"

"Get the hell out of here!" Military ordered Hal. "You're not involved in this discussion."

"Hell, this is no discussion," Freed stepped even closer. "This is a crucifixion! Nobody gets away with talking about my commander like that."

"Right on to that, man!" Starch said.

Military released his grip on my flight suit. Turning to face Freed, he put his most piercing stare in that direction.

Freed stepped closer. "No son of a bitch will talk about John deserving to die. I'll never let you get away with that while I'm around."

"So, it's perfectly all right to bang Alexander's wife?" Military was talking rhetorically now.

I scowled. "Nobody's been doing anything to John's wife."

"What a liar you are. I saw you sneaking over to see her the night John died. I saw you go inside. You didn't leave until morning. What were you doing in there? Changing diapers?"

"No, not changing diapers."

"Wait a minute," Freed looked at Military. "You were spying on Alexander's house, weren't you?'

Military ignored Freed. "Amity, you were poking Alexander's wife, weren't you?"

"Sorry, Suzy's not that kind of girl," I said.

Military turned to Freed, Starch, and now Wise, who had walked up to join them. With a finger pointed back toward me, he added to this character assassination."Here you have it, men. Amity killed his flight commander and is now screwing the man's wife. You can't get much lower than that!"

Freed turned to me. Military was unaware of the danger he was in.

"Rob," Freed said quietly. "Either you do it, or I will."

I looked at Hal then at Military. This nutcase had not missed a beat in his insults of the friends I loved the most.

Military continued to fume. "What makes it even more pathetic is that Amity can't help screwing up a piss eval. Maybe his limp dick couldn't do anything to satisfy that wife of Alexander's...."

"This is for John!" I said to interrupt. My right hook caught him bullseye on the point of his nose. Blood splattered as Military's head hit the floor.

Freed stepped quickly forward, helping Military back to his feet. "Here, Captain. Rob forgot to include all the poor Air Force bastards who are here because of assholes like you."

Freed's haymaker blow to an ear knocked Military to the floor once more. He lay there, unconscious and in a bloody heap. We all stared down at him, the anger showing in all our expressions. Finally, Starch stepped closer to look down at him.

"Is the bastard dead?"

"No." Freed looked closer. "He's still breathing. See?"

Bloody red bubbles gurgled from his nose with each exhale.

"Well," Starch said with more inflection than he was known for. "Hit the son of a bitch again!"

"No!" I quickly extended my arm to block any attempt. "Let's leave well enough alone."

I looked at Freed with a *"what the hell do I do now"* expression. Hal turned around with his back to the prostrate Military. "Does anybody know what happened to our leader?"

"I think he just kind of fell," Starch said.

I didn't like that idea. It implied there were witnesses. "I think, actually, we were all gone already. If this bonehead wants to fall, let him fall on his own time. I'm for getting the hell outta Dodge."

"Rob's right," Freed said. "Did anybody see what happened?"

As Freed surveyed the room, all of us shook our heads, then slowly, nonchalantly walked out of the Ragtop Flight room and headed down the hallway. Passing out the door to the open sky, the bright sun temporarily blinded my vision. The clouds had gone. The solar warmth felt good.

"Hal," I said, as we walked more quickly from the squadron building. "Does your hand hurt?"

He laughed. "It hurts like a son of a bitch!"

"You and John didn't tell me doing this could hurt."

"Sometimes, Amity, pain like this feels good. Real good."

36

THE NEXT MORNING GREETED ME with the joy of a spring in full bloom. I relished that internal surge of passion for life, with the knowledge that after every dreary winter the flowers soon returned. On this day, after so much tension the day before, I was hopeful. My flight commander, Captain Military, had called in sick.

It was with joy that I took off with Ted Ark for one of his final instrument rides. He was very good at his job now. In formation flights he was better than I ever hoped to be myself. Ark had even given me a few pointers. On instruments Ark was competent in nearly every aspect. In only one area had I been unsuccessful. I failed at getting either Ark or Fred Picks to do a decent penetration turn. We had climbed to altitude and were at the VOR. Approach Control cleared us for our rapid descent. At this moment I was seeing incompetence once again.

"Ark, get your nose down," I said. "We're at 3000 feet per minute."

"Sorry, sir. I'll just push the nose down here."

"Ted," I said in frustration. "Keep the nose down or, as you increase airspeed in your descent, the nose wants to come up. You know that by now."

I paused to take my mask off. Pinching my nose shut, I blew hard to force air into my ear canals and into my sinuses. Without doing this Valsalva maneuver, my sinuses were in an increasing partial vacuum whenever I descended. Penetration turns were always the test of my sinus condition.

At a proper 6000 feet per minute fall from the VOR, the vacuum it created could get terribly uncomfortable unless I forced the air back into my head.

I looked at the ground below us. We had drifted, as usual, way past the normal point where our penetration turn would commence returning us back to the VOR for what usually became a radar approach for landing.

"Ark, we're in Oklahoma right now," I said sarcastically. "No, sorry, Kansas."

"Sorry, sir." Ark forced the Tweet's nose down. Our airspeed and rate of descent increased immediately.

I gently pushed on the stick to keep the nose down for Ted.

"Use your trim, damn it! Get ready to make your turn... but watch that rate of descent. Keep her at 6000 feet a minute, or I'll flunk your ass."

"Yes, sir." But he failed to hold the nose down.

Our plane was creeping under 5000 feet per minute when Ark started the thirty-degree bank turn to return to the VOR. Turns always increased the rate of descent, so I was much happier.

I looked outside at the horizon. Something curious was moving. Was it an object in the distance? It wasn't an object, just a blur. The blur grew wider. In a fraction of a second the pop in my left ear signaled the damage. Then pain came like a rifle shot. I looked away as these odd sensations filled my head. It was the sound of the lining of my left frontal sinus separating from the skull cavity in a vacuum rupture. The pain of the implosion was like being stabbed in the eyeball with an ice pick all the way to the back of my skull. So intense was the pain that I went blind. I raised both hands to my helmet, then my whole body recoiled instinctively into a fetal position. I began to scream.

"Sir?" he said over the sound of my involuntary cry of agony. "What the hell?"

Ted Ark almost by instinct ripped his cardboard instrument hood off, levelled the aircraft to stop the descent, and climbed up in altitude a couple of thousand feet until the pressure evened out in my head.

"Sir, are you all right?"

"No," I moaned between rapid breaths. "I'm not all right."

"Sinus?"

"Yes."

"Is the pressure off?"

"I don't know, Ark. I can't think."

"Maybe you should pop your ears, sir."

Ark was right. I pinched my nose shut and blew against my closed mouth until my ears popped. My sinus did not feel any better. At least the ice pick-like pain was gone. I was scared. What if another sinus blew? How much gas did we have left? Could Lieutenant Ark get me back? I could not see.

"Ark," I said, still breathing hard. "You've got to get me down. I can't see!"

"Laredo Approach, Axon two-two."

"Axon two-two, I see you off course."

"Axon two-two is cancelling IFR," Ark said with authority. *"We are declaring an in-flight emergency. I am going to Maytime frequency."*

"Say again, Axon two-two." The radar controller confirmed. *"Are you declaring an emergency?"*

"That's affirmative. Cancel IFR. Axon two-two is departing your frequency."

"Roger, copy, Axon two-two."

Ark took the time to check the trim and our rate of descent. Next, he turned the IFF to 7700. He was headed visually back toward the base at a straight ahead drop of 100 feet per minute. My vision was slowly returning. The pain gradually left me with only a throbbing ache in place of the more specific sharp stabbing agony.

"What do I need to do for you, sir?"

"Just get me on the ground as best you can."

That was all I could think of. I was helpless, unable to think clearly. My fear of more sinus ruptures almost drove me mad.

"How much fuel do we have left?"

"We have over a half tank left, sir. I'll check the wing tanks."

"Slow to 125 knots, Ted. We need to stay airborne as long as possible."

"We're there already, sir. One-twenty-five."

"Good. Now just get me down without blowing up something else."

Ark said no more and took over like a pro.

"Maytime, Axon two-two, just departed Laredo Approach. We are declaring an emergency."

Word had travelled fast. To my surprise the unmistakable voice of Colonel Meneur came over the radio at Maytime. His presence meant the situation was serious.

"*Axon two-two. State the nature of the emergency.*"

"*Maytime, my instructor has had a sinus block on descent. He's pretty much incapacitated. Axon two-two.*"

"*Any problems with you flying back, Axon two-two?*" Colonel Meneur's voice was gruff with stress.

"*No, sir.*"

"*Are you a student, Axon two-two?*"

"*Yes, sir. Lieutenant Ark, sir.*"

"*Roger, copy. Axon two-two, listen carefully.*" The colonel instructed Ark. "*Head directly to the test track and orbit north of there until you can slowly reduce your altitude. When you get to traffic pattern altitude, we will clear you for a straight-in landing. Do you copy?*"

"*Maytime, we copy. Direct to the test track, orbit in a descent, then a straight-in approach when possible.*"

The test track was an enormous five-mile-long circular road that Uniroyal Tires used to test their products. Automobiles constantly circled day and night, serving as the biggest, most easily identified landmark in south Texas, especially at night.

I cautioned him. "Ted, he said orbit north of the test track. I don't want to hit anybody."

"Yes, sir. I copy that. You doin' all right?"

"Okay so far. You're doing a great job."

We got to the test track and orbited to the north for another fifteen minutes. I had never seen a student make such an exact, invariable 100 feet per minute descent before. I would have found it impossible to do myself under normal circumstances. While Ark orbited in a slow drop, I performed several more times my Valsalva maneuver and tried to think.

I knew this was the end of my flying career. It gave me a sense of relief, yet, I had a strong sense of regret. In my short life, this meant the end of my glory days. Nothing would ever be as exhilarating as the acceleration of takeoff or the Gs of a high-speed turn. The thrill of spins dropping me 10,000 feet in twenty seconds could never be equaled in any carnival ride. The status of being a pilot, whether deserved or not, was about to become only a memory. Like before college graduation, this meant my last days were to become goodbyes.

We reached pattern altitude without more stabbing sinus pain. Straight ahead lay runway one-seven. My last chance was at hand.

"Ark," I said. "This is my last chance to grease one on. I'm going to land this mother, okay?"

Ark relinquished the stick without comment. He understood. We came over the runway threshold, configured for landing, and touched down about as well as I had ever done. It wasn't a perfect landing. Hell, they never were.

"You taxi forward, partner." With those words, I instructed for the last time. "The fire truck will tell us what to do."

Ahead lay the huge fire truck and the ambulance, red lights flashing, both waiting for me. Out to greet me first was Doc Terra. I cut the engine on my side of the aircraft before he approached.

"Are you all right?" Terra leaned into the cockpit. Looking at me more closely, he continued. "Amity, is that you?"

"Afraid so, Doc," I used morbid humor. "I guess my six months is up early, huh?"

"Could be. Could be. Can you taxi back to the ramp or not?"

"I'll be okay."

"All right," Terra continued. "When you get back to the flightline, come over to my office immediately. Have someone take you if necessary."

"Will do."

"Okay, then. Get going."

I let Ark taxi back, park, and shut down the other engine. He could fill out the paperwork in the 781. I slowly climbed out of the cockpit and walked to the squadron building, back to a life that was never to be the same, once more.

37

ONE HOUR LATER I SAT staring at a black and white image, brilliant against a fluorescent light. Through experience, I could read the meaning of every light and shadow.

"Your sinuses are a mess," Doc Terra said, looking at the newest X-rays of my head. "How bad do you want to fly?"

"Not that bad."

"You need surgery on your frontal here." He pointed to my ruptured left frontal sinus on the X-ray. "But these maxillary sinuses are in the worst shape of all. Are your teeth still giving you problems?"

"Constantly. I've just sort of gotten used to the discomfort."

"We've talked about your surgical options before," Terra went on. "I think I know you pretty well by now. You want my medical advice?"

"Absolutely."

"After they work on your ruptured sinus," Terra said with metered emphasis, "don't let them do any more. Just tell them you want to be grounded and refuse any further surgery. I'll back you up."

"Thank you, Doc. My accident and the fire probably didn't help me, either."

"I'm sure that contributed but remember. For goodness sake, I wouldn't want them taking a hammer and chisel to my head. That's brutal work. I'm not sure that in the long run it would be that good for you. There are risks, you know."

"I agree. So, when do I go to Wilford Hall for surgery?"

"Next Monday this month you report. Tuesday, they operate."

I left at zero-dark-thirty that Monday morning in a military van driven by a two-striper. All the passengers were quiet, unhappy, and bound for some type of medical intervention. The statement that the Air Force owns your body and can do with it as they want surely was on the minds of all of us for the 150-mile ride to Lackland Air Force Base. After a thorough physical—including my first prostate exam which was an eye opener—I had my last meal at lunch before surgery very early next morning.

On Tuesday morning, I had suspicions that I was training a medical intern. Through my medicated stupor, I remember these bits and pieces.

"Okay, drill a hole. There's the clot. Don't touch the optic nerve. Insert the drain tube. See the fibrillation? Sew it up. Next!"

"Did you get all the fibrils out?" I was incoherently chattering at the end of the procedure.

"Yes, we did," the intern said. "Every one of them."

IT WAS WEDNESDAY MORNING. I laid back against the firm pillow of the bed at Wilford Hall Hospital in San Antonio, Texas, feeling alone and depressed after surgery. I had no discomfort, but I was afraid to move too much. It was my back reclining on a strange bed that caused me to finally shift my weight.

Not bad. I felt nothing.

I drew a hand up to feel the incision in my left eyebrow. A large dressing covered the wound. A small irrigation tube extended out of my head. I now had plumbing. The surgery had sounded like going to the dentist. They had opened the sinus up with a scalpel, then further widened it with a dentist's drill—except, it was not a tooth they were drilling but my forehead. Thankfully it was over. I lay there all afternoon, until medics brought me dinner. Ravenously hungry, I ate with gusto, then promptly threw it up. I was glad I had no visitors.

One day after my surgery the effects of morphine and other drugs had worn off. Feeling much better, I enjoyed a good breakfast. I had a chance to look at my quarters. It was a large ward of about twenty beds ringing the walls of a long rectangular room. Throughout the morning men were wheeled out for sinus surgery, then later wheeled back in. Nearly all the airmen came back looking beat up and unconscious. These were the patients undergoing hammer and chisel surgery on their maxillary sinuses to install what the doctors called "windows." At least my surgery had been under a local anesthetic. The "window" patients were given a general anesthetic then opened through an incision in the upper jaw between their teeth and their upper lip. A quarter-sized hole was hammered open on each maxillary sinus. These patients looked like hell and later told me they felt like it, too. They could barely communicate because of the gauze stuffed in their mouths and nose. In contrast, my comfort level had improved enough in one day that I wanted to talk to people, but no doctor came that morning when I was awake. My energy was limited, and I frequently dozed off. My eyes had just closed again when two familiar voices spoke to me.

"I think he's malingerin'. What do you think?"

"I think he looks like roadkill."

"Well, he always looks like that."

I was unaware that I had been sleeping. Slowly opening my eyes, I gazed upon two formless faces. It took a few seconds to gather my wits and focus on the two, their expressions filled with impish grins.

"Oh, no!" I said. "I've died and been sent to hell."

"No, sir," Fred Picks pointed to Ted Ark. "Worse than that. It's us."

I looked at the clock on the near wall. It was just past noon. My tray of food for lunch was next to my bed, untouched. "Why aren't you guys out at the flightline?"

"I guess you haven't looked outside, sir," Ark said. "It's WXOFF. The weather people said it would be cancelled all morning on account of heavy rain and fog. So, we decided to come up here and see how you were doing."

"Well, I'm doing okay. How about you guys?" I said. "You guys ever learn to fly?"

"Yes, sir," Picks said. "We start T-38s next week. Things are goin' well."

Ark chuckled. "We're done with T-37s."

I was a bit surprised by this. and it must have showed. "Please tell me you both learned how to do a penetration turn finally?"

"Not exactly, sir," Ark said sheepishly, his eyes averting my gaze.

I looked at Picks. He was looking at Ark. A guilty expression passed between them. I waited for a further explanation. They said nothing.

"What's going on here, guys? I'm reading more into this."

"Sir, don't let your lunch get cold," Picks said. "If you can't eat it all, I might help out."

"Here let me move this around for you." Ark turned the lunch tray across my lap. "You've got ham. Mashed potatoes. Peas. Red Jell-O. Um-um!"

"Okay, guys. I'll eat. You talk."

I picked up my fork to begin eating. I didn't realize how hungry I was until my first bite. I never understood the jokes about hospital food. It tasted good. As I chewed, I looked up alternately at the two students who glanced back as if I had caught them with their hands in the cookie jar.

"How the hell did you guys get so good all of a sudden?" I took another bite of lunch.

"We sort of tricked you, sir," Picks's face turned red in embarrassment. I had never seen Picks blush for anything.

"Tricked me? How?"

"We knew you were having sinus problems," Ark continued.

"Captain Alexander told Ark about it one day after he flew with him," Picks said.

"He told me it was pretty serious," Ark went on. "You might get in real trouble someday if we didn't take good care of you. So, we decided to take care of you."

"How?"

"Sir," Picks said, taking a deep nervous breath. "We can do penetration turns with no problem. We always have. Hell, they're easy."

"Yeah," Ark said. "You must have thought we were incompetent."

"Well, not really," I said sincerely. "I thought you were morons."

Fred Picks went on, ignoring my insult. "We got together and decided to intentionally shallow out our penetration turns because that's where we noticed you had the most problems."

I looked at the two in astonishment. I did not know whether to be angry or not. In my gut I knew it was their tribute.

"That's about the dumbest thing I've ever heard!" I said sternly.

"Yes, sir," Picks said.

"Sir," Ark said. "If I had to do it again, I'd do it the same way, maybe shallower. You're easy to fool."

"I'm easy to fool, huh?" I gave him an incredulous laugh. Now they bordered on insulting me.

"Yes, sir," Ark said, while Picks nodded agreement.

"I won't ever be fooled again, guys."

"We know, sir," Picks said.

I looked at the two of them. Their grins were gone, replaced by embarrassment. It was a pathetic sight.

"I just want you to remember one thing," I said calmly. "Nothing else matters. When you look back on these days and what you did, just don't forget what I tell you."

My two students looked at me, expecting the worst.

"That was really stupid of you two! It's the dumbest thing I've ever had to thank someone for. Thanks for trying."

My two students soon grew tired of watching me doze off and bid farewell, saying they were going to look up Honey before their return to Laredo. Finally left alone, I soon was dreaming of Honey and Boopsie, but in my fantasy this time, Suzy came to chase them away. This night she had no one else to run off, and so she stayed with me in my dream until morning.

38

THE NEXT MORNING, I WALKED down the long hall in my hospital gown to an Ear, Nose, and Throat doctor's office for further consultation. Major Webb removed the dressing from my incision to expose my irrigation tube. Then he hooked up a syringe full of saline to irrigate my frontal sinus.

"If you're lucky," he said, "you'll feel saltwater go down the back of your throat. Otherwise, we'll have to open you back up again."

I was lucky. I nearly choked on the saltwater that gushed from my throat into my mouth.

"I want to keep you here over the weekend. On Monday we're going to put windows on those maxillary sinuses. Then you'll be ready to fly full time again."

"Aren't there possible complications?"

"No," he said to my face. "Not really."

"It's the 'not really' part that I worry about."

"You can leave that decision up to me," Dr. Webb said in a tone of impatience. "That's my job."

He smiled with closed lips that mutated into a sneer. It was a look I sometimes observed in very rich or very high-ranking people. It said, "pity the poor humble masses." Dr. Webb wore black horn-rimmed Goldwater glasses resting on a magnificently sculpted nose. His dark wavy hair and his prominent chin gave him a Clark Kent look. His long white medical coat was pristine. He seemed too perfectly configured to be comfortable.

"I've talked to Doctor Terra, the flight surgeon in Laredo,"—I began on my well-rehearsed speech—"and he told me of several possible complications."

"Oh, he's just overly conservative."

"...and he said there was a risk of raw exposed nerves with chronic pain, and...."

"But *I'm* the specialist."

"...and it could change my voice to be more nasal...."

"Look...." Dr. Webb extended his hand toward me to stop my talking. "It's my word against his."

"Okay," I said, hoping he would say something more conciliatory.

"Okay, so you'll be scheduled for Monday at...."

"...Doctor Webb," I in turn interrupted. "I'm going to refuse any more surgery on my sinuses."

He was astonished by my boldness. "You're *what?*"

"I don't want surgery. I want to be grounded."

"This is unheard of!"

"But that's what I choose."

"You can't do this. The Air Force has paid good money to train you to be a pilot. You can't just walk away. It's against regulations."

"Oh, but yes, it is within my rights. I have that option, and I intend to take it."

"Is that so?" Dr. Webb blurted, then opened my chart and began to write furiously. "We'll see about that."

I sat still in the exam chair watching him write madly into my medical record. Halfway down the page his periods and dotted "i's" were gaining in violence as he punched holes in my chart. Near the end of the page Dr. Webb's neatly-groomed hair grew disheveled. He was using body English to add emphasis to each comment. I was waiting to see a drop of sweat form on his statuesque nose and drip off from his workout. He furiously turned the page and started a second but soon peaked, stopping at the end of the third line. He signed his name, folded the chart back up, stapled it shut, and turned to me.

"Here," he said, aggressively tossing my medical chart onto my lap. "Try to do something with this."

He stormed out of the room, leaving me with no instructions. I sat there a few minutes, wondering if he were coming back. Finally, a medic came in to ask if anything was wrong. I shook my head and went back to my ward, leaving the chart with the medic. I'll always wonder what Dr. Webb scrawled in that chart.

I left for home the next morning.

39

I ARRIVED FOR DUTY ONE week later after some rest and recuperation. Mondays do not set well with some people, as I soon discovered. Except for Cadet Mossare, my students had followed the rest of their class to the squadron down the road, which flew the supersonic, sexy, sweat-inducing T-38 Talon. That left too many days for Captain Military with nothing to do. He soon found me.

His nose still had a faint discoloration from my fist. I must have given him amnesia. He had not referred to it since it happened. That made him very dangerous.

"What's this I hear? The little wimp can't take it any longer? I think you're pathetic."

"Not exactly." I was bitter, seeing he still did not have the decency to spew his venom in the privacy of his office but instead chose a time in front of my peers.

"Still no sign of respect, I see. He just keeps on digging his hole deeper."

I looked at him. I did not speak. To do so was to egg him on. He stood over my table, his hands resting on the edge of the glass top. "Why are you not standing up when I'm speaking to you?"

"Two reasons, Military. One—I'm working. As you know, regulations do not require military courtesy while an airman is performing his tasks. Two—I have utter contempt for you."

Military showed no emotion as he listened to me. He just looked with hatred into my eyes. This hatred I could not understand. It was not worth the effort this ass was putting out to hate me.

"You're a screw-up, Amity. You know that?" He said into my face at very close range, his breath foul from the cigarettes he smoked. "You can't take a drug screen, you can't fly. You seem only capable of banging widows."

"Haven't we been this way before? I don't recall that this line of dialogue got us very far."

"Just mark my word, Amity. Your ass is mine. It's just when, not *if.*"

Wise gratefully interrupted us with a message. He stood by Captain Military and gave me my excuse to leave.

"Rob, Colonel Meneur would like to see you in his office, ASAP."

"Oops! Got to go." I stood up with relief. "I've got to go see a superior officer. Maybe he'll give me a medal."

"No, *Lieutenant* Amity." Military gave me an ugly grin. "He's going to bust your ass like I said I would do. So, go in there and have a good time. I'll be waiting."

I was fearful that he was telling the truth. With apprehension, I walked past my new flight commander toward an uncertain meeting with the Old Man. Sergeant Cervantes led me straight back to his spartan corner office.

"Colonel, Captain Amity is here," the first sergeant announced.

"Come in," Colonel Meneur ordered.

I marched over to the front of his desk, snapped to attention, and saluted with pride.

"Sir, Captain Amity, reporting as ordered."

"At ease, Rob. Take a seat and relax," the squadron commander directed. "I just got a call from Major Terra at the flight surgeons office."

"Yes, sir."

"Very interesting conversation, we had," Meneur's voice inflection sounded more like a set-up than merely a report of this conversation. "He told me you refused to undergo any further surgery to correct your sinus condition."

"Yes, sir. That's correct," I said cautiously.

"Why?"

I was not prepared to make any justification of my reasons to anyone. Certainly, I was not prepared to explain it to the colonel. I mentally stumbled, then decided that, if I was put in a corner, the truth would do me less harm.

"Sir, I've flown almost 800 hours. The last half of those have resulted in pain that I've lived with for the last year and a half. When Doc Terra examined me one time, he asked me why I was still flying. He told me that my sinuses were in the worst shape for someone still flying of anyone he had ever seen."

"Okay. That's what he told me. Go on."

This was encouraging. I looked at him, swallowed hard, and barreled on.

"Sir, just recently, Doc said I might last as many as six months before I would have to ground myself. I didn't last that long."

"I understand you had quite a severe episode up there?"

"Yes, sir. The most painful thing I've ever experienced. But my ruptured sinus can be repaired. Doctor Terra said the maxillary sinuses were what would do me in. He suggested I forget about flying... that the surgery would create a new set of problems. He said I was better off just staying on the ground. I agree with him, sir."

"Major Terra told me that the docs at Wilford Hall didn't like what you told them." His expression searched for a reply.

"No, sir. I think the man's name was Webb. Doctor Webb wrote a novel in my chart, then threw it at me. I don't know what it said, but it had to be bad."

"He probably wanted to practice surgery on somebody," Meneur said dryly, "and you screwed up his plans."

"I'd like to think so, sir."

"Have you talked to your flight commander?"

"Yes, sir. Captain Military knows. He's not very happy about it."

"Military. Everything pisses him off. His trouble is he's got a set of Air Force regulations stuck up his ass."

"No comment, sir."

For the first time, Colonel Meneur laughed. "No comment. No comment? I've got plenty of comment. How he's getting promoted to major below the zone is a mystery to me."

At that moment I could sense that my colonel just let the cat out of the bag. He didn't mean to, but he let it slip. I stood before him as speechless as a rock. My head was swirling with something to say, but anything that came to mind would be suicide. Although I chose silence, my expression said it all—and Colonel Meneur knew it.

The colonel paused to look at me. He reached in his desk drawer and pulled out a yellow file folder. From it he pulled out a single sheet of paper. "Captain Amity, it takes a lot of guts to do what you did. I admire you for being smart enough to be honest with yourself. You did the right thing. Nobody else I know who flies has that much common sense."

"Thank you, sir," I said with relief. "I just wish it didn't have to happen."

"Nonsense. You've done a good job under adverse medical conditions. You are to be commended."

"Perhaps, if I had been healthier, I could have saved John," I said before I knew what I was saying.

"What?"

"Maybe I could have prevented an accident. I might have been distracted. Maybe I didn't quit soon enough."

Colonel Meneur looked at me. He handed me a letter signed by him. "Speculation like that will kill you, son. You did better than most. Your suggestion is nonsense."

I looked at the letter but was too preoccupied to read it.

"You have to know that this endless war is winding down. This is a letter recommending that you be given early separation from active duty." He looked me squarely in the eye. "I know all about your career goals. Get out at the first available opportunity? Is that right? Did you really put that on your dream sheet?"

"Yes, sir."

He laughed. "Well, at least you were honest."

"Thank you, sir."

"If you want out, I think you've paid your dues. Think it over. This letter is not official, yet. If it's what you really want, I'll help you arrange it. Okay?"

"Thank you, sir. I'll think it over."

I stood up, saluted my commander, turned an about face, and started to march out of his office.

"Captain Amity" the colonel said.

I stopped and turned around. "Yes, sir?"

"One word to anyone about my little slip up about promotions and they will be calling you *Lieutenant* Amity. Do you understand?"

"Yes, sir. I promise to follow orders."

"Dismissed."

My mind was swimming with possibilities. A crowd had gathered at the squadron ops desk listening to the radio in noisy confusion. I spied Freed and Wise standing in the corner talking feverishly. Freed did not look as calm as normal.

I joined them. "What's up?"

"We're history!" Wise said.

"What do you mean, we're history?"

"They shut us down," Freed said.

"They're closing the base down!" Wise shouted.

"Laredo Air Force Base?"

"Yes." Wise waved his arms in the air. "Laredo, the Boston Naval Ship-yard, probably every place that voted for McGovern!"

I recalled that the city of Laredo had voted about eighty percent for George McGovern for President and that Massachusetts was the only state to send Electors to vote for the Democrat against President Nixon. It seemed very blatant to me. Now I knew why Colonel Meneur was so willing to recommend separation for me. He knew this would be my last duty station.

Amid the chaos, as every instructor milled in confused speculation about their futures, I spotted Captain—soon-to-be-Major—Military. He came up like a pouncing puma, heading for the kill.

"Well, Lieutenant Amity, I trust Colonel Meneur set you straight?"

"He asked me to tell you something."

"Oh?"

"Yeah. He said I had permission to speak my mind to you."

"What?" He sounded puzzled as I walked rapidly down the hall clutching Colonel Meneur's letter.

I turned around and continued while walking backwards, cupping my hands around my mouth like a megaphone.

"You can kiss my ass!"

40

FOUR WEEKS LATER CAME ANOTHER commander's call. It was also the day that Ragtop Flight IPs had planned to hold a wake for the promotion of Captain Military to Major Military. How he had been promoted, no one could figure it out. It was also a day to award several decorations of valor to newer instructors recently returned from Southeast Asia.

I spent the previous day trying to speed along the bureaucracy, wading through the muck and mire of military regulations, to speed along my own hasty separation from the service. I determined I had enough leave accrued to bug out now. I'd still be paid as a Captain, but I would be through with active duty as soon as I signed out today.

I entered my squadron building for the last time in full dress blues. I had already turned in all my flightsuits. My shiny captain's bars and pilot's wings overshadowed the pitiful array of ribbons I wore underneath. I had only three. They were the Howdy Doody Ribbon, the Good Guy Ribbon, and the Killer Ribbon. In order they signified that I joined the service, that I did not get booted out for four years, and that I could shoot a gun straight. Maybe someday my kids would be impressed. Nobody else was.

A few friends came up the hallway to greet me. My departure was bittersweet. John Alexander was dead. With Laredo Air Force Base being closed, all these friends would be scattered in every direction. Freed was preordained to be shipped to an out of the way, obscure, remote hellhole. Wise would do okay. He was a proven survivor. Jim Starchweather would most likely have fun, even if locked him in a closet, living out some chemically induced fantasy in his own mind. And Vic Nuñez, who was hungry for flight hours, would do fine if he got to schedule lots of flights for himself at his new base.

"How are you doing?" Wise greeted me with a grin. "Whoo-ee! Don't we look slick today?"

"I'm short, man." I laughed. "I'm a short timer for sure."

"You look good short," Freed said, in his usual supremely self-assured manner. "How short are you?"

"I think about twenty days. But that's all leave time. I'm checking out of this sinking ship today."

"You mean this is it?" Starch said. "Hell, who's going to listen to my stories? These jerks won't."

"Starch, I never listened to your stories,. They're too...."

"Full of bull?" Starch was being his own critic.

I just smiled. I noticed Nuñez and Freed, as always, quiet and attentive.

"Tell it to Vic or Hal. Maybe one of those stories will rev them up."

I walked down the hall with my friends to squadron ops, where Major Cooke sat placidly staring at the wall. Signing out on the leave sheet, a strong surge of emotion hit me hard. This was my home, taken away from me by circumstances. This base closing, my medical grounding, and the soon-to-be-Major Military, as my new flight commander, had all, in some fashion, ripped me out by my roots. I had to figure out what to do with the rest of my life in these next twenty days. All change is frightening. This was worse. I was frightened of leaving the very Air Force I had vowed to desert at the first available opportunity. Now that the time was here, I wanted to turn back the clock.

I looked at my friends and guessed that I would never see most of them during the rest of my life. This was it. Life goes on.

First Sergeant Cervantes came walking into the hall motioning us to step inside the Ragtop Room for commander's call. Colonel Meneur would soon follow.

"Captain Amity, you're late," It was the familiar growl of Captain-for-one-more-hour Military.

"So?"

"You never learn, do you, Captain?"

"You've learned to call me Captain," I said in mock amazement. "I guess it doesn't matter after today, though, does it?"

"To me it does."

"Well, Captain-for-one-more-hour, I guarantee you that you'll never outrank me. I'll always remember you as just a captain."

"We'll see. Get in here." He pointed into the student room.

I walked ahead of Captain Military and past my flightline buddies to my familiar table, now denuded of all its mementoes. Like everything else I valued as priceless, they were safely packed away in my car.

Our First Sergeant swiftly called the squadron's attention to the arrival of Colonel Meneur. Captain-for-less-than-one-hour Military called the officers to attention, as Major Cooke looked on in puzzled amusement.

"Be seated, gentlemen," the colonel said before he was halfway through the door.

Captain-for-only-fifty-minutes Military stood at the ready with his cigarette lighter. Colonel Meneur started to speak, looked at Military standing there, then frowned.

"Oh, sit down, Captain," the colonel growled. "I don't smoke any more. Neither will anyone else. It's stupid."

Military crawled backwards like a kicked puppy dog to his front row seat. An audible groan came up out of the ranks as more than half of the officers put away their cigarettes and lighters.

"We've got several items and persons to give away or to kick upstairs today," Colonel Meneur began, "so let's get started."

He shuffled some papers around on the podium, finally asking his first sergeant to find the proper ones for him.

"Major-designate Military, would you please step forward," the squadron commander ordered.

Captain-for-less-than-forty-five-minutes Military marched up like a Prussian drill master and stomped his feet to attention. Major Cooke stepped up with medal in hand as Colonel Meneur read the citation.

"Captain Military is hereby awarded the Distinguished Flying Cross for achievement...." Meneur read on while, I'm sure, holding back a reflex to puke.

Freed whispered to me from his table, "He got that flying the T-38?"

I just shrugged my shoulders in bewilderment. Colonel Meneur took the medal from Major Cooke and pinned it on the rigid Military, then received a smart salute.

"Captain Military is hereby awarded the Airman's Medal for Heroism...." the colonel read anew.

I turned around and looked at the instructors behind me. They all looked as if they were here only because there was a gun held to their heads.

"This was the one for flying the T-37," Freed whispered.

Colonel Meneur again pinned a medal on the chest of my flight commander. After another humorous salute, he stepped back to read again.

"Captain Military is hereby awarded the Meritorious Service Medal for meritorious service...." Colonel Meneur read again—etcetera.

"Captain Military is hereby awarded the Air Medal for meritorious achievement while... blah... blah... blah...."

"I think I'm going to throw up," Freed whispered a little louder.

"Did we really punch out a guy like that?" I whispered back.

Colonel Meneur droned on.

"Captain Military is hereby awarded the Air Force Commendation Medal for meritorious achievement for duties performed as flight safety officer, the squadron awards and decorations officer...."

The whole room burst out in contemptuous howls of derisive laughter, as Colonel Meneur persisted in reading the citation without interrupting his cadence. Captain-for-almost-thirty-minutes Military continued to stand rigidly at attention, seemingly unfazed by the uproar, while the colonel pinned the fifth and telling medal on his chest.

"Now we know how to get an asshole promoted to major," Freed said for the whole room to hear.

Amid the laughter and insults, it was Colonel Meneur who seemed to laugh the hardest of all.

41

"SERGEANT CERVANTES," COLONEL MENEUR CONTINUED, after Captain-for-fifteen-more-minutes Military had sat down. "Show in Missus Alexander."

"Yes, sir." Our first sergeant dutifully opened the door as the whole squadron respectfully stood up *en masse*.

This was a surprise to me. Suzy stepped inside, dressed beautifully in a classic white blouse and lavender skirt with a chain belt. She reminded me of an attractive 1969 *Life* Magazine photograph of a long-haired brunette strolling down a city sidewalk, sunglasses atop her head. From the hall, baby Sean cried in protest. Ramona Nuñez held him, gently patting his back to comfort the little boy. Colonel Meneur motioned to John's widow to step over beside him at the podium. Suzy caught my eye and gave me a broad smile.

"Captain Amity," Colonel Meneur said. *"Report!"*

I was shocked but managed to stand up to report to my commander. Stepping up smartly, I saluted Colonel Meneur, then glanced at Suzy with confused, questioning eyes.

"It is most appropriate that we have Missus Alexander here today," Colonel Meneur said, "and we all extend to her our deepest sympathies for the death of her husband and our fine friend, Captain John Alexander."

"Thank you." Suzy nodded her head in recognition.

"This tragedy," Meneur continued, "the result of factors beyond anybody's control, produced evidence of the finest traditions of the United States Air Force."

Colonel Meneur nodded to Major Cooke, who stepped forward with another medal. "Captain Robert S. Amity is hereby awarded the Airman's Medal for heroism."

I flushed with the jolt of those words. I had never considered myself a hero. I had done nothing consciously to turn myself into one, but I listened as Colonel Meneur read on.

"...upon ejection from his aircraft, First Lieutenant Amity, at great risk to his life, pulled his fellow crewman from the flames of the wreckage, thus sustaining injuries of his own. The actions of First Lieutenant Amity reflect great credit upon himself and the United States Air Force."

Major Cooke handed the Airman's Medal to Suzy, who pinned it on the pocket of my dress blue uniform. Tears began to stream slowly down from our eyes as she kissed me softly on my cheek. The officers present, who had never sat down, clapped their hands with such feeling that I found myself hoping it would never end. Colonel Meneur stepped forward to congratulate me. I gave him my best military salute, just as I saluted Major Cooke who followed. Golden opportunity fell in my hand as Captain-for-just-five-more-minutes-*OH-PLEASE-HELP-US* Military stepped up, medals dangling, to congratulate me.

He stood at attention and extended his hand as I had seen Prussian generals do it in old Hollywood movies. "Congratulations."

"Thanks."

"Captain Amity," he whispered. "Will you salute me?"

"No."

"I don't believe you understood me."

"Yeah! I know what you want."

"Then, let's do this thing right."

I continued to speak quietly. "No thanks."

"In case you haven't noticed," he roared. "I'm giving you a *direct order*."

"So?"

The room had abruptly grown silent.

Major-designate Military plucked his two gold maple leaves out of Major Cooke's hands to show me.

"Do you know what these mean?"

"Well, actually, Major-to-be, *sir*," I began. "I bet I know more about where those leaves came from than you do."

"No, no!" he growled. "I don't think you get my point!"

"But I think I do."

"I think this has gone far enough," Colonel Meneur said.

"Please, Colonel Meneur, sir," I hastily said. "Please. If I may be so honored and allowed to continue, I think this has some bearing."

He was lost for words, so I went on.

"I've been doing some studying up on the subject, you see," I said, so far uninterrupted. "Most ranks and their insignia have origins earlier than Christ."

Major Military's eyes told me that I had hooked a live one. I continued.

"The idea of using stripes of increasing numbers to indicate rank among enlisted men originated in the early days of Greece and Rome. The stripes symbolized formations of troops. The number of stripes signified the number of men under a soldier's command. Of course, they were made of cloth, which, like the troops to a certain extent, were expendable."

Sergeant Cervantes rolled his eyes in amazement. He knew bull when he heard it. The officers were still content to listen, so I went on.

"Of course, the concept of officer's insignia originated even earlier than that. Take the gold bar. The bar symbolizes the straight and narrow path, while pure gold is very malleable and can be formed in a particular way, much like the second lieutenant is used to fit the needs of the Air Force. Then with more experience, the first lieutenant is logically less changeable but must usually still follow a very restricted and narrow path in his career… thus, the silver bar is less malleable than the gold but the same shape."

I could not believe almost-Major Military was falling for this, so I continued.

"Then you take two silver bars. The silver signifies less change, while two parallel bars are a symbol for infinity. The sky is the limit, you might say. Then, of course, the colonel carries the rank of the silver eagle, signifying the ability to soar to even greater heights. Finally, the highest possible ranks are the stars, which our generals wear to signify the highest... the ultimate in achievement and prestige."

"Wait a minute. What about *my* rank?" Major Military interrupted to ask, holding up his soon-to-be-pinned-on gold oak leaves. "What does the gold leaf signify?"

"Oh! I almost forgot. The leaf comes from the Renaissance.... From marble statuary, we learned that they used the leaf to cover their pricks."

Almost-Major Military stood still, his jaw wide open, as I snapped to attention. I raised my hand to salute him, but instead, rotated my thumb to my nose and fanned my fingers, while he stared dumbly at me. Suddenly, the officers broke out in a pandemonium of laughter that fed on itself with increasing volume.

Colonel Meneur came close to my ear and spoke in a stern voice. "That was good, but get the hell out of here before I have you court-martialed."

I saluted the colonel sharply, hastily did my best possible about-face, took Suzy by the arm, and marched out of my flight room forever.

After a few separation formalities, I would be free to pursue my dreams again. What first began as shame, I now viewed with pride. I was a changed man, no longer so sure of my earlier fundamental beliefs. My earlier suspicion of military life was now changed by experience. My fellow airman were not the mindless madmen marching in lockstep that my college acquaintances said they were. They were no different than any other Americans. Some were good. Some were bad. Others were smart. Many were smarter. All had feelings—triumph or regrets, bravery or fear, joy or sorrow. All had strengths and weaknesses. They were men that I admired now, above all groups in my life. Those whom I first misperceived to have selfish motives were now and forever my close friends. In only a few years, I did a one eighty in my perceptions of life, love, and service to my country. I now cherished my time in the Air Force.

Truth be told, I missed it already.

Amid the echoes of men's laughter coursing down the long hallway, we found John's baby boy at the end of the hall, sleeping peacefully in the comforting embrace of a veteran mother. Suzy took the slumbering child once more into her arms and to her breast. Gently holding her waist, I escorted the two of them through the door outside into a radiant light.

High above was a dazzling mixture of blue sky and white cumulus clouds, imperceptibly exploding overhead. The firmament was not a flat canvas but an enormous array of three dimensions. Miles of rainless sky boiled with clouds from the power of a resplendent sun. The vapor trail from a lone jet underlined the blue sky latitudes away. Suzy lifted her gaze heavenward, then again to me. With her *Life* Magazine look, she reflected the wonder of it all in her brilliant warm smile.

KENT McINNIS is an Oklahoma-born chronicler of people, places, and good times, lives with his wife, Cheryl, in Oklahoma City. He served as an Air Force primary jet instructor pilot during the last five years of the Vietnam War.

For the next 33 years he worked in the pharmaceutical industry while pursuing his hobbies of writing, American history, and flying. After retiring in 2008, Kent assumed the position of Chairman of Westerners International, an organization with chapters on three continents dedicated to making the study of Western American History fun—"no stuffed shirts allowed." He stepped down nine years later to return to writing full time.

Kent is past leader of Order of Daedalians (a military pilot fraternity), Chisholm Trail Corral (a Westerners chapter), and Rio River Rat Pilot Training Class 7106. He also chaired three high school class reunions. He is active in the Indian Territory Posse (another Westerners chapter) and the Oklahoma City Men's Dinner Club.

In his spare time Kent travels by car with Cheryl to see America at ground level, visit their three grown children, and savor the joys of freedom in this great country.

Find Kent at RioRiverRat@cox.net or on Facebook.